THE EXTRAORDINARY LIFE OF

THE MAN WHO
CAUGHT CRIPPEN

Joe Saward is a journalist and writer. He began his career working in motorsport, travelling from race to race around Europe, before joining Autosport magazine in London. A pioneer in the new electronic media he created the award-winning "Business of Motorsport" electronic newsletter in 1994, the grandprix.com website and Grand Prix +, motorsport's first e-magazine. He now runs his own F1 blog. In 2007 he published "The Grand Prix Saboteurs", the untold true story of motor racing stars who became British secret agents fighting with the French Resistance during World War II. He was named Author of the Year by the Guild of Motoring Writers.

MORIENVAL
PRESS

First published in 2010 by Morienval Press

1 3 5 7 9 8 6 4 2

Morienval Press,
4 rue des Trois Couronnes,
60127 Morienval, France.

www.morienval.com

ISBN 978-0-9554868-1-4

Typeset in Hoepfler Text

Printed and bound in the United Kingdom by
Lightning Source
Chapter House
Pitfield, Kiln Farm,
Milton Keynes MK11 3LW

And in the United States of America by
Lightning Source Inc
1246 Heil Quaker Boulevard.
La Vergne, Tennessee 37086

THE EXTRAORDINARY LIFE OF
THE MAN WHO CAUGHT CRIPPEN

JOE SAWARD

FOR MY FATHER

ACKNOWLEDGEMENTS

Much of the information in the book comes from Henry Kendall's own notes and journals and from family records. Some of the stories mentioned appeared in "Adventures on the High Seas" by Henry Kendall, which was published by Hurst & Blackett in 1939. There was also considerable research work which included the Canadian Pacific Archives in Montreal, the Queensland State Library and State Archives in Brisbane, the Lloyds of London Historical Collection at the Guildhall Library in London, the Merseyside Maritime Museum and the archives of the New York Times.

I would like to thank the following for their help: Gus Funnell, John Winrow, Jo-Anne Colby and Tom Ehman.

Joe Saward
Morienval, August 2010

"As long as men will travel on the water, the sea-gods will take their toll. They will catch good seamen napping, or confuse their judgment by arts well known to them who go to sea, or overcome them by the sheer brutality of elemental forces."

Joseph Conrad

ATLANTIC CANADA

QUEBEC
PROVINCE

EMPRESS OF IRELAND * * FATHER
POINT

NEW
BRUNSWICK

* QUEBEC CITY

MAINE
(USA)

NOVA
SCOTIA

SAINT JOHN *

BAY
OF
FUNDY

* HALIFAX

* CAPE SABLE

BELLE ISLE STRAIT

GULF
OF SAINT
LAWRENCE

NEWFOUNDLAND

SAINT JOHN'S *

LUSITANIA *

CAPE RACE *

NORTH ATLANTIC
OCEAN

CHAPTER ONE

The old man was dying. It was to be expected at the age of 91, but Henry Kendall clung on stubbornly to life. He did not want to let go. His children knew that the time had come. And their children too. Everyone knew that it was just a matter of days.

But what a life he had lived. He should have died many times over in the course of his adventures. He had survived wild storms and shipwrecks, torpedoes, murderous villains, scorpion bites, a marauding leopard, cannibals, sharks, fevers, flying bombs and even, so they said, the curse of the notorious Dr Crippen.

Yet, in the end, it was old age that was going to claim him.

Old age and memories.

We all travel through our lives with reminders of those who have gone before, but Kendall had been accompanied on his journey by many more souls than most. There had been friends and family members, of course, and those who had been killed in the wars in which Henry had played his role. As a mariner he had known many others who had died before their time; or had simply disappeared in the vast oceans, their fate never certain.

In the final hours of his life, in the Trinity Hospice on London's Clapham Common, Henry Kendall faced up to the ghosts that had haunted him for so long. For half a century he had lived with the knowledge that a thousand people in his care had been lost on one awful night in 1914. Yet he had survived.

Kendall, a sea captain from head to toe, had meant to go down with the ship. That was how it should have been. But fate, or God, or whatever, had not allowed it. Only two of the seven deck officers on the RMS Empress of Ireland had survived that dreadful night - and he had been one of them. He had lived on, and with him had lived the memories and the questions; the "what ifs" that would come to him at the dark times.

The Court of Inquiry after the accident had ruled that the sinking of the Empress, in the St Lawrence Estuary in Canada, had not been his fault. Everyone involved had been trying to do the best they could. Courts of Inquiry cannot blame the sea gods and others got the blame. Kendall was sure that he had done the right things, but he knew that the actions of the different parties had combined to create a disaster. He had told himself over and over that he could have done nothing differently, but the questions remained. Could the collision have been avoided? Could more people have been saved? Each time the demons came Kendall forced himself to move on; to be his usual self. He played the role, and was what people expected him to be. But time and again he would relive the events on the night that the Empress went down.

That day - in May 1914 - had begun for him in picturesque Quebec City, where the Empress was moored in the shadow of the majestic Chateau Frontenac hotel, one of one series of luxury chateau-style establishments that had been built by the Canadian Pacific Railway as it tried to attract high-spending travellers for its trains and steamships.

Although there was much tension in international affairs at that time, people around the globe still lived in a world of illusions. The effects of industrialisation on warfare were still to be fully understood. The maelstrom, the mud, the waste and the hopelessness of the Great War were discoveries yet to be made. Things were different then.

Henry Kendall was a hero of the age of illusion.

People need heroes to reflect the finest qualities of mankind and to inspire them. Heroes are symbols of the hopes and dreams of millions of normal people. In the Nineteenth Century Britain found its champions from among the men in the red tunics who fought and died for the great British Empire. The Victoria Cross had been created for them. Yet heroism was not just about fighting savages with spears and saving the colours from the enemy. It was also about facing the unknown. The world had made heroes of the explorers who disappeared into Africa; who climbed great mountains; or who struggled and died on their way to the North and South Poles. Although the globe was largely charted by that stage, those who went to sea were still considered to be a breed apart. Most people never travelled far from their homes. Going beyond the horizon, out into an empty sea, was an act of courage and of romance. Nature was a powerful adversary. It had yet to be de-constructed by science. Nature was not seen as beautiful, as it is today, but appeared instead to be a constant threat.

Sailors revelled in their status. They developed symbols to show off their courage: wearing earrings to indicate that they had rounded Cape Horn. For centuries they had told wild tales of supernatural beasts and mountainous storms, of deserted islands where savages ate other human beings. There was no-one to challenge their claims and, no doubt, the dangers and the hardships were magnified by some. Yet sailors were still seen as adventurers. Everyone loved a sailor.

As mankind reached for the skies and pushed the limits with aeroplanes and automobiles a new generation of heroes would be created, but in 1914 aviation was still seen as the sport of madmen. It was true that as early as 1866 the writer Jules Verne had imagined that man could one day go to the Moon in a machine and his predictions in "From the Earth to the Moon" would prove to be astonishingly accurate, but space travel was beyond the comprehension of the man in the street. The Moon, they used to say, was made of green cheese.

The advent of the great steamships had begun to open the way for safer, faster and more predictable travel, but the men who commanded these ships had learned their trade in sailing ships, in the old fashioned way. Kendall had spent 25 of his 40 years at sea. He was one of the best and brightest of the officers working for the Canadian Pacific Railway, and the youngest captain on any of the big Atlantic liners. He had every reason to be proud as he prepared for his third voyage as commander of CPR's flagship vessel, the Empress of Ireland.

He had taken command of the ship just four weeks earlier, on May 1. She had been docked in Halifax, Nova Scotia, on Canada's east coast. This was the Empress's winter terminal in the Americas, as ice in the St Lawrence Estuary meant that between October and April it was too dangerous for the big liners to travel to their summer terminals in Quebec and Montreal, 400 miles further to the west. In the winter months that journey had to be made by train. Kendall had taken the Empress across the Atlantic to the port of Liverpool, his adopted home, and, as the ice in Canada had by then melted, they had headed back to Quebec, through the treacherous Belle Isle Strait into the Gulf of St Lawrence, and from there up the St Lawrence River to Quebec City.

There they remained for a week, in the docks beneath the Chateau Frontenac, the ship towering above the wharf, a 14,000-ton floating palace. During that period Kendall and his officers oversaw the loading of 2,600 tons of coal, the fuel that was needed to get them back to Liverpool. There were 1,100 tons of cargo, including 318 bags of mail bound for Europe. In the safe aboard the ship there were no fewer than 212 bars of silver, worth more than $1 million, a very considerable sum of money in 1914. The ship's official name was RMS Empress of Ireland, RMS standing for "Royal Mail Ship", a much sought-after designation which implied speed, quality and efficiency.

"My world was perfect," Kendall wrote. "The international tensions in Europe were getting ever more noticeable. We were living on borrowed time, I suppose, but we did not know it then."

In May 1914 the world was laughing at the cinema's newest star, Charlie Chaplin, who had won the hearts of millions a few months earlier with his portrayal of a bumbling but good-natured tramp. Chaplin helped the world forget its problems: German military might, symbolized by the giant Zeppelin airships, was growing. The Irish were much in the news and were granted Home Rule by the British Parliament. Suffragettes were demanding votes for women. There was revolution in Mexico. The barriers of the rigid old Victorian world were beginning to break down. The rigid class system in Britain was being shaken more and more. George Bernard Shaw's play Pygmalion, which had just opened in London, portrayed Professor Henry Higgins, a patrician, wagering that he can pass off a Cockney flower girl, Eliza Doolittle, as a refined society lady, with just a few months of training. Higgins succeeds in his task, but is smitten by the girl, although she rejects him because of his bullying ways and marries a poor young man instead. Although the blurring of the lines of society was still a new concept, there were many more people willing and able to travel. Shipping companies continued to divide up the social classes, but Lords and immigrants travelled on the same ships, albeit on different decks.

The officers of the ocean liners transcended social class. They may have grown up as deckhands on sailing ships, but in 1914 they mixed with high society. Kendall had grown used to the lifestyle. He had served on liners for more than 15 years. He had been Chief Officer on the Empress in 1907 under Captain John Forster and had been reunited with many old friends when he rejoined the ship in Halifax. By his side on the first run across the Atlantic was Mansfield Steede, a 41-year-old Irishman, who had been at sea since he was 14. He had been with the Empress since she was built in 1906.

"It was a happy ship," Kendall remembered, "and, while luxurious, she was not a par with the great liners trading on the New York run. But to me that day she was the most beautiful ship I had ever seen. I cannot explain the thrill I had as we headed out into the Atlantic. Here I was in charge of a 14,000 ton floating hotel, with her crew of 420, her 550ft of handsome length, her saloons and music room. And her 18 knots."

There were more than 1,000 passengers, although the ship was still not filled to capacity, except in Third Class. Second Class was only half full, despite a contingent of 171 members of the Salvation Army, who were travelling to London to take part in an International Congress.

If there had been the demand, the Empress could have taken three times as many First Class passengers as it had for that voyage, but the select group of travellers on this trip included three notable people: Sir Henry Seton-Karr, a celebrated lawyer and Member of Parliament, who had developed a taste for travel and big-game hunting. He was returning home from a hunting trip in British Columbia; and then there were the actors Laurence Irving and Mabel Hackney.

Irving was the son of the celebrated actor/manager Sir Henry Irving and not only acted but also wrote plays. He and his wife Hackney had been on tour in Canada and, keen to return home, had gone ahead of the rest of the company.

Preparations for the voyage were completed by 4pm on Thursday, May 28. Half an hour later the ship began her 96th Atlantic crossing.

"As darkness fell on the St Lawrence River I remember thinking that it was cold for that time of year," Kendall recalled. "Standing on the bridge of the Empress I could see the bright lights of the liner below me as I listened to the lilting music drifting upwards through the skylight above the Music Room. I intended to stay up until we were clear of the St Lawrence River, before handing over to my chief officer. He was a good man. We were about the same age and had both been at sea for all of our adult lives."

It was after midnight before the Empress reached Father Point, where the St Lawrence Estuary is 30 miles wide and ships tended to hug the southern shoreline to be able to see the lighthouses and hear the foghorns, lest visibility become a problem. From the Empress they could see the Father Point lighthouse blinking in the darkness and soon the Eureka, a pilot boat, came out to meet the ship and fetch Adelard Bernier, the pilot who had been navigating from Quebec. Once the pilot had disembarked Kendall handed over command to First Officer Edward Jones. The order was given to go full speed ahead.

A few minutes later a lookout reported that there was a ship on the starboard bow, about six miles ahead. Kendall had not yet gone to bed and returned to the bridge to see what was going on.

"Up ahead there were the distant lights of an incoming ship," he wrote. "I went out onto the deck and round to the stairs leading to the upper bridge. I checked the ship's position with the prismatic compass. There was no danger and I returned to the wheelhouse below."

The other ship was heading in to Father Point to pick up a pilot and was closer to the shore than the Empress and so Kendall planned to cross the path of the incoming ship and then turn onto a parallel course and pass starboard-to-starboard without any danger.

Everything seemed to be in order.

"Just then I saw a swirl of fog - one of the most lethal hazards of the St Lawrence - as it began to roll off the land and onto the river," Kendall remembered. "Two years before our sister ship, the Empress of Britain, had collided with a Norwegian collier in the fog not far from that point. I did not want a repeat of that.

"The incoming ship had disappeared into the fog. To be certain that there would be no danger I ordered the engines to be put full astern and gave three short blasts on the ship's whistle to signal to the other ship that I was going astern."

The other ship replied with a single long blast, indicating that she was going to continue on her course.

The ship out in the fog was the SS Storstad, a 6,000-ton Norwegian coal freighter. She was heavily loaded and riding low in the water. She boasted a reinforced bow that was designed for breaking through pack ice. At that moment the Storstad was under the command of Chief Officer Alfred Toftenes. The 33-year-old Norwegian said later that before the fog rolled across the river they could see from the lights that there was a large liner ahead on the port bow. He claimed that he could see the liner's green starboard light and then caught a glimpse of the red light on the port side, just as the fog arrived. This suggested to him that the liner was going to pass on the port side, between his ship and the shore.

"I walked out onto the navigating bridge to see if I could see better," Kendall recalled. "The ship had stopped moving and so I ordered two blasts of the whistle to signal to the other ship that the Empress was not moving. Then I checked the compass to see if we had drifted. All was well."

Toftenes responded with another long blast of the horn but then, assuming the Empress to be on his port side, ordered the Third Mate Jacob Saxe to steer the Storstad sharply to starboard, thinking that this would give the liner more space.

Kendall was out on the starboard side of the navigation bridge, staring into the fog, hoping to catch a glimpse of the other ship passing between the Empress and the shore.

What he saw was something that would stay with him for the rest of his days.

"The incoming ship was there, steaming straight towards us," he remembered. "It was going to hit the Empress at right angles. I knew instinctively that there would be a collision, but I thought that perhaps if I could turn the ship, the angle of the impact would be a glancing blow. I rang full speed ahead on the engine telegraph and ran back to the wheelhouse and ordered the wheel be put hard over to starboard."

Kendall grabbed a megaphone and ran out on to the navigation bridge once again, bellowing "Go astern! Go astern!" in the direction of the oncoming ship.

At that same moment Thomas Anderson, the Storstad's captain, appeared on the bridge of his ship. He saw the Empress ahead in the fog and ordered the engines to be put into reverse. The startled Toftenes sounded three long blasts of the ship's horn to warn the Empress.

No warning was needed. Kendall had already instructed First Officer Jones to begin preparing the lifeboats and then he watched in awe and horror as the Storstad slid at unabated speed into his ship.

"The impact was terrible," he remembered, "a sheet of fire was produced as metal hit metal. There must have been a huge gash in the side. I wanted to save my ship and in order to keep her afloat, I decided that the bows of the other ship must remain wedged in the side of the Empress. I grabbed the megaphone once more and shouted through the darkness for them to keep their engines going full ahead."

Kendall and Jones both agreed later that although the Empress was going full ahead, there had not been enough time for the ship to begin to move forwards, but any hope there might have been of plugging the hole in the side of the liner disappeared in seconds. The Storstad's engines were going full astern and the smaller vessel was more responsive and began to move backwards. The two ships pulled apart, leaving a hole 14 feet wide and 25 feet deep in the side of the Empress. Within seconds the freighter had disappeared into the fog.

It has been calculated that, in the minute that followed the impact, 60,000 gallons of water per second surged into the liner. The mathematics are chilling. Sixty thousand gallons of salt water weigh 230 tons, so in the first 30 seconds after the collision the Empress took on in the region of 6,900 tons of water - almost half her own weight. Six thousand nine hundred tons of water fills around 285,000 cubic feet. The Aft Boiler Room was instantly flooded and water burst through the connecting doors into the Forward Boiler Room. There was no time to close them. The two boiler rooms - which combined to form a space of 300,000 cubic feet - were filled with freezing water within 90 seconds. Then water began to pour along the corridors into the Third Class accommodation.

Although the order to close the watertight doors had been given just before the collision, within a minute of the impact the Empress was listing nine degrees to starboard. This meant that the task of closing the heavy doors became almost impossible as the crewmen struggled to wind the weight uphill. On the lower decks crew members would have been swept away by the mass of water.

Kendall hoped that there was still a chance to run the Empress into the shore and thus keep her afloat, but the water reached the boilers almost immediately. The only reports from the engine room were terrified noises echoing through the voice pipes.

There was no steam. The Empress of Ireland was doomed.

Chief Officer Steede appeared on the bridge in his pyjamas and Kendall ordered him to send an SOS message, only to be told that Steede had already issued the same order. The First Class passengers, who had cabins near the top of the ship, began emerging from their quarters, although they reacted slowly, unaware that the impact had been so devastating. Those in the Third Class cabins had virtually no chance of survival, unless they left their cabins within the first minute of the impact.

Leaving the bridge in Steede's capable hands, Kendall went to the boat deck and began to oversee the release of the lifeboats. It was a race against time. As the Empress listed more and more the boats on the starboard side of the ship were soon just a few feet above the water, while those on the port side were quickly at an angle that meant that it was impossible to launch them. First Officer Jones was working to release one of the boats when he lost his footing and slid into the river. In the end the crew was only able to launch four lifeboats. At the same time the increasing list caused the deck gear of the liner to begin to break loose from its mountings. Many of those who did make it on to the deck were swept away by flying machinery. Others were crushed to death. To make matters worse the ship's electrical system failed, plunging everything into darkness and ending all wireless transmissions. The word, however, had been picked up immediately and help was on its way within minutes.

Kendall returned to the bridge to direct operations and

Steede went down on to the boat deck, only to be swept away by flying machinery. Henry witnessed the death of his friend.

Within a few minutes Kendall was hanging by one hand on the rail on the port side of the navigation bridge, using the other hand to hold the megaphone, into which he shouted orders to what was left of his crew. In reality there was nothing to be done. Water soon began to pour into the open portholes of cabins which had been low down on the starboard side. The people who were on the deck found it hard to keep their footing. Many slid helplessly across the deck and into the freezing waters. Others found themselves trapped in a V between the cabins and the deck on the port side as the ship tilted more and more. People clawed their way up to the railings and clung on. Others took to the water, fearing that they would be dragged under when the Empress sank.

Twelve minutes after the impact, without any warning, the Empress of Ireland lurched violently to starboard and fell on her side. As the ship went over Augustus Gaade, the chief steward, and the purser Alexander McDonald both witnessed Captain Kendall being hurled into the water.

"My grip on the bridge rail was hopeless against gravity," Kendall recalled. "I had meant to go down with my ship, but it was not to be. I was flung out into the dark freezing water and I went deep. When I rose to the surface, lungs bursting, the ship was gone. There was nothing but fiercely frothing water and cries in the darkness. A piece of wreckage rose to the surface from beneath me and I grabbed it and clung tight to it. I don't know what I was thinking then, in that dreadful numbing cold, but I remember the feeling that I must do my utmost to save as many people as I could."

The Empress was still afloat, lying on her side, barely above the water level. Some of those on the port side clambered on to the hull. There were explosions in the darkness as the boilers blew up. The water quickly began to rise up and in less than two minutes the great ship slipped finally beneath the water. As the Empress disappeared eyewitnesses saw Second Officer Roger Williams sucked into one of the funnels as he tried to swim away.

It had been just 14 minutes since the Storstad had hit the Empress.

CHAPTER TWO

They say that when one is close to death, one's life flashes before one's eyes, but as Henry Kendall fought to stay afloat in the icy waters of the St Lawrence Estuary, his mind was not on the past.

The truth was that he did not know very much about his early years, nor about his ancestors. He had been told that many years earlier, long before he was born, his father had inherited a Bible that had once belonged to a Captain John Kendall. It was said that it had been washed ashore after Kendall had drowned in one of the thousands of shipwrecks on the rugged coast of Cornwall. The scavengers had the good grace to make sure that the Bible was returned to his family, but no-one knew much more than that.

There had been a Captain John Kendall in 1826. He was the commander of the Mary Francis, a sailing ship that left New Brunswick in Canada, bound for Liverpool with 21 passengers and crew aboard. There had been a storm so violent that the Mary Francis was damaged to the point that she was no longer controllable and was simply drifting at sea. Such was the plight of the passengers and crew that, as a survivor Miss Ann Saunders later recalled, "we were reduced to the awful extremity to attempt to support our feeble bodies a while longer by subsisting on the dead body of the deceased - it was cut into slices, then washed in salt water, and after being exposed to and dried a little in the sun, was apportioned to each of the miserable survivors".

Only Captain Kendall and five others survived, saved at the very last moment by the dashing Lord Byron (a cousin of the poet), the captain of HMS Blonde.

Whether this is the same John Kendall who drowned off the Cornish coast was not something that Henry's father Joseph knew, but the Bible was his prize possession until he accidentally left it on a train and it was lost forever.

Kendall is a common enough name. Some think it is Scottish, but it originates from the town of Kendal, in what was once called Westmorland, in the north-west of England. Originally it was little more than a village where the River Kent ran through a valley - or a dale as they call them up there. Over time lazy tongues turned Kent Dale into Kendal and the settlement grew, mainly because it was on the main road to Scotland and because the hills above the town were well-suited to sheep. The local farmers would descend to Kendal to sell their wool, which was big business back then. To the north of Kendal the Pennine Hills, which form the backbone of England, spill across from the east into the Lake District. The road to Scotland thus has to climb up from 150 ft above sea level in Kendal itself to around 1,500 ft in the craggy hills above Borrowdale. Kendal was a good place to stop before the climb.

It was a town that people travelled through on the way to somewhere else. This made the people of Kendal less frightened of the world beyond the horizon and they travelled more than most. Thus the name spread north and south. By the middle of the 19th century there were Kendalls all over England and in 1847 Joseph Kendall was born in Exeter, Devon, in the south-west. He grew up in the cathedral city and, in time, became a white-smith: a man who worked with soft metals, such as lead, tin and pewter. A blacksmith works with harder, darker metals. The key difference between the two trades was that a white-smith was not tied to his forge and could travel from place to place, plying his business.

In his late teens Joseph Kendall began moving around the country, finding work where he could. By 1868 he had gravitated to London where he met and married Mary Eaton, who worked as a seamstress. Mary was just 16, but they soon had their first child, a daughter called Elizabeth. The following year a son was born. He was baptized Joseph, after his father, but he died when just a few weeks old. Two years passed and in 1872 there came another daughter, baptized Alice. In 1874 there was another son, named Henry, after Mary's father Henry Eaton.

The family was always on the move, but when Henry was born they were living in Chelsea, which was not the exclusive London suburb it is today. Joseph had turned his skills to fitting gas systems in expensive London houses. Times were still hard and soon after Henry's birth the family moved to Tunbridge Wells in Kent, where Henry Eaton had established an organ-building business. Eaton had fought in the Crimean War and Mary's brother, also called Henry, was a veteran as well. The brief respite may have provided Mary and Joseph Kendall with financial stability for a period but they soon moved on, heading to Liverpool where the shipbuilding trade was booming and there was work for whitesmiths. The Kendalls settled in Birkenhead, across the River Mersey from Liverpool.

Before 1730 the city traded mainly with Ireland, but the increasing number of colonies provided raw materials - such as cotton, sugar and tobacco - that transformed Liverpool into the chief port of the British Empire. Nearby Manchester developed into the centre of the world's manufacturing industry, its steam-powered mills producing high quality goods that were then shipped out to the colonies. The merchants of Liverpool initiated a triangular trade taking the Manchester goods to Africa, transporting slaves to the Americas, and then shipping the produce from the plantations to Britain. When transporting slaves was made illegal in 1807, the merchants looked instead to India, where the monopoly enjoyed by the East India Company ended in 1813. The competition to get products back to England meant that speed became a factor and so bigger and better ships had to be built. Thus Liverpool became a centre for shipbuilding. Birkenhead was the site of the Laird Brothers yards, which produced large iron sailing vessels and warships. Prosperity brought growth: in 1800 Liverpool was a city of 77,000 people; by 1900 the population had grown to 700,000 and it had become the chief port of the British Empire.

The Kendall family soon put down roots and in 1880 another son, named Charles was born. He died young, for life in the big cities was never healthy. Young Henry was stronger and as he was growing up he was often dressed in sailor suits - a fashion at the time. He was referred to by the family as "Jack the Sailor".

"Whether this attire had anything to do with any lifelong ambition for the sea, I don't know," Henry remembered, "but I have the feeling it influenced my mind greatly."

Henry Eaton's wife - Henry's maternal grandmother - was a Scot, born in Paisley, near Glasgow, into a family named Kidd. In later years Kendall liked to suggest that his grandmother was a descendant of the 17th century pirate Captain William Kidd, who originated in Greenock, not far from Paisley. It was possible. Certainly Kendall was a roving and energetic spirit. He was forever clowning about, throwing himself around, twisting himself into knots.

"I looked upon the world as a playground," he recalled. "My mother always said that I caused her more worry than all her other children put together. I was naturally mischievous."

It was not long before the family moved across the Mersey and into Liverpool itself. They settled in the Kensington district and Henry went to school in nearby Fairfield. He was soon amusing his friends with his contortions, becoming known as "the Indian rubber kid", although his antics did not go down well with his teachers.

"It was apt that the headmaster's name was Thrasher," he remembered. "The cane was going all day long like a Maxim gun."

On January 3, 1885 everything changed for the Kendall Family. Thirty-eight-year-old Joseph died, leaving Mary and the children penniless. Henry was 10. The family needed money and so the boy was sent out to work. He did many different jobs, beginning as an errand boy for shops up and down Prescot Street and then serving behind the counter. The fishmonger was particularly helpful, providing the family with fresh fish on Fridays and Saturdays. At the end of the year he was also able to find work at the Royal Alexandra Theatre on Lime Street, where he appeared as a contortionist in the Christmas pantomime. The leading lady was Marie Loftus, one of the biggest stars of music hall at the time. Kendall used to tie himself in knots and jump through windows. It was three months of work but during that time Henry decided on his future career.

"My youthful wanderings on Sunday mornings took me around the Liverpool docks, when everything was quiet," he explained. "I would inhale the smell of spices and other Oriental goods. One day I made up my mind to lead a sailor's life."

His mother was violently opposed to the idea, but life was not easy for the young widow, and Henry was resolute. In the end she accepted his wishes. She had, in any case, decided that it would be best for the family to return to London, taking her daughters with her. She asked the local vicar if he could recommend Henry for a place on the training ship Indefatigable, which was moored at Rock Ferry on the Birkenhead side of the Mersey.

The Indefatigable was one of four such school ships. The first had been the Akbar which began operating in 1856. She was a reform school ship to which boys were sent by a magistrate. Three years later the Conway put down anchor nearby. She was a training ship for boys from wealthy families. The two ships were joined by a third in 1863 when the Clarence arrived, another reform school ship, although her inmates had to be Roman Catholics.

As none of these catered for the underprivileged youngsters who had not turned to crime, in 1865 a group of merchants led by John Clint established an educational trust designed to help destitute and orphan boys from Liverpool. They negotiated the loan of the Indefatigable from the Royal Navy. She had been one of the last wooden frigates, built in Devonport in 1848. She had retired from active service after just nine years and then spent eight years in the Reserve Fleet.

Ship-owner and banker James Bibby spent £5,000 to convert the ship into a training vessel, which boasted a classroom and accommodation for 200 boys on the old gun deck. They slept in hammocks. In addition to their seamanship training, the boys received normal schooling. The ship later acquired a floating swimming bath in which the pupils were taught to swim. Once they had completed the course the staff of the Indefatigable arranged places for them aboard Merchant Navy ships.

Henry joined the Indefatigable on June 7, 1887. He was 13 years old, stood 4 feet 6 inches tall and weighed 74 pounds. He would stay on the ship for the next two and a half years.

The Indefatigable was under the command of Captain John Groome. He was 65 and lived on board with his wife, four instructors and a maid.

"I never saw such punishment meted out to boys," Kendall remembered. "The old skipper was the greatest villain that ever trod a ship's deck. He gloried in it and never a kind word ever passed his lips. After a boy received punishment and after the Sunday service at 8pm, the boy with hopes of easing the position would approach the skipper asking for forgiveness. The answer a boy always got from the swine was: 'I'll forgive you, but by God I won't forget you!'.

"After 12 months I ran away, escaping by the skin of my teeth, and after hiding out for two weeks under the worst conditions, was collared. I expected to be hung, drawn and quartered on my return. Such was not to be for during my absence the boys had revolted, the Captain and his officers (who were just as bad) locked themselves in their quarters while the boys threw everything overboard and were bent on doing the same to the Captain and his officers. News got ashore and a party of ship-owners who were the committee arrived in a tug. An inquiry was held. The brutal marks on the boys were examined, which made the committee members almost faint and as the ship had such a good image they didn't want it to get into the papers so within a few days the captain and all the officers were dismissed and a new staff appointed. Things were far better."

There are no records of this revolt - such things were covered up in Victorian times - but Groome resigned and a new Captain called Bremner arrived.

"I could not forget the past and what I had been through," Kendall said. "My only thoughts were to get out of that ship and start an active life at sea in anything that would float."

By the middle of 1889 Kendall was reaching the end of his time on Indefatigable. That summer Thomas Ismay, the owner of the White Star Line and one of the founders of the Indefatigable trust, organized for all 200 boys to attend the Naval Review at Spithead, near Portsmouth, working as crew aboard the brand new White Star liner RMS Teutonic. This was a great honour as the Teutonic was the newest and most exciting ship of the era.

From 1870 onwards there had been intense competition between the different shipping lines to win the Blue Riband, the award for the fastest Atlantic crossing. In 1872 the White Star liner Adriatic achieved an average speed of 14.53 knots. By 1889 that record had been broken 13 times and the Inman Line's City of Paris has raised the target to over 20 knots. Speed was of great importance because it helped a firm bid for the lucrative mail contracts that were available at the time from the various governments. The competition for the British Government contracts was intense, as moving mail quickly around the British Empire was of vital importance. These contracts generally included terms which gave the government the right to requisition mail ships for military purposes if that was required. Such arrangements were very profitable for the shipping firms, but resulted in the government making more and more demands and in 1880 the major mail carriers were forced to agree to the Armed Cruiser Convention, which dictated that they built liners that could be transformed rapidly into armed cruisers. The White Star Line commissioned two new ships from the Harland and Wolff yards in Belfast: the Teutonic and the Majestic. These were designed to challenge for the Blue Riband and at the same time could be converted into fighting ships under the terms of the convention.

The Teutonic was launched in January 1889, was fitted out by the summer and headed immediately to Spithead and, crewed by the boys from the Indefatigable, she created much interest at the Naval Review.

The event that year had been designed as a celebration of the close links between Britain and Germany. It is often forgotten in the light of what happened in the years that followed, but the royal families of the two European nations were intertwined. Queen Victoria was married to a German and her daughter, also called Victoria, had in turn married Frederick, the Crown Prince of Germany. He had become the Emperor in 1888, although it was a brief reign for he died after just a few months and his son, Victoria's grandson, Wilhelm took over at the age of just 29. That summer the new Emperor arrived in England aboard the imperial yacht Hohenzollern, accompanied by a fleet of 12 warships, which then travelled to Spithead to see the Naval Review in his honour.

The Kaiser met his Uncle Albert (Princess Victoria's brother) who was then the Prince of Wales and would later become King Edward VII, and the two attended the Review together. The German made no secret of his respect for the Royal Navy and expressed a desire to one day build a fleet of his own. On August 3 the Kaiser went aboard the Teutonic and inspected the boys from the Indefatigable. He was impressed by the ship and was heard to remark that "we must have some of these".

The Review itself had to be postponed because of poor weather and the Teutonic left Spithead before the big event in which 20 battleships, 35 cruisers, 18 gunboats and 38 torpedo boats, along with more than 20,000 British sailors, saluted the royals. The Teutonic was by then in Liverpool having her guns removed in preparation for her first transatlantic voyage on August 7.

The Kaiser went on to Aldershot and inspected the British Army in a parade that featured 27,000 soldiers. After a quick trip to see his dear old grandmother - Queen Victoria - at her favoured residence at Osborne on the Isle of Wight, he sailed back to Germany.

A year later the Majestic took the Blue Riband with a speed of 20.5 knots and soon afterwards the Teutonic went even faster, although in the summer of 1892 she would be outrun by the City of Paris. The Teutonic's visit to Spithead was deemed to have been significant for the Kaiser set in motion events that would result in the launch of the Norddeutscher Lloyd Line's Kaiser Wilhelm der Grosse, the first four-funneled liner in the world, in 1897. This would raise the Atlantic record to 22.3 knots and gave a clear indication of Germany's ambitions to take its place in the maritime world. Both Britain and Germany began building bigger and better liners. And bigger and better battleships.

Kendall and the other boys from the Indefatigable may not have appreciated it, but the Kaiser's visit that day would shape many of their futures.

CHAPTER THREE

The Age of Steam took much longer to turn the shipping world on its head than one might have expected. Wind is free and while steam power provided a more reliable means of getting a ship from one port to another, the cost of the coal consumed meant that the early steamers could not compete with sailing ships over very long distances. The first important innovation that made steamers more efficient was the iron hull. This was lighter than the traditional wood and thus required less coal to move a ship. In the 1860s the arrival of multi-cylinder steam engines and steel hulls, plus the opening of the Suez Canal, meant that steamships finally became efficient enough to challenge sail.

As Kendall and his chums from the Indefatigable paraded on the deck of the Teutonic in 1889 they could not have imagined what was to come. They might have marvelled that the French had built the vast Eiffel Tower, as part of the Universal Exposition in Paris. They would, no doubt, have been interested that two Germans - Gottlieb Daimler and Wilhelm Maybach - had built a gasoline-powered "automobile". In the United States of America, George Eastman started selling a portable camera which captured images on film rather than on a plate of glass and Thomas Edison was working on an idea to create moving pictures.

None of the apprentices had ever heard the name Marconi and the Wright Brothers were still complete unknowns. There were still vast tracts of land around the globe that had yet to be explored. The Wild West might have been largely tamed and Buffalo Bill was touring Europe with his Wild West Show. But Butch Cassidy was still robbing banks and the last great Land Rush was taking place in Oklahoma.

In a world before flying machines, the combination of trains and fast ships was the best way to travel, a fact that was underlined by the publication in 1873 of Jules Verne's classic novel "Around the World in 80 Days" in which Phileas Fogg, a wealthy English gentleman, wagers £20,000 that following the opening of a new section of railway near Jubbulpore in India, which linked Bombay to Calcutta, it would be possible to circumnavigate the globe in under 80 days, using railways and steamships.

More importantly, steamships and railways became the most efficient way to send mail, a much more lucrative activity than transporting passengers or freight. As a result railway companies began buying steamships and shipping companies began investing in railways.

In the summer of 1889 Kendall's time on the Indefatigable came to an end. A place was found for him as a cabin boy on the City of Berlin, a liner owned by the Inman & International Line. Once a leading shipping company, it had been unable to find enough money to replace its ageing fleet, and had gradually been swallowed up by the rival American Line, a subsidiary of the giant Pennsylvania Rail Road company.

Twenty-five years before Kendall joined the ship, the City of Berlin had been the largest civilian ship in the world, apart from Isambard Kingdom Brunel's extraordinary SS Great Eastern. The City of Berlin had engines that were capable of producing 3,200 horsepower, sufficient to power the 5,500 ton ship to a speed of 14 knots. In 1875 she won the Blue Riband. Four years later the ship became the first to be fitted with electric lighting in the cabins, but by the time Kendall stepped aboard for the first time, the City of Berlin was dwarfed by the new generation of bigger and better machinery. The City of New York and her sister ship the City of Paris were 10,500 tons and could cross the Atlantic at an average speed of 20 knots.

In 1887 the City of Berlin was laid up for a lengthy refit at the Laird shipyards in Birkenhead, being fitted with the latest triple expansion engines and having the cabins rebuilt, but the ship was like an actress who was past her prime. Cosmetic changes would do only so much. Henry Kendall did not, of course, look at the ship in such a light. To him she was a magnificent vessel. He was young and green.

Before he joined the City of Berlin Kendall visited London to see his mother and his sisters. Mary was still firmly opposed to him going off to sea but she had little choice. Everyone, even his Uncle Henry who had just returned from fighting in Sudan, turned up at London's Euston Station to see him off on December 4, 1889.

"My mother felt a terrible grief at parting with me," Kendall remembered. "My luggage was placed in the van and as the last goodbyes were said my mother pushed up the window as the guard blew the whistle and said: 'Whatever you do now that you have started sea life, never drink intoxicating liquors, never chew tobacco and never be tattooed.' That was a tall order, but as it was said at a time when it was most likely to be stamped on my brain, I gave a promise and I was determined to keep it.

"When the train got well under way I noticed that the other occupant of the compartment was making himself comfortable for the night by stretching himself out on the opposite seat. When fairly settled, he looked at me and said: 'Well, my boy, you are bound away to sea and, within my hearing, you have made promises to your mother which I doubt you will ever keep'. Naturally I asked him why I would break the promises and he replied that he was a sailor himself, had been at sea for 20 years, and was on his way to join a ship at North Shields. A sailor's life, he said, was too full of temptation to avoid breaking such promises. He added with a grin that if you don't drink when you are ashore in a foreign port with your shipmates they will pump it down your throat with a syringe.

"As regards being tattooed, he said Kendall would not be able to resist the temptation. Tobacco, he added, was part of the food, especially when one is beating around Cape Horn on a dirty night'.

"He was certainly a Job's comforter," Kendall remembered.

The City of Berlin was under the command of Captain Francis Land, who had spent 17 years with the company. He had captained the City of New York and the City of Brussels, although the latter had sunk after a collision in the Mersey.

In the winter of 1886 the City of Berlin had hit an iceberg but Land played his role perfectly, being described as having been "cooler than the iceberg". A year later he was back in the news when the City of Montreal caught fire, 400 miles from land, en route to Liverpool with a cargo of cotton. The crew had fought the blaze through the night but in the end it became clear that there was no choice but to abandon ship. They were lucky in that a steamer called York City and a German barque appeared soon after the lifeboats were launched. Only one boat was lost and that was because those aboard had not followed Land's orders. Thirteen people disappeared but The New York Times reported that "the other survivors consider the fate of the occupants of the lost boat as a judgement for their cowardice". Land and his crew were highly commended.

The Captain's energy was reflected in a saying of his crew. "Sailing on the City of Berlin is not so bad," they used to say. "Land is always in sight". To the young Kendall, this imposing figure was a larger than life character, and his first real role model of what a sea captain should be.

The City of Berlin sailed for New York on December 5, 1889. She stopped briefly at Queenstown, in Cork Harbour, on the southern coast of Ireland, and then steamed on to arrive across from the three-year-old Statue of Liberty, which for millions of immigrants symbolized the start of a new life. It was little different for young Kendall. There were just three days in the port before the ship sailed again and, after spending Christmas Day at sea, she arrived back in Liverpool in time for the New Year celebrations.

That winter the gales in the North Atlantic were some of the most violent for years. There were hurricane force winds, driving snow and rain. The extent of the ice fields and the number of icebergs sighted were both unprecedented. Many lives were lost as the ships were whipped by icy winds and big waves that broke over them. If one was swept overboard in such a storm there was no chance of survival. Conditions were so bad that it was impossible to launch even a lifeboat.

It was not much fun for a novice.

"Whoever wrote the song 'Life on the Ocean Wave' did not do so aboard a ship in the North Atlantic in winter," Kendall remarked.

He soon concluded that this was not what he dreamed of doing and decided that on his return he would try to find a job on a ship going east, where the climate was warmer and where the British Empire offered more exotic discoveries. Within a week he had visited the offices of the Blue Funnel Line in the India Building on Water Street and had been signed up as a cabin boy on the SS Agamemnon. She was bound for Japan.

The wide-eyed cabin boy was dreaming of warm waters and flying fish and not much interested in the history of the ship, but the Agamemnon had been a significant ship in her day. Launched in 1866, at a time when steam ships were still struggling to compete with sail, the Agamemnon had been the first vessel to be fitted with engines that featured multiple expansion chambers. At the time the marine designers knew that they needed to increase the pressure of the steam in the engines if they were to get more power, but this was reckoned to be dangerous, as the sea water that was used tended to leave deposits in the boilers and clog the piping, which caused explosions.

Liverpool merchant Alfred Holt had been trained as a railway engineer and saw no reason why marine engines could not produce more power at a lower cost. In 1864 he convinced his brother Philip to sell their fleet of small steamers that had been doing a decent business between Liverpool and the West Indies and they invested the money in a new company which they called the Blue Funnel Line. They built a fleet of new steamers, designed for trading between Liverpool and China.

The problem was solved with the invention of a condenser which recycled fresh water. Thus the boiler pressures could increase significantly and the 2,280-ton Agamemnon was the first ship to be fitted with Holt's new engines. She quickly proved that steamships could travel faster and further than ever before. In 1869, for example, she carried 2,000 tons of tea from China in just 77 days, her coal consumption never exceeding 20 tons a day. That one cargo paid for more than half the cost of her construction. The Holt Brothers had known when they began building the Agamemnon that the Suez Canal would soon open and that this would cut 3,300 miles from the trip to China and reduce the voyage time by at least 10 days. They also knew that sailing ships would not be able to use the canal, as it was too narrow for them to manoeuvre and towing them through was too slow.

What they did not foresee was that the Suez Canal would increase the competition, notably from the Peninsular and Oriental (P&O) line, and as rival firms adopted the new steam technologies, the Blue Funnel fleet quickly lost its advantage. Newer ships were larger and faster and the Agamemnon was handicapped by the fact that Holt had included other innovations that did not work as well as the multiple expansion chambers. The major problem was that he reversed the positions of the rudder and the propeller and this made the Agamemnon rather difficult to manoeuvre.

By the time Kendall joined the ship, the Agamemnon had been steaming the oceans for 23 years and had been passed on to Anne Holt, the sister of Alfred and Philip, who was a successful businesswoman in her own right, a rare thing in Victorian times.

The ship sailed from Liverpool at the end of March with a cargo of the finest Manchester goods, bound for China and Japan. Kendall's desire for warmer weather was at first thwarted. The ship ran into storms in the Bay of Biscay, but as the Agamemnon steamed along the coast of Portugal the weather began to improve and Henry found himself in exactly the kind of conditions he had dreamed of seeing.

And then, rising up ahead of the ship, were The Pillars of Hercules, with the mighty Rock of Gibraltar to the north and the hill of Abyla above Ceuta, on the southern side of the straits, in Morocco. They steamed through into the Mediterranean and hugging the coast of Algeria, the Agamemnon continued east, bypassing Oran, to arrive in Algiers, where she paused to load coal.

If Kendall had been expecting to see camels wandering the streets he would have been disappointed for the city had a distinctly European feel to it, apart from the many mosques. Away from the port area was the ancient town, in which congregated a motley throng of Arabs, Moors, Jews and Europeans, but the crew was not allowed ashore and Kendall had to be content to watch from afar.

Departing Algiers, the Agamemnon headed for Tunis and Cape Bon, passing close to the rugged island of Pantelleria, an old volcano that rises from the sea in the middle of the Sicilian Strait. From there it was on to Malta and then across to the coast of Cyrenaica and the Nile Delta.

The Suez Canal began at Port Said. Dug by a French corporation, which was part-owned by Isma'il Pasha, the Ottoman khedive (governor) of Egypt, the canal had been opened for just 20 years, but was already recognized as having key strategic importance to the British. When Prime Minister Benjamin Disraeli took office in 1874 he discovered that the khedive was heavily in debt and was negotiating to sell his shares in the Suez company to the French government. Disraeli was appalled at the idea and moved quickly to borrow £4m - a vast sum at the time - from Baron Lionel de Rothschild, in order to buy the shares. Having done that he then faced the task of convincing parliament to agree to fund the purchase!

In the end Disraeli won the day and the khedive's financial problems were such that he soon had to accept Anglo-French control of his treasury and other important services. This led to a nationalistic backlash in Egypt, led by Urabi Pasha, and a revolt began in the summer of 1881. The British, who by then had William Gladstone as Prime Minister, decided to take advantage of the situation to protect their interests. A British fleet was sent to Egypt where it bombarded and then occupied the city of Alexandria. In September 1882 this force defeated Urabi's army at the Battle of Tel El-Kebir and thus Britain gained complete control of the Suez Canal, and a permanent military garrison in Egypt. Although nominally part of the Ottoman Empire, Egypt was effectively controlled by the British.

This created problems in Sudan, which had previously been ruled from Cairo, and Muhammad Ahmad, known as the Mahdi, gathered an army, started a revolt and drove out the British. Trouble would flare up again in 1898 when Horatio Kitchener was sent to reconquer the region, but when the Agamemnon steamed slowly through the canal, the area was at peace.

The Suez Canal passes through the desert to a series of lakes before reaching the Red Sea at Port Tewfik. It was already a very busy thoroughfare but, as not all ships were fitted with searchlights, most vessels stopped each evening to avoid the risk of collision. Without stops the journey would take 15 hours, but it usually took two days.

Once in the Red Sea the Agamemnon headed onward, bound for the coaling port on Perim Island in the Straits of Bab-el-Mandeb, known to the Arabs as "The Gate of Tears" because of the difficult waters in the straits. From there it was out into the Gulf of Aden and across the Arabian Sea towards Colombo, on the island of Ceylon, which had been a British crown colony for almost a century. From there the voyage then took them across the Bay of Bengal to the Straits of Malacca and Singapore, where there was cargo to be unloaded and coal to be loaded. There were also new passengers and then the Agamemnon put to sea again, bound for China.

Many of the passengers on this leg of the voyage were Chinese, returning to their homeland after working in the tin mines of the Straits Settlements, which were at the time the largest tin producers in the world. Some were ill and Kendall soon began to learn about the problems presented by deaths at sea.

"The ship was supplied with plenty of coffins," he recalled, "but as it was against Chinese customs to be buried at sea, we had to resort to embalming."

The route took them across the South China Sea to Hong Kong and they continued from there to Shanghai. The final leg of the voyage was across the East China Sea to Japan and the ship's final destination at Yokohama.

This was a very international city at the time and boasted an English language newspaper and a district called Kannai, where foreigners lived separated from the locals. Although there was cargo to be off-loaded and a new cargo and coal to be taken aboard, there was time for Kendall to marvel at this fantastic world before the Agamemnon began the long trip home, steaming across the Inland Sea from Kobe. At Nagasaki the ship was coaled by Japanese women. Young Henry discovered that the unmarried girls had white teeth while those who were married had their teeth lacquered black to make them unattractive to other men. While there he indulged in a little trading, swapping a pair of his trousers for three canaries, three bird cages and a tea set.

When they reached Hong Kong he witnessed yet another strange tradition. The ship was loaded with Chinese workers heading to the tin mines of the Straits Settlements. It was the custom that as soon as they were at sea the workers would be given an advance of their wages by the mining companies. This was paid in Chinese silver dollars. Immediately this had been done a number of the passengers would leap overboard and attempt to swim to the shore with their money - not all survived.

In Singapore the Agamemnon picked up passengers bound for Liverpool, including the captain of a coastal steamer who was going home on leave. He died before the ship reached Acheen Head, at the northern end of the Straits of Malacca, and Kendall took part in his first burial at sea.

The return journey followed the same route they had taken until they reached the English Channel where they were diverted to Ijmuiden in the Netherlands to unload cargo, before returning to Liverpool by way of Dover. They arrived in the Mersey on June 15, 1890. Kendall had seen tropical seas and flying fish and had not been disappointed with his trip but the captain had told the impressionable youngster that if he wanted to be "a real sailor" he must serve on sailing ships.

As they headed up the river all the church bells of Liverpool were ringing, Kendall decided that he was going to take a step back in time.

CHAPTER FOUR

Captain Turner Russell, the Marine Superintendant of the Blue Funnel Line, was nearly 60. He had served at sea for more than 20 years, winning the annual tea race from Foochow to Gravesend in the Achilles, at such a speed that Alfred Holt refused to believe the ship was in London, until the news was verified. Kendall sought an audience with Turner and the old sea dog saw potential in the cabin boy. He agreed to do what he could to find Henry a position on a sailing ship. It would have to be with a different company as the Holts did not have any sailing vessels in their fleet.

A few days later Kendall was called to see Turner and was informed that a position had been secured for him as an apprentice on a windjammer called the Iolanthe, which travelled to wherever cargos could be found, usually making very long voyages to remote destinations, as these were difficult for the steamships.

Russell explained that the ship had been laid up in the port of Middlesbrough for several months for repairs and suggested that Kendall use the time to visit his family in London. It was not until late July that Henry boarded a train at Euston Station, bound for Middlesbrough.

He was met on arrival by the son of Captain George Stanton.

"He was a young chap of about 14 who had been sent to show me the way to the ship," Kendall remembered. "Of course I asked him what kind of a fellow the skipper was and, in fact, put a thousand questions to him about the ship. He tried to answer them all. On our arrival at the ship my kit was heaved on board by the watchman, who quickly acquainted me with the fact that he would be delighted to drink my health. Needless to say it was not long before he was doing just that at the nearest pub with the tip I had given him."

Kendall's next duty was to report to Captain Stanton.

"Never will I forget those moments as I walked aft to do so," Kendall remembered. "He was walking up and down on the poop deck and had just finished his breakfast. He gazed at me - as only skippers can gaze. As I approached him I said that I had come to join the ship as an apprentice. 'Yes,' he said. 'I know. Now get all those brass buttons off your fine clothes and get into dungarees and get to work as soon as possible'. He appeared very gruff but I was fully resigned to my fate and took everything as a matter of course. I found out afterwards that the skipper was a red-hot Nova Scotian, we used to call them Blue Noses, and was notorious for hard work and discipline. He could swear for half an hour at a time without using the same word twice."

The Iolanthe was a classic windjammer, an iron-hulled sailing ship with three masts and square sails. These elegant vessels had dominated world trade in the middle of the century, but as the steamships became more competitive, the windjammers were forced on to routes on which coal and water were not readily available. There were no longer any regular routes for such ships. They travelled to wherever they were needed, mainly on runs to Australia and the western coast of the Americas. Crews were taken on for each individual voyage and were paid off quickly, in order to keep down the costs. Working on a windjammer was a life of much variety, with different ports, different routes and different shipmates. It was exactly what the curious Kendall wanted.

He soon learned that it was also a very tough life. The food was poor, there was much dangerous work to be done up in the rigging and, in addition, there were the pressures of learning to how to work with the other crew members. It was a hard school, but it meant that a sailor had to learn to get along with everyone else.

The Iolanthe was in Middlesbrough loading specially-manufactured steel rails and sleepers which were required to build a 94-mile railway between the remote northern Australian port of Normanton and the goldfield town of Croydon. The country was so barren that there were few trees for sleepers and frequent flooding would wash away the ballast. There were also termites which, the engineers believed, would eat away any wood. They decided it was impossible to use normal wooden sleepers and traditional gravel ballast so George Phillips designed hollow steel sleepers, the bases of which could be packed with earth. As a result floods would have no effect as the waters simply flowed over the rails, and there was little need for maintenance. An order for the Phillips Sleepers was placed in Middlesbrough, the centre of the world's iron and steel manufacturing at the time. Loading the Iolanthe with the sleepers took three weeks, during which time Kendall learned about the ship.

Captain Stanton then disappeared to Liverpool to recruit a crew. He wanted a black crew because it was cheaper and because he believed that black men were stronger and better at handling the ship in bad weather. This was a common belief at the time.

In those days a crew at sea was divided into two teams, known as watches. They were named Port and Starboard (left and right in nautical terms) and would take turns to man the helm, trim the sails, navigate and keep a look out. Captains were constantly looking for ways to make their ships more efficient, and Stanton believed that it was best to have the two watches in competition with one another and so picked his crews accordingly. One idea was for the two watches to be of different races with the Port watch consisting of black men and the Starboard team being made up of white men. This was known as a "checker board crew". Stanton, however, had a more refined idea. He wanted a black crew, but picked American blacks for one watch and West Indians for the other.

"They were a very fine class of men, but not very much in love with one another," Kendall recalled. "The First Mate was a German by birth, but had become a naturalized British subject. He was not a bad fellow. The Second Mate was a big raw-boned Shetland Islander and a brute from the word go. The Third Mate was the Captain's son and was very much following in his father's footsteps as regards being a hard case.

"I was the only apprentice - which was rather hard. The steward was a Tynesider and would not part with much and the cook was a happy-go-lucky chap you did not worry about much. The carpenter was a chronic growler, but they were certainly all good men in their own spheres."

Early one morning at the beginning of August, the Iolanthe was towed down the River Tees by a tug and set adrift in Tees Bay. Kendall was enthralled as the crew scaled the masts and unfurled the huge sails. The wind filled them and Henry felt the age-old sense of excitement as the ship began to edge forwards. He heard orders being barked from below and the sails were trimmed and a course set: north towards Scotland.

A steam ship heads to its destination by the most direct route, but a sailing ship goes with the winds. It might have been a shorter journey to go south to the English Channel, but Stanton knew it was best to get out into the Trade Winds in the Atlantic as quickly as possible.

"The sea was comparatively smooth," Kendall recalled. "As I gazed up aloft at the thousands of yards of canvas which were spread above me, I really felt that I had then begun my sea life. Gradually the evening stole upon us and the sun disappeared behind a bank of clouds. Many craft were passed during the night, mainly fishermen who were trawling in the vicinity of the Dogger Bank. Throughout my watch below I would listen to the tinkle of the ship's bells noting the hour through profound stillness, broken only be the gentle splash of the water against the iron sides of our vessel."

On a sailing ship life was dictated by the bell. Each day the two watches were on duty for three four-hour periods. The first began at midnight and continued until four o'clock, and so on throughout the day until four in the afternoon when the fifth period was split into two "dog watches" which were each two hours. This meant that both watches could eat dinner at a sensible time and would start the next 24-hour cycle on a different pattern to the previous day. This provided variety in what was otherwise a monotonous life. The ship's bell was rung every 30 minutes and in the course of each watch the number of bells increased until "eight bells" was reached, indicating the end of the four hour watch.

The other watch would then take over.

That first night Kendall was called on to the deck for the morning watch at four o'clock.

"It was glorious night," he remembered. "The moon was shining brightly at the time and rendered all effects at sea clear to view. I felt a great change coming over me for the glorious sea air was working on me. My appetite was increasing, though our rations were scant, and I managed to enjoy a good biscuit."

The diet on a sailing ship was basic. Crews were usually healthy, but they were always hungry. Each sailor had a pound of hard biscuit each day, with salt beef one evening and salt port the next. Every week each man was given 14 ounces of brown sugar, seven ounces of butter and seven ounces of marmalade. On Sunday, Tuesday and Thursday they were each issued with a half pound loaf of bread, which was considered a great luxury. Each day they were allowed four quarts of water. This was to be used for tea, coffee, pea soup or simply to be drunk.

They washed in salt water.

Because they had limited access to fruits or vegetables the sailors were required by law to drink lime juice every day, in order to prevent suffering from a lack of Vitamin C, also known as scurvy, a condition which could be fatal. It was this tradition that caused Americans to refer to British sailors (and indeed the nation as a whole) as "Limeys".

During each watch the sailors spent much of the time up in the rigging, doing a variety of different jobs. When they were off duty they slept, read (if indeed they could read), played dice or cards, carved, drew, practiced tying knots or made ropes by spinning threads of cotton yarn. While doing this they often told one another stories and thus was born the expression "spinning a yarn" for story-telling. There was also much singing. Sea shanties were work songs, the rhythm of the music being used to synchronize movements and to lighten the burden. Often the sailors used "call and response" songs, with a shantyman singing one line and a chorus of sailors singing the response.

They lived in cramped conditions, slept in hammocks and in heavy weather had to work in clothing that was constantly wet. In such difficult conditions there was much camaraderie, but problems also developed that blew out of proportion, particularly during longer voyages. Captains, however, were unwilling to allow the crews ashore for fear that they would not return to the ship.

For the young Kendall, the early days were just as he had imagined. They headed north to the Pentland Firth, the stretch of water that separates the Orkney Islands from the northern tip of the Scottish mainland at John O'Groats. They picked up the Trade Winds without too much difficulty and then changed the sails, bringing down the heavy sheets which was used in the windier latitudes and replacing then with older sails to avoid the heavy ones being worn out as they rubbed on the masts as the ship ran in and out of calm patches. A good voyage to the Equator was around 21 days, but that depended on what happened in the Doldrums, the area near the Equator where the winds tended to be light.

It took the Iolanthe 30 days before she "crossed the line". This event was cause for a double celebration. The tradition was that those who had not crossed the Equator before had to pay tribute to Father Neptune, the god of the sea; and it was a month after they had sailed from Middlesbrough, which meant that the sailors were once again earning money. The custom at the time was for the crew to receive their first month's pay in advance. This was spent before they boarded the ship and so for the first month they earned nothing. The end of this period involved a ceremony called "burying the dead horse".

The first ceremony involved those who had not crossed the line having their heads shaved and being dipped in a canvas bath filled with sea water.

"Most of the crew did not seem to care whether they had crossed the line before or not," Kendall remembered. "They all had a go as part of the day's fun."

The second celebration involved the effigy of a horse being hoisted to the yardarm with a sailor on its back. A shanty would be sung, there would be three cheers for the captain and for the sailor on the horse. The line holding the horse would then be cut and the effigy would drop into the sea while the rider, attached by a separate rope, would be lowered to the deck as the crew sang "Blow the man down", a favourite sea shanty. The captain then called the crew aft and issued them each with a tot of rum.

They picked up the Southern Trade Winds soon afterwards

and ran down the western part of the South Atlantic until they were in the vicinity of the lonely islands of Tristan da Cunha, 37-degrees to the south of the Equator. Stanton then turned the ship to the south-east and they edged southward into the Roaring Forties, where strong currents and blustery winds would whisk them to the south of the Cape of Good Hope and out into the Indian Ocean. The further south they went the quicker the passage would be, but most ships stayed on the northern edge of the 40th parallel, in order to reduce the risk of running into ice floes and bergs.

They passed the Cape of Good Hope on their 74th day at sea, and headed out into the loneliest shipping lanes in the world.

CHAPTER FIVE

In the southern Indian Ocean there are few islands. This is because the sea floor is to be found on average more than 12,500 feet below the surface. In places it descends to 24,000 feet. Beneath the waves, in the freezing darkness of the ocean, great mountain ranges rise up, but such is the depth of the water that only a handful of the peaks reach the surface. These remote outcrops of land are usually underwater volcanoes, rising from a fault in the surface of the earth where two of the earth's plates collide. The two most significant islands are Amsterdam and St Paul. They lie 1,800 miles from the nearest land, close to the 38th parallel, and are the top of an unseen ridge beneath the waves. They are inhospitable places and their jagged rocks have caught many a ship unawares in the night. The survivors of such wrecks, if there were any, would be washed up on a savage shoreline and forced to survive by whatever means they could, hoping that someone would eventually come to their rescue. Many ships passed, but very few stopped. The one value of these dangerous islands was that, in the days before modern navigational techniques, they served to confirm that a ship was on its correct course.

The Iolanthe first spotted the imposing Amsterdam Island, which is just a few miles across but rises in places to nearly 3,000 feet above the sea. Landing there was not an option as there are steep cliffs on all sides. In the centre of the island is a plateau where explorers found an abundance of wood. Attempts had been made to settle the island at various times, but each had been abandoned, although in the 1870s a group of settlers had left sheep and cows behind and they had survived, living wild. The islands had supported important colonies of seals, but by the time the Iolanthe arrived hunters had killed so many that the species was almost extinct. The islands were thus considered useless and for 40 years no nation had even bothered to claim them. The French would do so just a few months after the Iolanthe's visit.

The ship pressed on another 50 miles until St Paul Island came into view. This, too, boasts steep cliffs, rising in places to 600 feet above the sea. It has several dramatic offshore stacks, but careful navigation enabled a ship to reach a small circular bay on the eastern side of the island. This was the crater of an old volcano that had been flooded by the sea, and was protected from the predominant westerly winds. The result was a steep-sided lagoon. Entrance from the sea had been blocked by sand bars that had formed across the bay, but ships were still able to drop anchor on the leeward side of the island and send boats to the beach. Twenty years earlier an iron-hulled ship called the HMS Meagara had foundered on the reef at the entrance and for two months 400 men had lived on the island. They had built a number of very basic stone huts on a small area of flat land, close to the entrance. As there was nowhere for the crew to escape to, Captain Stanton decided that it would do no harm to stop for a while to give men a chance to get off the ship and to put their feet on dry land for a few hours. The other sailors told Kendall wild stories of how the island had once been used by pirates and that, no doubt, there was treasure to be found in its caves. The only treasure that Kendall could find was a multitude of fish and spiny lobsters trapped in the lagoon.

This adventure was one that delighted the sailors, for St Paul is one of the few places in the world where one can catch a fish and, without removing it from the line, drop it immediately into a thermal spring that lies next to the lagoon. For an uncomplicated lad from Liverpool, this was a memorable experience.

"The fish were excellent and abundant," said Kendall. "The glittering St Paul rock cod, weighing six to eight pounds, was much welcomed as the ship's menu had become inordinately monotonous. And there was no little pleasure in the catching and the cooking of these fish."

For a few hours the crew explored the island, but then it was time to return to the ship and they set sail once again, heading east towards Australia. The wind blew strongly, sometimes with hurricane force, accompanied by hail, sleet and even snow squalls. These continued until Stanton decided it was time to edge further to the north in order to reach Australia's lonely North West Cape. They arrived off the cape on their 95th day out of Middlesbrough and there was finally an opportunity to dry their clothes as the ship sailed into sunnier waters. But as the weather improved the winds dropped and they found themselves stuck in the doldrums.

"For days on end we lay without even a breath of wind," Kendall remembered. "The heat was intense and the sharks numerous. There were so many that one could not count them."

For the next 60 days the Iolanthe crawled up the deserted northern coast of Australia. There were endless beaches but Stanton warned the crew that this was inhospitable country and the chances were that they would be speared by the aborigines, who were still attacking white men on a regular basis, or that they would fall prey to sharks or crocodiles. This greatly reduced their urge to swim or to go ashore to see what the land had to offer. The Iolanthe had been at sea for five months, apart from the one day on St Paul Island, and there was much tension. Everyone, from the captain downwards, was unhappy. There began to be problems amongst the ship mates, who were sick of the sight of each other. There were arguments and even fights. Stanton's idea of competing watches was beginning to backfire on him.

On the 140th day of the voyage Kendall was sitting reading by the main hatch. It was a Sunday and he was explaining parts of the story to a West Indian seaman called Louis, who came from the island of Martinique. Another West Indian by the name of Allyce approached and joined in, asking about the book and taking a look at it. For reasons that Kendall did not understand this caused an American black called Smith to join the group. He has been sitting nearby, whittling with a knife and making a model of a ship.

"Smith came around to Allyce and asked why he was speaking to me," Kendall remembered. "He said: 'You have been getting on to me for speaking to the boy and you are doing it yourself'. Allyce did not say anything. He put the book down and punched Smith in the eye. There was a scuffle between the two men and I got up to get out of the way. Little scrummages on board the ship were common enough and I did not think anything of this until I realized that Smith had stabbed Allyce with his knife. I saw the blood.

"Without a moment's hesitation, Smith turned to us and came at Louis and me with his knife. I can never explain why he did this but I do know that I never ran so hard in my life."

Fortunately other sailors raised the alarm and all hands were called on deck. Allyce was carried to the Captain's quarters to receive whatever medical aid Stanton could provide. There was no ship's doctor and Allyce had three stab wounds in his chest, one just below the heart. His life was hanging in the balance.

Captain Stanton questioned Smith about the fight and he explained that Allyce had hit him first. When the captain asked Kendall and Louis if this had been the case, they told the truth and Stanton decided to leave Smith at liberty. This was a dangerous development for the only two witnesses to the fight.

"We soon heard that he had sworn to fix us before reaching port," Kendall said. "We told the captain this, but it made no impression on him. He simply gave orders that we were never to go up aloft with Smith, in case he tried to knock us down."

Soon afterwards the winds suddenly came up and the ship sailed finally into the Gulf of Carpentaria. They arrived at their anchorage at midnight on the 166th day of the voyage. They were three miles out from the lightship and 12 miles from the mouth of the Norman River.

"The sails were cleared up and all hands were sent aloft to make them fast, Louis and I being careful not to go up the same mast as our friend Smith," Kendall remembered. "We had just finished making fast the topsails and were moving out to fasten the yard arm section when Louis made an awful gurgling sound. He was about to fall so we grabbed him and held him there, one hundred feet above the deck."

Louis was unconscious. Kendall and Stanton Jr carefully moved him towards to the mast and, by cutting down some rope, were able to secure it around the West Indian and he was lowered to the deck below where Captain Stanton treated him.

"My pal was then stretched out on the deck and a mirror was used to see if he was breathing," Kendall said. "He was dead. Imagine my feelings! Here was I, the only witness left. The villain had seen one go and I wondered if by fair or foul means whether I would be next."

Morning came and the low Australian coastline was visible in the distance, although it was impossible to take the ship any nearer because of the shallow water. They had to wait for a tender that came out down once a week from Normanton. She had been down the day before they arrived so they knew they would have to wait another six days.

"At nine o'clock that morning Louis's corpse was sewn up in canvas and weighed down with a bag of coal," Kendall recalled. "It was impossible to keep the body in the tropical heat for six days so poor Louis would have to make do with a sailor's grave. Ten o'clock struck and an impressive scene began. Louis was carried along by his shipmates on a hatch grating. A brief service took place while I tolled the ship's bell, then the body was committed to five fathoms of water. The Skipper entered Louis's death in the official log book as being due to heart disease. But everyone began to wonder whether Louis had been poisoned by Smith. A healthy 30-year-old rarely drops dead from heart disease.

But dead men, of course, tell no tales.

All that day the crew was hard at work knocking down the wooden supports that had been built to keep the cargo from shifting during the voyage.

"At 6pm the crew stopped work and at about 8.30pm I turned into my bunk," Kendall remembered. "I slept in a small compartment on the forward deck and after what had happened I made it a practice of locking my door. About 10.30pm I was awakened by some person quietly trying to unlock my door with a skeleton key. I quietly jumped up and gazing through my porthole which was close to the door, I observed the murderous villain. He was trying to get in to fix me. I let out a yell and asked who was there and the alarm scared him and he cleared away into the darkness to his berth."

It was a stormy night.

"We had both anchors down," Kendall said," but the seas were sweeping clean over the ship. About one in the morning all hands were called, the cargo had shifted and the steel rails were playing havoc down in the hold. As I came out of my room I had to take every precaution to get safely aft. As I held on to the rail, watching for my opportunity, the moon broke through the clouds for an instant and I saw the murderous Smith behind the main mast, waiting for me. I did not know what to do, but as I hesitated a huge wave broke over the ship and swept me aft where I was picked up by the Third Mate. I told him what I had seen and how the villain had tried to pick my lock."

Towards daylight the wind died down and the sea returned to normal. The Iolanthe had lost one of its anchors and 500 feet of chain, but the second anchor had held firm. The lightship had broken adrift and had been swept into the mangrove swamps along the shoreline and had been wrecked.

Captain Stanton placed Smith under surveillance for the next few days and finally the river steamer came out from Normanton. She brought fruit that was eagerly devoured by the crew. Smith and Allyce were then taken aboard and the captain went with them up the Norman River to Normanton. Smith was put in jail and Allyce taken to the hospital. The next morning Smith was remanded in custody for a week, pending the arrival of the witness.

"It was a happy day when the tender came down and I had to go to town," Kendall recalled. "I had been caged up on the ship for nearly six months. No-one but a sailor can imagine that feeling. No wonder they say that a sailor ashore is a sailor on a spree!"

The Norman River reaches the Gulf of Carpentaria about 25 miles from the town of Normanton, as the crow flies. But the river is running slowly through the wetlands close to the sea and curls backwards and forwards on itself, which means that the boat journey from the mouth of the river to town is actually around 70 miles. The river is fringed with mangrove for much of its route but behind this are extensive salt flats and wetlands. This is alive with dangerous wildlife, not least the giant salt water crocodiles that can grow to more than 20 feet in length and can weigh up to 1,700 pounds. These fearsome predators are capable of killing monkeys, kangaroos, wild boar, small water buffalo and, of course, human beings. They have incredibly powerful jaws and are surprisingly fast given their size and weight. They wait for their prey in the shallows at water's edge and drag their victims into the river.

It was evening by the time Kendall arrived in Normanton and was put into the same hotel as Captain Stanton. The following day he made a statement to the police and it was decided that Smith would go to trial when the court was next in session. This was not due to happen until the middle of April. There was to be more waiting and so Stanton and Kendall returned to the ship and the process of unloading the railway lines continued.

The judge eventually arrived by steamer and the tender that was taking him to Normanton called at the Iolanthe to pick up the Captain and Kendall and they all made the trip up the Norman River. Justice Charles Chubb and his officials had a busy schedule ahead of them. The grandly-named Supreme Courthouse was, according to Kendall, "more like a cowshed than anything else" but court could hold about 100 people and when the court was in session people from the neighbouring areas came to town and Normanton was very lively all week.

Justice Chubb was an Englishman, born in London in 1845. His father was a solicitor but decided to emigrate with the family when Charles was 16. Once in Australia, Chubb followed his father into the legal profession and rose quickly through the ranks. He was a member of the Queensland state parliament, then the state attorney-general and a Queen's Counsel by the time he was 48. At the end of 1889 he retired from politics and was posted to Townsville as the head of the northern district of the Supreme Court of Queensland. As Kendall would find out, he had a love for Latin quotations, but found this of little use in the rough and ready courthouses in Australia's wild north.

The first case that day was to consider an attack that had been made on the local police constable. It was followed by a case against a man who had been accused of "carnally knowing" a girl aged 10 and leaving her with "a nameless disease".

The third case was to consider Smith's attack on Allyce. This had become rather more sensational when it emerged that Allyce had died of his injuries. Young Kendall was called before the court and told his story but even the youngster was less than impressed by the members of the jury.

"They were the scrapings of the place," he said later. "If the truth be told I should think they had committed worse crimes than any of the prisoners."

Once the evidence had been presented the jury retired, probably to the local bar, and returned not long afterwards with the decision to acquit all of those accused.

It was a shock for Kendall, who had expected more from the justice system.

"One of the jury told me after the case was over that they never liked to see any of the boys go to prison," Kendall recalled. "Normanton had a pretty clean record and with jurymen like that it was not really a surprise."

As Henry waited outside the courthouse for Captain Stanton to give him orders, Smith emerged and, with a less than pleasant look on his face, approached Kendall and whispered that the boy had better watch out - he would kill him at the first opportunity.

CHAPTER SIX

Kendall was frightened, but Captain Stanton offered no consolation. He told Henry that he could do as he pleased until the early evening, when he should be at Normanton wharf to catch the tender back to the Iolanthe. Smith was somewhere in the town and would probably find some drink in the course of the day. He had killed Allyce and, Kendall believed, had used some kind of poison to murder Louis. The idea of returning to sea on a ship with a man who was intent on murdering him was terrifying. If he returned to the ship there was no guarantee that Captain Stanton would do anything to help. The captain had avoided trouble by burying Louis's body as quickly as possible and Kendall did not want to follow his friend to a watery grave.

The alternative was desertion, but for a lad of just 17 that was a desperate remedy. If he ran away he would become a fugitive and might never be able to return to England. If he was caught he knew that he would face imprisonment. There were no guarantees that he would ever be able to return to his old life, which was all that he wanted to do.

When Henry looked at the options it was clear to him that the choice was between life and death. If he ran away his life would be different, but the risks were fewer and there was always the possibility that he might one day explain what had happened and return to his chosen profession. The more he thought about it, the more it was clear that running away was his only choice. He concluded that it would be better to leave as soon as possible so that if there were any searches when he failed to turn up at the wharf in the evening, he would not be found in the town. The Iolanthe would remain off the coast for some time, unloading the railway lines and sleepers, and so he knew he had to leave Normanton.

"I decided that I would clear out and made tracks into the bush," Kendall recalled. "Croydon was the only place I had heard of and so I determined to get there at all costs."

He had no idea of what to expect on his route, but he knew that the railway that was being built was going to Croydon and so he would be heading in the right direction if he followed the tracks south out of Normanton. He did not know how far the railway went, but reckoned that when the rails stopped, the chances were that the ground had been cleared in preparation for the arrival of the new sleepers. If the railway stopped in the middle of nowhere he would decide what to do when he got there.

The advantage of following a railway line is that trains can only climb very gentle slopes and so Henry knew that the route would be easy and that there would be bridges on which he could cross the rivers.

Normanton was built on an ironstone ridge, the first high ground inland from the coast. To the south lay vast plains of flat, dusty, savannah grassland. There were occasional small trees. These dry prairies stretched from the Great Dividing Range in the east to the Northern Territory in the west and continued south until the vegetation petered out in the deserts of central Australia. The region was drained by a number of slow-flowing wide rivers, which spread out into separate channels with small islands or sand bars between them. Now and then, where there was no water, there were arid tracts of dusty desert. There were a few isolated hills, but almost no settlers as even prospectors and sheep farmers struggled to make a living in such unforgiving country.

Kendall set off immediately and ran for several miles before deciding that it was best to conserve his energy in the heat of the afternoon. Initially the railway lines kept to the lower ground, skirting around the hills to the south of Normanton and staying close to the Norman River. Then the dusty tracks that ran beside the rails headed off to remote sheep stations and only the railway remained, branching off to the east into drier country. There were occasional ponds and waterholes and a number of streams to be crossed but, to begin with, these presented no problems. Fresh water was readily available, but food was scarce, although Kendall soon found that there was a plum-like fruit growing wild on some of the trees which he discovered later was known as the wangai. Towards the evening, as the light faded, Kendall was miles out into the bush. The alarm was raised in Normanton when Captain Stanton, Smith and the other passengers gathered that evening to board the Dugong, but Kendall was nowhere to be found.

When it was dark and too dangerous to go on moving, Henry climbed a small tree and finding a suitable place to sleep was able to doze, hoping that any predators below would not be able to find him. In the morning he continued on his path, hoping that no-one was out looking for him.

The railway which Kendall was following was originally intended to go due south to the copper mines at Cloncurry, where it would link up with the Great Northern Railway that had been planned from Townsville, 500 miles to the east. In November 1885, however, that plan was changed when a major gold strike was reported on a cattle station called Croydon Downs, about 100 miles to the south-east of Normanton. Three months later the area was declared a goldfield by the Queensland Mines Department. Prospectors began to flock to the region and within a matter of months there were more than 100 mines in operation. In the course of 1887 the population of Croydon jumped from 2,000 to 7,000. At that moment the gold seams looked as though they would go on forever and the decision was taken to divert the railway. By the spring of 1891 more than half of the route had been completed.

What Kendall did not know was that there were serious floods in his path. The region had suffered a bad drought in the late 1880s but in January 1890 rain had returned with a vengeance. Almost four feet of rainfall had been recorded in the four months that followed. The majority of the rivers drain northwards into the Gulf of Carpentaria but these had overflowed in many places. There was further heavy rain early in 1891 and Kendall found several places where the railway lines simply disappeared into lakes of standing water. In total more than 12 miles of the railway was underwater, to a depth of between six and 16ft. Trains were running as far as the flooded area but then passengers and goods had to be ferried across the floods by boat. When he reached such points Henry skirted the waters until the rails re-emerged again.

"It was almost an unexplored country," he remembered. "It had bewildering bush and trackless deserts, sudden floods and devastating droughts. I had heard of squatters hacked to death in the night by the aborigines, whole families wiped out in a single night, although women as well as men were ever ready for these treacherous attacks. All of this came to me on my journey, but I really had no choice but to go on."

On occasion he stopped and cooled himself down in a lake, but he was worried too about the crocodiles he had heard about when he visited Normanton. Eventually the railway stopped but, as he had hoped, the path beyond that had been cleared in preparation for the arrival of the new rails and Phillips Sleepers that were aboard the Iolanthe. He was confident that he would eventually arrive in Croydon. There were around 30 miles with no rails but after travelling for three days and two nights, Kendall began to see the first tent communities, which had sprung up near the mines that surrounded Croydon. He was greeted with curiosity by the miners, but they fed him and put him to work.

"There were no difficulties finding work," he said. "Nor any lack of kindness. If you could not work there were plenty of friends to see that you did not run short of food."

Gold rushes the world over have tended to attract single men of many nations, all desperate to get rich quick. The absence of womenfolk meant that their society had few refinements, bad language was the norm and fighting common. A percentage of the diggers were runaways or felons and so a goldfield was a relatively lawless place. At the same time the population was willing to accept anyone who turned up without too many questions being asked.

Kendall discovered that there were a series of tented villages around the town. These had evocative names such as Golden Gate, Tabletop, Gorge Creek, Golden Valley and Homeward Bound. There was a big Chinese community, not only digging for gold but also providing services for the miners. The diggers worked hard and played hard. Every Saturday a stage coach, run by Cobb & Co, would arrive in Croydon from Granite Creek, with all the latest news from the East Coast. Hundreds of miners would head into town to see if there was any mail - and to let off steam. They liked to drink, dance and watch music hall acts. There was much alcohol. Croydon was a den of iniquity.

As there was little timber in the region, the buildings were constructed from corrugated iron. Despite this Croydon boasted a hundred or more places where one could buy liquor and around 20 hotels, some more respectable than others. There were seven stores, five banks and two newspaper offices, one publishing The Golden Age, the other The Mining Times.

There were also a few women, "recently arrived from Paris", who had turned up in Croydon, attracted by the lure of the gold and the demand of hundreds of lonely men. Officially they were dancers and actresses but when the sun went down they plied a different trade.

It was all new and very exciting to Henry Kendall. After trying his hand at mining he quickly concluded that it would not make him a fortune, so he did other jobs that provided the miners with the things they needed, remembering the old adage that if you want to make money in a gold rush, the best way to do it is to sell picks and shovels. Being a clean-living young man, he did not spend much, for there was little he wanted to buy.

In the course of the weeks that followed Henry met a fascinating selection of people from all over the world. These included several runaways like himself, although they had come mainly from ships on the East Coast and had travelled the 250 miles to the goldfields in the hope of striking it rich. One, who claimed to be the son of an English bishop, had jumped ship in Cooktown six months earlier. He was 20 and the young Kendall, still only just 17, found himself with a suitable companion. The pair then hooked up with an Irishman in his early twenties and, tiring of the life in Croydon, the trio decided to "go walkabout", to see what life would throw at them and to make their way east, through the endless grasslands towards the Great Dividing Range and the Atherton Tablelands. From there it was just a short trip, through pleasant countryside, to the port of Cairns on the Pacific Ocean. Kendall hoped to find a ship which could take him home to England so he could begin his career again.

His two companions told him that travelling to Queensland was relatively easy, but they had not considered the effect of the flooding and they quickly found that large areas were still underwater. On the second day out from Croydon the land rose before them and they crossed the watershed into the basin of the Gilbert River. Later that day they chanced upon a sheep station beside the road.

"We asked for food and rest for the night," Kendall recalled. "This was never refused by an Australian. The farmer had a very fine house with two or three outhouses close by, mostly for the shearers who came during the sheep-shearing season. We were told to go to one of these houses and that the servants would bring us food. Two fine girls appeared with a splendid supper and we certainly enjoyed their company. My pal the Irishman seemed rather unwell, but he did his best to entertain the girls and later, when they had gone back to the house, confessed that he was madly in love with one of them, who also came from Ireland.

"When morning came I found my Irish friend was delirious with swamp fever. He remained that way for days. The Irish girl stood by him night and day. I think she had been smitten also. It was over three weeks before he finally began to recover and during that time I was kept working around the place."

As the Irishman became more aware of his surroundings he and the Irish girl began to talk and, inevitably, the conversation turned to their homeland as they began to compare notes about their lives.

"Suddenly she fainted away," Kendall remembered. "She was brought round with water and we asked her what was wrong. She said that she had discovered that her patient was none other than her own brother, whom she had not seen for eight years. She had left Ireland as a girl of 10 with one of her aunts and had sailed on the British India Company's steamer Quetta. She spent six years in Brisbane with her aunt, and then decided to go her own way, and had arrived at the farm a year earlier. The Irishman had not been home for six years and although he knew that he had a sister in Australia, he did not know

Kendall reckoned that his desire to become a sailor was the result of Sunday walks in the Liverpool docks (above), when he was about 11 years of age. He recalled the exotic smells from the goods that had been unloaded. He learned the arts of seafaring on the school ship Indefatigable, an old war ship which he joined when he was 13. She was moored off Rock Ferry in the River Mersey (right). Two years later he went to sea as a cabin boy on the Inman & International Line's City of Berlin (below), sailing between Liverpool and New York.

When he was 16 Kendall sailed to Australia as a member of the crew of the Iolanthe, delivering railway sleepers to the remote town of Normanton, in the Gulf of Carpentaria. Having witnessed a murder, he jumped ship, afraid that he too would be killed. He ended up in Port Kennedy (above), on Thursday Island, working in the pearl industry. Pearl divers worked from small boats, with air pumped manually to them through hoses. The pumping was done by the other crew members (left). The divers collected pearl shells which were then hauled to the surface and cleaned by their workmates, who searched each shell for the rare pearls (below).

Kendall made money in the pearl industry and was asked to finance the return to Europe of a Norwegian barque, called the Rollo (above). The ship's captain had run out of money and needed funding. Henry worked as a crewman during the voyage home. This was eventful, with the Rollo rounding Cape Horn with only one mast intact. Kendall went on to serve on the windjammer Liverpool, racing back from India to Dundee once a year with a cargo of jute from Calcutta (below). The windjammers were the last serious competition for steam ships.

Henry switched between steam and sailing ships on several occasions early in his career. After his adventures on the windjammers, he turned to an African coastal steamer called the SS Bathurst (above). She became involved in the Ashanti Campaign in 1895, when the British Government needed troopships to carry an army to subdue King Prempeh. The soldiers landed at Cape Coast Castle (left) and marched inland to the Ashanti capital of Kumasi. Kendall then switched back to sailing ships and served on the Mashona (below), a 2,300-ton four-masted barque which took him to San Francisco, in 1896, just as the Yukon Gold Rush began.

Henry married Minnie Wright Jones (top left) in June 1896. They had four children, although their first born, a boy called Evelyn, died as an infant, when Henry was away at sea aboard the Ditton (top right) on a voyage to San Francisco and Portland In 1900 Kendall was an officer on the SS Lusitania (above), which was a much smaller ship than the more famous liner that followed. The ship ran on to the rocks on the Avalon Peninsula in Newfoundland (right) but the crew managed to get everyone ashore without any casualties.

The steamers of the era required large amounts of coal, which meant that they could only operate in range of ports with access to mines. This held back the development of steam ships until more efficient engines were invented. In far-flung ports facilities were poor and coal was delivered in baskets, which made loading difficult.

where she was and had never thought of meeting her."

This extraordinary coincidence convinced the Irishman to stay on the farm with his sister and the farmer was happy to offer him a permanent job. Kendall and the bishop's son decided that they wanted to move on and set off again, heading east towards the Gilbert River. It was by then well into the dry season, the heat was intense and the road dusty. When they reached the river their hearts sank. There was still extensive flooding and the water was too deep and too fast-flowing to wade through. In addition the rivers were filled with debris and dirt. Any attempt to cross would be foolish.

There was little to eat and it made no sense to stay and wait for the floods to subside. Even if they did get across the Gilbert River they had no idea what to expect in the unknown territory beyond. There were, the bishop's son said, a number of settlements on the way but these were a long way apart and there were other rivers to cross. And that was all before the Great Dividing Range.

The option was to go back to Croydon and from there go to Normanton and try to make it to the east coast by stowing away on a ship. By doing that they would at least know what to expect. Kendall knew that the monthly steamer arrived at the mouth of the Norman River on a certain date and was met by one of the Normanton tenders. There was an exchange of passengers, goods and mail. This took place in the early morning and often began in darkness. He also knew that the tender would depart from the Normanton wharf in the evening, so there was a good chance that they might be able to slip aboard under cover of darkness. The wharf was clear of the town and there were no houses nearby and so they could hide without too much difficulty.

He had also travelled the country between Croydon and Normanton and knew what to expect. If they had waited another month or two they might have been able to ride the train from the goldfields to the coast. As the floods went down the work began again and the last 27 miles of track was laid in just 11 weeks, using the rails that had arrived aboard the Iolanthe. The railway would open in the middle of July 1891. The bishop's son decided when they reached Croydon that he would be happier staying there and so Kendall was alone once again as he made the trip back to Normanton. He skirted the town and hid near the wharf until the evening that the tender was due to depart.

"I did not want to be seen as I thought that my Captain, if he was still in town, would hear about it and I would be seized and taken back to the ship," Kendall said, "So I sneaked onboard and made myself scarce."

The Dugong slipped quietly down the river in the darkness and arrived alongside the mail boat at four o'clock the next morning.

"I managed to get on board the steamer and found a place to hide while everything was bustling with the passengers and goods being exchanged," Kendall remembered. "The two ships then parted and away we went and I could see my old sailing ship lying at anchor not far away with her lights burning. Every minute was widening the distance between us and lowering the risk that I would be caught. When her light finally dipped below the horizon I felt a huge wave of relief."

By dawn they had left the Iolanthe far behind and Kendall decided that it was time to declare his presence to the captain of the steamer, which he had discovered was called the Yaralla. She was a 480-ton two-master that was operated by the Australasian United Steam Navigation Company, and plied her trade around the coast of Queensland.

Emerging from his hiding place, he walked calmly along the deck until he reached the wheelhouse. The Chief Officer recognized him immediately, as they had made a trip together from the Iolanthe to Normanton with Judge Charles Chubb. Kendall explained his situation and the old sailor commiserated. He said that it would be up to the captain to decide what to do with the stowaway. It was a nervous wait of four hours before Kendall was granted an audience with Captain Ussher.

Kendall saluted and told Ussher the whole story. Ussher visited Normanton once a month with the steamer and so was already well aware of Kendall's disappearance after the trial.

"He asked me my intention and I told him that I would be satisfied if he could land me anywhere on the east coast of Australia. I would look after myself," Kendall said. "But he replied that this was not possible. He could not take me past his first port of call without being open to the charge of harbouring a deserter. He said that he would land me on Thursday Island in the Torres Strait group of islands. Although I implored him to take me further he said he could not, because he would be in trouble if Captain Stanton ever heard about it."

As it turned out the Iolanthe would remain in Normanton until October before setting sail bound for the port of Newcastle in New South Wales, a cargo of coal having been secured that the Iolanthe would take to Taltal in Chile. She would take 75 days to sail from Normanton to Newcastle, passing around the west coast of Australia. The journey was so lengthy that the ship was even reported missing. She would not begin the voyage home until February 1892.

Captain Ussher was kind enough to allow Kendall to travel as a Second Class passenger at no cost but he had to do his duty. In the days that followed Henry related his tale to some of the other passengers on the Yaralla and one even offered to pay his fare to the east coast, but Ussher would not be moved.

Kendall would be landed on Thursday Island.

CHAPTER SEVEN

It was at about six in the morning when Henry Kendall heard the lookout of the Yaralla cry out: "Land Ahoy" when he sighted the first of the islands in the Torres Strait two days later. Normally such a shout would bring a moment of joy, but Kendall was filled with a sense of dread.

"I thought of the famous picture of Napoleon standing on the deck of the British ship as he was being taken into exile and caught his first glimpse of St Helena," he remembered. "I reckoned he was no worse off than I was."

Despite his fears, Kendall was happy to be away from the Iolanthe and more than a little curious to see the islands on which he was going to be marooned and he watched intently as the ship approached. The first was Crab Island, lying close to the mainland on the starboard side. Away to port was Woody Wallis Island, covered with small trees and partly obscuring Red Wallis Island behind it. Already these had been dwarfed by the sight of the much larger Prince of Wales Island, on the port side, which was separated from the mainland by a narrow channel called the Endeavour Strait, after the ship in which Captain James Cook had explored the islands in 1770. Other Europeans had been there long before Cook, with Luis de Torres reckoned to have been the first to sail through the islands in 1606.

At around the same time a Dutch ship called the Duyfken, under the command of Captain Willem Janszoon, had sailed south from New Guinea and sighted land on the western coast of the Cape

York Peninsula, in the Gulf of Carpentaria. The crew believed that this was a southern extension of New Guinea and although the Duyfken sailed into the Torres Strait, the appearance of so many islands seemed to convince them that there was no way through. That was probably not surprising given the dangers. The Endeavour Strait was dotted with small islands and rocky outcrops which were extremely hazardous for ships, particularly as there were also strong currents. Even if one did survive a shipwreck there were other dangers in the waters: sharks out at sea and in the shallows saltwater crocodiles. If one reached land it was entirely possible that the natives would attack. A number of shipwrecked seamen had been murdered in this way, notably 28 men aboard the schooner Sperweer which was found aground on Prince of Wales Island in 1869. That same year a pearler called the Catherine Seymour was reported to have been attacked by natives, and a total of 22 people were killed with spears. Others were taken prisoner. There had been violent punitive raids as a response, but only three years before Kendall arrived a lugger called the Tam-O-Shanter had disappeared without trace. There was a strong suspicion that the crew had fallen into the hands of cannibals living on the islands, who had sunk the boat and eaten the sailors.

The Yaralla edged towards the Endeavour Strait, staying well clear of shallow waters on the port side. She then rounded Entrance Island and headed for a gap called Boat Channel between Prince of Wales Island and Horn Island. There were small islands and rocks to be avoided but gradually the ship edged towards a low island ahead of them where there was a jetty jutting out into the bay. There were two floating hulks which were used as mooring points. The Yaralla tied up alongside an old Dutch ship called the Baron Sloeth Van de Beale. The unloading process began.

"I was beginning to think that Captain Ussher had forgotten me," Kendall remembered, "but about five minutes before the Yaralla was ready to sail, he sent for me, wished me all kinds of good fortune, and added that he had written to the ship's agent on the island, asking him to do what he could. Standing on that old hulk, I watched the mail steamer cast off and begin her southern course. The world seemed full of loneliness and uncertainty."

The island, he was told, was called Thursday Island and

to the east one could find Tuesday and Wednesday Islands as well. They were 25 miles off the coast of Cape York, the northern-most tip of the Australian mainland. At that time Australia was not yet one nation. Different regions wanted to control their own destinies and in 1859 Queen Victoria had decreed that Queensland should be granted the status of an independent British colony, rather than being governed from Sydney. For the next 40 years Queensland ran its own affairs, under the watchful but distant guidance of the Colonial Office in London.

In those days northern Queensland was wild and uncharted country and north of Cooktown, at the foot of the Cape York Peninsula, it was considered to be extremely dangerous, not only because of the predators and the climate, but also because of the threat of murderous attacks from the aborigines. When James Cook first landed from the Endeavour in 1770 there were no problems with the locals, but as more settlers arrived so the natives felt more and more threatened.

In 1862 Sir George Bowen, the first Governor of the colony, took a voyage north along the coast towards Cape York, aboard a steamer called the Pioneer. He was looking for a suitable seat of government for the northern part of Queensland and duly telegraphed the Colonial Office in London with the proposal that a settlement be established close to the cape itself, at a place that would be called Somerset. The plan was for a coaling station, a trading post and a harbour of refuge. John Jardine, the magistrate of Rockhampton, and a detachment of marines were sent north to begin work on the construction of the port. Jardine proposed sending his own sons, Frank and Alexander, overland with a herd of cattle and horses, to establish a cattle station at Cape York, in order to supply the needs of the new settlement. With eight others to help them, the Jardine brothers took 10 months to fight their way to the cape. By the time they arrived there were only 12 of the original 42 horses and 50 of the 250 cattle left alive. On the way they had waged war on the aborigines, killing at will and earning Frank the nickname of "Debil Debil", because of a tendency for violent behaviour. It was reckoned that he alone killed 80 natives in the course of the journey. Despite this bloody record, Frank was named as Police Magistrate in Somerset in 1868. He built himself a fine residence and played host to the many visitors, all the while retaining his reputation as a violent and dangerous man.

At the same time, Captain William Banner, an experienced commander of trading ships in the Pacific, was sailing the Torres Strait, in search of new groves of sandal wood. He noticed that the natives on one of the islands he visited were wearing strings of pearls. The children were even using pearls to play marbles. Banner suspected that there must be a good supply of pearls in the local waters and set his men to find them. It was not difficult. The pearl shells were everywhere, even in the shallows.

Man has always given pearls a high value. They are exceptionally rare, with only one or two being found in every ton of shell taken from the sea. Few of them are perfectly round and until man discovered the secrets of pearl farming, the value of a perfect pearl was enormous. The pearlers, however, found that they could also make decent money by selling the pearl shells - known as mother of pearl - which was used in Europe and America as inlay for decorative furniture and snuff boxes, for knife handles, fans, combs and for shirt buttons.

The trade was sufficiently good that before long the real money was found to be in the mother of pearl. Actual pearls were looked upon as a bonus.

At first Banner and his men were able to pick up large quantities of pearl shells without needing to dive for them, and they returned to Sydney with 50 tons, reckoned to be worth £7,500 (around £600,000 at modern prices). The following year another crew collected 41 tons of shell in just two months. It was easy money but, as easily accessible shells were quickly exhausted, divers were soon required and thus the word got out that there was money to be made in the Torres Strait. What amounted to a Pearl Rush began. In 1872, largely to protect the pearl industry, the Colony of Queensland annexed the southern islands in the Strait.

By then Frank Jardine had been replaced as the government agent and his successor, Henry Chester, refused to allow the pearlers to settle on the islands. By 1877 Somerset was the home harbour for around 100 pearl luggers and schooners, all of them working in the Strait. That year Sir Arthur Kennedy, a colonial administrator who had previously served as Governor of Sierra Leone, Western

Australia, British Columbia and Hong Kong, arrived in Brisbane to replace the ailing William Cairns. Kennedy began to reorganize the way Queensland was run and concluded that Somerset was the wrong place from which to govern the Torres Strait. He believed that in order to increase British influence in the region, it was necessary to have a permanent presence on the islands. Thursday Island provided the most promising site, as it offered a deep water anchorage, protected on all sides by other islands. It was also right on the major shipping routes from Australia's east coast to Asia and Europe.

Construction began on what would become Port Kennedy, with a series of government buildings being erected. A Harbour Master and a Shipping Master were appointed to organize the activities in the port and the town soon began to grow. Kennedy decided that it was best to extend British jurisdiction to all the islands in the Torres Strait. This secured for the British control of an important shipping channel. In the years that followed the Queenslanders began to suspect that Germany was trying to expand in the region. The western half of New Guinea had been administered for many years by the Dutch but none of the European powers had shown much interest in the eastern part of the island. The Queensland Premier, Sir Thomas McIlwraith, received word that Germany was about to stake a claim on the region. He did not wait for London to act and instructed Chester to take possession of the land to the south of the island's central mountain range. The move took the diplomats in London by surprise. German emissaries denied any such ambitions in the region and so Britain's Colonial Secretary Lord Derby repudiated Queensland's claim. He would soon realize that this had been a mistake, and that the Germans did have colonial ambitions. These were discussed at the Berlin Conference in November 1884, which was convened to deal with colonial disputes in Africa. As a result, Germany was granted sovereignty over the lands to the north of the central mountain range of New Guinea and islands to the north of that, while Britain took control of the south. As this was being sorted out, Port Kennedy was growing in importance, becoming a coaling station for British, Dutch, Japanese and Chinese steamers.

Early in 1885 an important new figure appeared on the scene. The Hon John Douglas, a nephew of the Marquess of Queensberry, was appointed as the government resident of the Torres Strait and Northern Queensland. He would play an important role in the development of the region for the next 20 years.

Educated at Rugby School, he emigrated to Australia at the age of 23 with £2,000 (£160,000) with which he and his brothers intended to buy land. They bought a 64,000-acre farm in the Darling Downs and using this as their base, Douglas began to involve himself in local politics while his brother Edward ran the business. John married and moved to Brisbane in 1863 after Edward decided to sell up and return home. Although John was insolvent by 1872, he was named Premier of Queensland five years later. After three years in office he was forced to resign in a scandal after he leaked secret documents to the press, believing that the public had the right to know what was going on. In the years that followed he made a living as a journalist before travelling to Britain in 1884, angling for an appointment in the Imperial Service. He was offered the post of government resident and police magistrate on Thursday Island - although he was known by everyone as "Governor". Within a few months of his arrival in 1885 he had survived a shipwreck on one of the reefs. Then his wife fell seriously ill. At the end of the year Sir Peter Scratchley, the British representative in New Guinea, died of malaria and Douglas was given the job of running the protectorate as well as his role on Thursday Island. For three years he ferried back and forth while his family moved to the Australian mainland.

One of Douglas's first actions was to allow the pearl industry to operate on Thursday Island, and he began selling plots of land to those involved in the business. In the three years that followed the population shot up to more than 500 people, with many more working on the nearby islands. In addition to the indigenous Torres Strait Islanders there were Europeans, Japanese, Chinese, mainland Aborigines, South Sea Islanders, Malays, Filipinos, Indians, and even a number of Africans and Arabs. He returned full time to the island at the end of 1888.

Life was not easy because his wife had developed a serious problem with alcohol which resulted in often violent behaviour and on several occasions the Governor sought police protection from his own spouse.

Douglas enjoyed huge power in the islands but his influence was generally benign and he showed a real interest in the development of the region. He followed orders sent from London, including the rather bizarre command to build a fortress on the island - in order to be ready if the Russians invaded.

At the time the Great Powers of Europe were busy building their empires, and the Colonial Office in London concluded that the construction of the Trans-Siberian Railway from Moscow to the naval base in Vladivostok was a sign that Russia was looking to expand in the Far East. They feared that the Russians might try to take over Australia, and so Douglas oversaw the construction of Green Hill Fort. When Kendall arrived on the windblown jetty in Port Kennedy in 1891, he had no idea that he was standing in a place of such strategic significance.

The town did not look much. There were luggers moored here and there and a new jetty was under construction, but the town itself was small. There were around 100 houses, built of weatherboard with corrugated iron roofs. Behind them were the low hills in the centre of the island, dotted with a few trees. And it was hot. Very hot.

Clasping Captain Ussher's letter, Kendall made for the collection of buildings that faced the harbour, in search of Vivian Bowden of the Burns Philip trading company.

Burns Philip had started out with a single store in Brisbane nearly 30 years earlier. After 12 years James Burns joined forces with shipping agent Robert Philip in Brisbane and moved into shipping, expanding the company rapidly on land and at sea. By the late 1880s Burns Philip was the dominant trading company in the South West Pacific.

The shipping office was easy to find and Kendall was duly introduced to Bowden. Ussher's letter was handed over and once he understood Kendall's circumstances, Bowden said he would see what could be organized. Ussher had strongly urged him not to send the runaway back to Normanton. Kendall was instructed to live in one of the old hulks in the harbour until employment could be found.

Once he had settled in, Kendall began to explore Port Kennedy. The Government Residency was a large bungalow on a hilltop overlooking the town. The other government buildings were below it. These included the police station, which was manned by a Mr Simpson, one of the early settlers. There were no roads but rather sandy tracks. The central part of town featured no fewer than four hotels, the newest being called The Grand. This was reckoned to be the finest building in the whole of Queensland and had only just opened for business.

The Thursday Island Hotel, the first to be established, was run by Thomas McNulty and his wife Maggie, known to all as "the Irish Queen". She was a kindly woman who took an interest in Kendall. The Royal Hotel, run by a Captain Pearson, had originally been in Cooktown but had been dismantled in 1887 and shipped to Thursday Island to be rebuilt. Although there was much drinking done on the island, the population was generally well-behaved.

There was a hospital under construction with Dr Arthur Salter as the island's medical officer. The town boasted a library, a school of arts which doubled as the town hall, a school and a Catholic church.

In addition to Burns Philip there was one other store than had been established the previous year by Captain Edmund Brown and his wife Marjory. They had a small daughter with the unusual name of Quetta. Kendall soon learned the story of the little girl. Fifteen months before his arrival on the island, the SS Quetta, a British India steamship bound for Europe, had hit an uncharted coral needle in the Mount Adolphus Channel, 20 miles to the east of Thursday Island, in the middle of the night. She had sunk in just five minutes. One hundred and thirty-three lives had been lost, many passengers drowning in their cabins, as the rock had torn a hole that extended through six different compartments.

The people on Thursday Island were alerted to the disaster the following morning when survivors rowed a lifeboat to Somerset and a telegraph message was sent to Douglas. He immediately ordered Captain David Reid, a former officer of the British India line, to take the government steamer Albatross to the scene with food and clothing. Dr Salter, Captain Wilkie and the missionary Albert Maclaren were all onboard. It was followed within an hour or two by the Merrie England, the New Guinea government steamer that was also based on Thursday Island. By the time the two ships arrived at the scene there were few survivors in the water. That evening the

Albatross found a girl who had been swimming for 36 hours. When they lifted her from the water, her arms continued to move as though swimming.

Among the other survivors was a baby girl, who was claimed by no-one. She had been plucked from the ship by one of the stewards who had handed her to a crewman called "Smiler" Clark before going back to look for more survivors. No-one knew to whom the child belonged and as she was too young to speak, she could give no clue as to her identity. It was assumed that her entire family had perished and in the end it was agreed that Captain Brown and his wife would adopt her. She grew up on Thursday Island, known to all as Quetta Brown. In his wanderings on the island, Kendall found that a church was being built as a memorial to the shipwreck.

The island had little fresh water. There were no natural water sources and so water had to be boiled before it could be drunk. There was no agriculture, but Chinese settlers grew vegetables on the island opposite and these were sold in Port Douglas. Otherwise the population lived on canned goods, fish and oysters.

Although it was a rough and ready town, it was a pleasant place for Kendall to be and was no worse than what he had experienced in the Croydon goldfields. The penniless runaway was struck by the kindness of the island folk and he was soon doing odd jobs. After a few days, he received word that Bowden wished to see him. There was an opportunity to become a member of the crew of one of the pearl luggers working out of Port Kennedy.

Would Henry like to try his hand in the pearl industry?

CHAPTER EIGHT

The Torres Strait, between the northern shores of Australia and the coast of New Guinea features around 150 islands and sand cays. They stretch out in the east as far as the northern tip of the Great Barrier Reef, and beyond that to Mer, Dauar and Waier, a remote trio of volcanic islands known collectively as the Murray Islands. These rise steeply from the sea and, compared to the sandy islands of the Strait, are fertile, offering not only fish and turtles to eat, but also many different fruits and even corn and sweet potato.

The cays in the Strait are less well provisioned, and are what romantics might describe as desert islands. In Kendall's time there was a small amount of wild fruit to be found, but attempts at farming had largely failed. Most of the islands had been abandoned, leaving the houses that had been built to fall into ruin.

Henry's employer was a remarkable man. Born on the island of Rotuma, a tiny volcanic dot in the ocean, 300 miles to the north of Fiji, he was the son of a king. This gave him considerable status amongst the white men and he was one of the few non-whites to own a pearl diving boat. The islanders had few rights at the time. Even more remarkable was the fact that the captain was married to a white woman, the widow of an English captain, who had been drowned on the reefs in the Strait.

In the early days of the pearling industry many of the boats were crewed by South Sea Islanders, who had been brought to Australia - sometimes against their will - to work either in the sugar plantations of Queensland or in the pearl industry. This "blackbirding" trade was a highly profitable business in the 1860s, the traders visiting the islands and offering the chiefs gifts in exchange for some of their people. Often they were happy to sell their own.

In other places the natives were only too willing to travel. The Rotumans, for example, were a friendly nation and the blackbirders found that they were more than willing to sign up as crew members. In other places there is no doubt that some of the traders were not entirely scrupulous and kidnapped islanders, luring them aboard the ships and then trapping them in the hold and sailing away, later selling the unfortunates to the highest bidders when they reached the shores of Queensland.

"I met a good many blackbirds," Kendall said, "but never once did I hear them speak unkindly either of those whites who had taken them or of those planters who worked them. They were humanely treated and, assisted by missionaries, their lot was by no means unhappy."

Kendall clearly felt that life as a lowly paid workman was better than scraping an existence as a cannibal on a remote island.

To Henry the captain was "a decent chap", and his crew boasted islanders from a wide variety of backgrounds with two Rotumans, two from Tanna Island (part of modern Vanuatu) and two from Jesus Island in the Solomons. The crew was completed by Kendall and the captain.

The two-masted lugger on which they sailed weighed around 16 tons, and the crew worked hard. They started at dawn and laboured until dusk. Normally there would be two or three divers underwater at the same time. The rest of the crew kept watch, working the air compressors and handling the shells collected. The air compressor was little more than a large box with wheels that had to be turned constantly, to push air through hoses to the divers. The diving equipment was rudimentary, but as they were working most of the time in relatively shallow water, between 36 and 72 ft, it was sufficient. The diving was much more difficult in the Darnley Deep, where the depth of the sea increased to 250 ft.

On a normal day, the lugger would drop anchor above a pearl field but rather than being completely secured, the boat was allowed to drift slowly with the current, dragging the anchor along behind it.

This meant that the work could continue without the boat needing to be moved. The divers would remain underwater for long periods, often three hours at a time, coming up only for their meals. They placed the pearl shells that they gathered in large baskets that were left on the bottom until they were full and then hauled to the surface. The crewmen on the lugger took turns working the air compressor and tending the air lines, watching to make sure that air bubbles were rising and communicating with the divers by tugging on a lifeline Around half an hour before dusk the divers would be called to the surface. Their gear would be cleaned and stowed away. The air pipes would be inspected for damage and the machinery would be oiled. Then the lugger would sail to a sheltered spot beside one of the islands. While dinner was being prepared, the remaining shells would be cleaned and searched for pearls, and then the crew would settle down to an oyster curry and rice as the warm night descended. These carefree evenings, gazing up at the stars, would remain some of Kendall's fondest memories of his days in Australia.

Pearl diving was an extremely hazardous occupation and hundreds of divers were killed in the Torres Strait during the pearl boom. Some drowned because of problems with their air supply, others died from the bends, a condition that occurs if a diver rises too quickly to the surface after a long period under the water. When working in the high pressure underwater environment, nitrogen is absorbed by the diver's body, rather than being expelled by breathing. If the pressure on the body reduces too rapidly, this nitrogen forms tiny bubbles in the blood and tissue and these can cause a variety of problems ranging from rashes and pain in the joints, to dizziness, breathing problems, blood clots and even death.

Each year a couple of the pearl divers would fall victim to sharks and occasionally, if the pearl boats were working close to the shore, a saltwater crocodile would strike. There were also scorpions and tropical fevers which caused the deaths of many people because medical help was many miles away, and they could not get to the doctors quickly enough.

The small pearl boats were also vulnerable when storms whipped up in the Strait, while underwater coral, ragged coastlines and sand bars caused many wrecks. In the months before Henry arrived on Thursday Island, three luggers and a schooner were lost in this way. To make matters worse, there were still cannibals who lived on the shores of New Guinea, who were happy to dine on a little "long pig", if it was available.

They worked hard, but the crews of the pearl boats would get some time off, usually because of poor weather. It was not always possible to send the divers down as the tides sometimes made the waters murky, which increased the risks dramatically. When that happened and the divers refused to work, the luggers would sail to one of the islands where they could find drinking water. At low tide, when the waters dropped below the level of the reef, the lagoons would be filled with fish unable to get back to the sea. The crews would fish with spears and then settle down on the beach and feast on barbecued fish. If they were lucky there would be able to gather delicious pumpkins, yams and custard-apples. When the fruit was ripe, flocks of Torres Strait Pigeon would appear and the sailors would be able to pick them off with their Winchester rifles.

From time to time on these lazy days they would encounter local residents and Henry was particularly impressed by an old sailor who had settled on one of the islands, where he lived with his six wives. They were all local women, who speared his fish, grew his vegetables, prepared his meals and all seemed to get on very well with one another, smoking pipes together and chatting merrily in their own language. Kendall found it hard to understand such a lifestyle and refused to accept that the old seaman was right when he said that "this knocks spots off going to sea". Henry was still filled with the desire to travel and see the world.

Each voyage in search of pearl shell lasted about a month, during which time the crews usually managed to collect around two tons of shell. Once there was no more room on board the lugger, they would sail back to Port Kennedy. Prices had dropped since the early days when William Banner had been able to get £150 a ton (£12,000 at modern prices), but two tons of pearl shell would still raise £100 (£8,000). As wages were not high, the profits were impressive. The bigger companies would send the luggers back out to sea after just a few days, but it was the divers who called the shots with the smaller independent operators. When they had money in their pockets the bars of Thursday Island were kept busy.

So too was the jailhouse. There were many extraordinary characters to be found on Thursday Island in that period, but Kendall particularly enjoyed the friendship of a sailor called Price, an American of mixed race, who had been shipwrecked in the Coral Sea and had then moved from island to island until he arrived on Thursday Island.

Price was a good sailor but, like many others in Port Kennedy, he liked to drink. When he had drank too much he ended up getting into fights and smashing things up. As a result, Price was well-known to the Governor, who had become fervently opposed to all alcohol because of his wife's drinking problems. This meant that Price spent a great deal of his time in the Port Kennedy jail, which he liked to call "Simpson's Boarding House", after the jailkeeper of the day. The prisoners did not have a bad life. They were fed and had somewhere to sleep. They worked in the gardens of the Governor's residence. Price was often be seen amongst the many plants and flowers. On one occasion the Governor entertained Lord Thomas Brassey, a celebrated politician and traveller, for breakfast. This was generally considered to be the best meal of the day, as it was cool in the morning. Brassey brought a case of fine 80-year-old brandy with him and it was not long before Price found this. Within a few hours he had been discovered in a very contented state, having helped himself to a couple of bottles. He had two months left to serve on a "drunk and disorderly charge" and so the Governor decided that Price would be sent off to sea as a crew member on the government yacht, known as the Albatross. This went from island to island, making sure that all was in order. By the time the Albatross returned to Port Kennedy only a few days of Price's sentence remained. He was looking forward to being free again, but when the rest of the crew was allowed to head into town, Price found himself alone on the yacht. He could hear the happy sounds of folk in the bars and the temptation proved too much. He took a small dinghy and rowed to shore, and was greeted as a hero when he appeared at his favourite drinking establishment in full prison garb. He set to work to make up for lost time. It was not long before the local constabulary heard that an escaped prisoner had appeared in one of the bars and officers arrived to apprehend him.

With a shrug and a wave Price was marched off to jail once again, content to shoulder whatever punishment the Governor saw fit to give him.

Even Kendall was dragged into court on one of his visits to Port Kennedy after a member of his crew was accused by another of having stolen £3 (£240). One of the Rotumans was called in as a witness and was asked, before he gave evidence, whether he was a Christian and could thus swear an oath on the Bible.

"No sir," he replied. "I am a Wesleyan."

For some minutes the court was in an uproar of amusement but Kendall soon learned that the locals were not as uneducated as most of the white men liked to believe. From talking to his shipmates he discovered that the Rotuman islanders had a most unusual social structure and that every six months they would elect a new "king". This meant that most Rotumans were able to say - in all honesty - that they were related to royalty. The white men were impressed by such things and so the captain of lugger had used this to his advantage. He was not at all worried if they had misled themselves into thinking he was someone important.

During one of his visits to Port Kennedy Kendall was introduced to owner's wife. She was an Englishwoman who had lost her original husband in one of the many wrecks in the region and had decided to marry a local. She took a liking to Henry and enlisted his help to try to convince her husband that it would be best if he registered his vessel in her name, in order to ensure his long-term security. It was always possible, she argued, that the boat would be taken from him by the authorities if they needed an extra vessel. Kendall agreed that there was some sense to this argument for the islanders had few rights at the time, despite the efforts of Governor Douglas, who did much to improve their lives

Henry thus convinced his boss that this was the best course of action, something he would regret doing when the lady in question decided that she would join the crew for the next voyage, in order to discover what her husband was getting up to when he disappeared off to sea. After a few days watching the men working the pump, scanning for air bubbles and cleaning pearl shells, she became very bored and Kendall noticed that she had a well-developed taste for strong drink. As the days went by he realized that her chief source of nourishment appeared to be brandy. When she was not drinking, she spent most of her time trying to convince Kendall that she was related to the Lord Chancellor, Baron Halsbury. This was a subject that held little interest to Henry, who was not much impressed by fancy titles.

The owner's wife also had sudden fits of anger and would openly abuse her husband in front of his crew. At one point she insisted, as owner of the ship, that they sail to the New Guinea coastline, in order to recruit an extra crewman, who was needed because she was not doing any work. If nothing else, Kendall concluded, it would be a change of scenery and something a little different from the daily grind. The voyage across the Strait took them three days, during which time Kendall discovered that the quality of the seamanship of those on board was not what he was used to. He spent much of his time in the bow, scouring the seas ahead for any sign of underwater obstacles. The navigation was rudimentary and when they finally arrived on the coast of New Guinea, they found nothing but jungle.

As night was falling they dropped anchor and settled down to sleep, only to discover that the jungle was filled with thousands of mosquitoes, which descended on the boat in a cloud and left them all badly bitten. The sailors were terrified of malaria - a real killer at the time - and as soon as daylight came, they raised the anchor and sailed on. Further along the coast they came upon a small island, which boasted a rocky beach in front of the dense jungle vegetation.

They lowered the dinghy and Kendall, the captain and his wife set off towards the shore, to see what could be found. They were wary because they knew all the stories that did the rounds on Thursday Island about the cannibals of New Guinea, and had no desire to end up in a cooking pot. They were still some way from the beach, when a group of around 50 natives burst from the jungle and rushed into the water, whooping and waving. Henry kept the boat out of their reach, but then spotted a man on the beach in a white suit, waving a straw hat in their direction in what appeared to be a friendly manner. They decided that it was unlikely that a cannibal would wear a white suit and a straw hat and so cautiously approached the beach. As soon as they were within reach of the islanders, the boat was seized by the crowd, lifted clean out of the water and carried up the beach. They then had to shake hands with the entire tribe, one after another. This was quite an experience as many of the natives wore no clothing at all. They had bones through their noses and multicoloured tattoos all over their bodies. The women were topless and had decorative scars, ornate woven basket caps, necklaces and rather dramatic earrings.

The man with the straw hat was finally able to introduce himself and explained that he was a missionary and had been sent from the Straits Settlements to convert cannibals to Christianity. He had enjoyed considerable success and was gradually convincing them that God was not keen on cannibalism. After hearing this news the visitors were able to relax a little, although the missionary went on to explain that despite his best efforts, the tribe remained at war with several others in the area. They needed all the men that they could muster and no-one was available to work in the pearl industry.

The tribe seemed genuinely friendly and sent the lugger on its way, laden with a selection of local fruits.

Henry discovered that the captain's wife had been somewhat marked by her experience and had understood that it was simply good fortune that they had encountered a friendly tribe. She immediately decided that there was no great urgency to find another crew member and they were ordered to head back to Thursday Island. It was back to stories of Baron Halsbury and empty brandy bottles until a sufficient number of shells had been gathered to justify returning to Port Kennedy. They were happy to see the back of the captain's wife. She in turn was happy to be home, her thirst for adventure having failed to match her thirst for brandy.

CHAPTER NINE

Aside from petty crime and the occasional assault committed by the Governor's wife, there was little in the way of news on Thursday Island. There was no sign of any Russian invasion, although Green Hill Fort would soon be completed and, no doubt, the locals slept easier in their beds as a result. The quiet lifestyle of the islands had much appeal, but it meant that The Torres Strait Pilot was not a very interesting newspaper. Nonetheless this journal appeared each week from an office in Port Kennedy, its four pages listing the comings and goings.

One day, soon after his return from a pearl diving trip, Kendall was reading a copy of the newspaper, while relaxing at the Thursday Island Hotel. He was astonished to read an item that said that if the runaway Kendall would present himself at the office of the Torres Strait Pilot he would learn something to his advantage. Young Henry became quite excited and asked Mrs McNulty what she thought it could be, dreaming that perhaps a distant relative had died and he had been tracked down, so as to inform him that he had inherited a vast fortune.

Inevitably, Maggie McNulty already knew the answer. The owner of the Pilot was tired, she explained. He had decided to take a holiday and wanted to travel south to visit family in New South Wales. He needed to find someone who could read and write to run the newspaper in his absence. The number of candidates available was, therefore, somewhat limited, as most of those on the island were busy or did not have the necessary skills. The newspaper owner was hoping that Kendall might be the answer to his problem.

The idea of launching himself into the newspaper industry appealed to Kendall, and he rushed to the office to find out how much the owner would be willing to pay. He discovered that he had not been the first visitor and was told that his captain's wife had already dropped by and, keen to hold on to the useful young crew member, had mentioned to the newspaper proprietor that if he left the publication in the hands of young Kendall, he would not be the owner by the time he returned from his holiday. The publisher was having second thoughts about the idea.

It seemed that Kendall was fated to remain a sailor.

A few days later, the lugger departed on another pearling trip, the captain seeming rather keen to get away from his wife for a while. On this occasion they sailed to Cape York - the northern tip of the Australian mainland - and began diving in the area of Albany Island. This gave them the opportunity to call in at Somerset, which had declined considerably in importance by that time. Frank Jardine was still there, but the old tyrant was calmer by then. He had two sons and two daughters, all with the beautiful Samoan princess Sana Solia who, legend had it, had visited Somerset 20 years earlier on a missionary boat bound for New Guinea. Jardine had been enthralled by the striking young woman and after the ship had departed decided he could not live without her. He gave chase in his cutter, all but kidnapped the princess, despite protests from the missionaries, and took her back to Somerset.

Perhaps it was this sort of behaviour that had led to Jardine being removed from his post as Police Magistrate a couple of years later, although Sana Solia seemed happy enough with the arrangement and they were soon married. When the government base was moved to Thursday Island, Jardine had acquired the old government residence, a gracious house on top of the cliffs, and he lived there with his family, making a good living in the pearl industry. Visitors were served food on silver plates that had been made using the metal from Spanish coins, from a hoard he had found one day on a trip to one of the reefs. Kendall noted that the princess, who was by then 44, was still a startlingly attractive woman and the children made a good-looking group.

In the course of this trip the crew of the lugger encountered a number of aborigines when they anchored near the shore and Kendall spent many hours in their company.

"They often informed me that being a white man I should make very good food," Kendall reported. "Their frankness in this matter was amazing."

On the whole, however, he found the natives to be a rather sad and sorry group. Each carried a blanket in the centre of which was printed: "A gift from Queen Victoria to her Queensland Subjects", and each year the authorities handed out new blankets to each native. They held the old queen in high esteem. They were no longer violent as they had been in the 1860s and 1870s, having been worn down by the vicious behaviour of some of the settlers.

There were still other dangers for a young man.

"One evening I was stretched out on the deck enjoying the darkness when I suddenly felt a sharp pain between my thumb and forefinger," Kendall related. "I had been bitten by something. I summoned the crew and one of them pricked the place where I had been bitten with a knife and began to suck the poison from my hand. After doing that they took a piece of wood from the fire and cauterized the wound and then placed a tobacco leaf over the injury for protection. While this was going on lights were found and a scorpion was discovered. It had probably come across from the shore when they had cut some mangrove for firewood."

Kendall was frightened. He could feel the pain spreading up his arm and when eventually it reached his chest he was terrified he would die in agony, hundreds of miles from medical attention. He paced the deck all through the night, unable to rest because of the pain. But as the sun began to rise he felt the poison beginning to subside, although it would not be until the following evening that he felt fully recovered from his ordeal.

When they returned to Thursday Island with the next load of shells, they found the town preparing for a two-day fair to celebrate the arrival of the Australasian Auxiliary Squadron on its way to Sydney. The squadron consisted of four Pearl Class cruisers, each weighing 2,500 tons. They were named the Mildura, the Ringarooma, the Tauranga and the Wallaroo. They had been financed by the colonies, but were crewed by the Royal Navy. In addition, there were two torpedo boats called the Boomerang and the Karrakatta. The local population offered them a warm welcome although Price did his best to disrupt celebrations, by picking a fight with a large bluejacket. It was the shortest fight of Price's career as he was laid out with one punch by the sailor.

There were to be other adventures for Kendall out on the reefs. On one occasion Kendall was left behind on the lugger while the other crew members took the dinghy to a nearby island. He decided to join them and rather than wait, chose to swim the short distance from ship to shore. As he swam he was vaguely aware that the crewman on board was shouting to him, but he continued to swim without looking back and reached the shore unharmed. It was only later when he returned to the boat that he discovered that a shark had appeared behind him. It had followed him for some distance before turning away and heading off to look for other prey. Kendall never knew why the shark did not attack.

On another occasion they were spearing fish in a lagoon when Kendall felt a large fish touch his lower leg. He looked down and saw that it was a shark. He drove his spear into the water as hard as he could, more in fear than anything else. He then watched with astonishment as the spear was torn from his hand and took off through the water like the periscope of a submarine, to disappear out to sea.

Back on Thursday Island, Kendall was introduced to a Norwegian by the name of Captain Mangor. He was the commander of a ship that was moored 150 miles away on Raine Island, out in the Great Barrier Reef. He had been rowed in one of the ship's lifeboats to an island off the coast of Queensland and from there had caught a coastal steamer to Thursday Island. He had lost two men overboard during his outward voyage from New York, by way of Port Natal in South Africa, and was looking for replacements to help him get the ship home to England. He was loading guano. The problem was that Mangor had run out of money and needed to buy stores for the return leg of his journey. He was looking not only for a crewman, but also for a financier. Kendall had spent little during his time on Thursday Island and had collected £60 (the equivalent of £4,800 today) for his pearl diving activities. He was also the proud owner of four decent-sized pearls, which would fetch a good price in London. Mangor promised to pay him £3 a month to be Third Mate on the ship, if Kendall would lend him the money to buy the stores needed. Kendall was enjoying his life in the Torres Strait, but he had been away from home for more than a year and did not know when he might get another opportunity to return home. He was concerned also that his mother and sisters would be worried about what had happened to him. He discussed the offer with Bowden, who recommended that Kendall seize the chance in order to get back to clear his name. An agreement was drawn up and signed by Kendall and Mangor, with Bowden as the witness.

Bidding farewell to the islands was not easy, for the people of Thursday Island had made Henry's time there a period he would remember for the rest of his life. He might have stayed on, invested in the pearl industry and made himself a fortune, but he had bigger ambitions. He still wanted to travel the world and to become an officer in the merchant navy. He no longer wanted to be a runaway.

The coastal steamer took Kendall, Mangor and their supplies out from Port Kennedy and across to Cape York. From there it headed south along the coast, towards Cooktown, stopping off at a number of settlements along the way. Eventually they reached the Hannibal Isles, three tiny islands encircled by a reef, with a sand bar at the northern end. The islands were covered with small trees and bushes, and camped on the beach were some of the men from Mangor's ship. They had been living off fish and turtle meat. They packed up quickly and were soon ready to depart for Raine Island, 60 miles to the east, on the outer edge of the Great Barrier Reef.

"As I saw the coast sink from view, I realized that my Australian exploits were at an end," Kendall wrote. "And I repeated to myself the country's motto 'Advance Australia' and blessed her people. In my estimation there are no better and finer people on this earth than the Australians: man, woman and child. It is the only country where true hospitality lives."

Although the waters inside the Great Barrier Reef are shallower and calmer than in the Pacific Ocean itself, it was still a long and arduous journey to Raine Island in a small lifeboat. The crewmen in the boat with Kendall and Mangor spoke not a word of English, but once the coastline of Australia had disappeared, they were looking to the east. Having never been that far from Thursday Island, Kendall did not know what it was they were looking for, until a strange stone tower appeared on the horizon, indicating that they had reached their destination. The 60ft stone tower might have been a lighthouse had there been any means of powering a light. It had been built in 1844 by convicts, who had hewn the rock from the island itself and found timbers in nearby wrecks. Their creation could be seen for 12 miles in all directions and was designed to help ships locate a channel through the reef. But the Raine Island Entrance became redundant very quickly when a new passage through the reef was discovered further to the north.

As they drew closer to the island Kendall could see the Rollo, sitting offshore. Then he picked up the pungent smell of tons of dried seabird droppings. These had been built up over centuries by the thousands of birds, generation after generation, which had used the island for their breeding. Guano is rich in phosphorus, an essential ingredient in most fertilizers. It was thus considered to be of great value. Mining of the island by the JT Arundel company had started the previous year, with around one hundred Chinese workers sent to Raine. They had built a jetty and even constructed a railway system to transport the guano from the quarries in the centre of the island to the ships. In just 12 months tens of thousands of tons of guano had been removed from the island. It would not be long before the supply was exhausted, the mining company would pack up, and the island would be left once more to the birds and the turtles.

Raine is not an attractive island. It is low and flat, a tiny sand and coral cay measuring just 80 acres. There was not a single tree. At the north-western end of the island the workers had built a camp. The only other thing of note was a single grave, belonging to Annie Eliza Ellis, the mother of the JT Arundel manager Albert Ellis, who had died earlier that year.

"Reader! Be Ye Also Ready" were the menacing words engraved on the stone.

The Rollo was an iron barque of 900 tons. She had been built 15 years earlier by the Currie Line in Melbourne and had only recently been sold to the London shipping firm of John I Jacobs &

Co. She had been loading guano for almost a month and there were 500 tons in the hold. The Rollo was a three-master with a crew of just 11. It was a multinational crew with the Norwegian Captain Mangor, a Swedish First Mate and a Second Mate from Denmark. The cook and the steward were Russian Finns, the carpenter German and the rest of the crew a mixture of these backgrounds, plus a couple of Portuguese. They stayed on Raine Island for Christmas Day and then on December 29 put to sea, setting a southerly course towards New Zealand, where they hoped to pick up winds to carry them across the southern Pacific to Cape Horn.

Their route took them down the outside of the Great Barrier Reef and then out across the Tasman Sea towards Lord Howe Island. From there the plan was to skirt around New Zealand's South Island.

The weather was pleasant but as they sailed down towards the Roaring Forties the winds became stronger, the temperatures dropped, and Kendall remembered that life at sea was not always as romantic as he imagined when idling away time on Thursday Island.

And then, just as he was beginning to have doubts about his decision, there rose up ahead of them the impressive Lord Howe Island and Ball's Pyramid, to the south. These were the most spectacular islands he had yet seen, with cliffs rising vertically from the sea to a height of 1,800 feet, the jagged leftovers of ancient volcanoes. The world, Kendall reminded himself, was filled with such amazing sights.

As they neared New Zealand the weather turned bad and a violent storm broke the mizzenmast. It was a setback, but Mangor decided that he would simply take a slower route and not go as far to the south as he had originally planned. They headed for the Cook Straight, the narrow body of water between New Zealand's North and South Islands. From there the Rollo headed on into the southern Pacific. At the top edge of the Roaring Forties, the ship was able to make good time without fear of ice. The winds can be so strong in the region that they become a hazard and, as the ships get closer to South America, the waves become larger, as hundreds of miles of uninterrupted sea allow them to build in size. The spray and the waves meant that the crew found it impossible to keep dry. No longer was there sunshine to dry their clothing, although the Rollo had a pig aboard, known to Kendall as Dennis, and the crew used the heat from the animal to dry their clothes. Dennis lived a comfortable life, insulated from the low temperatures. As a result of this particular talent, Dennis saved his bacon - at least until the ship returned to warmer climates.

As they neared the South American mainland, Captain Mangor was faced with a dilemma. To get through to the Atlantic Ocean, a ship had to drop down through the Roaring Forties and into the latitudes known as "The Furious Fifties". There was no avoiding that, but then Mangor had a choice. There were several sheltered routes that ran through the many islands of the Tierra del Fuego archipelago. These were famously treacherous. There was little room for manoeuvre, and winds, known as williwaws, came off the land and could throw up a squall and dash a ship on the rocks. With the Rollo's reduced ability to steer because of the loss of the mizzenmast, Mangor concluded that the only sensible course of action was to descend 250 miles further to the south and go around Cape Horn in the open sea. Out in Drake Passage there was more space to manoeuvre, but the task of breaking through the world's most feared piece of ocean with a damaged ship was not going to be easy.

One might even say it was terrifying...

CHAPTER TEN

Where the Atlantic and the Pacific Oceans meet, the seas can be extremely violent. The large waves from the Southern Ocean suddenly become shorter and taller, as beneath the surface the seabed rises dramatically within a few miles from 13,000 to just 55 feet. Waves at Cape Horn can rise to 100 feet. These are the world's most violent waters. The temperatures are freezing, the winds howl, and ships are lashed by rain, sleet and snow. The giant waves crash down on vessels, sweeping away anything that is not tied down. And there are icebergs, huge chunks of ice that have broken off the ice fields of Antarctica and have drifted northward. Ships need lookouts, but with such vast waves and flying foam, it is hard for them to see anything. There is the constant danger that a wave will sweep a man away into the water.

Voyages in either direction are dangerous, but travelling from west to east is considered easier than heading into the prevailing winds, blasting from the south-west. In the days of sail, ships would often struggle to get through or be blown back out into the Atlantic. Below 40-degrees south, the sailors used to say, there is no law. Below 50-degrees south there is no God. Rounding the Horn was a terrifying experience, even for the most seasoned of sailors. The tradition was that those who had made it through would wear a gold earring to show the world. They joked that the earring was to pay for their burial if their body one day washed up on a foreign shore. Hundreds of ships were wrecked in these waters, and thousands of sailors were drowned. There were rarely survivors.

The ships ploughed through the waves as best they could. The danger came if a ship turned broadside as a giant wave arrived. If that happened the vessel could be rolled over. Anyone on deck, or in the rigging, would be lost. Others would be injured. In the worst case, a ship would simply fill with water and sink. The winds were often so strong that the sails would rip at the seams and then be torn to ribbons. Fittings for ropes would be ripped from the wood by the forces and any poorly tied knot would be wrenched apart. A ship without sails would quickly turn broadside and be at the mercy of the waves. In such moments the crew would have to rush from their shelter, climb the rigging and do whatever was possible to fix the problem. They could not hear one another above the howling winds. They were paralysed with cold, unfed and exhausted. It was impossible to eat or sleep in such seas. Men would suffer frostbite and fall to their deaths, there were broken arms and legs.

Time and again the ship would climb a giant wave and at the top would hang in the air for a terrifying moment before crashing down into the trough behind. At these moments the rudder would be clear of the water. The danger was that a ship would turn broadside before the rudder could correct the movement. And all the while the vessel would be pummelled by the waters. The seams of the hull would open and crews often found themselves pumping out water to keep their ship afloat.

"On our arrival off the Horn we lost our main mast," Kendall said. "The Rollo had just the lower mast standing and we had to make the best of it. She was leaking like a basket. We were a floating wreck."

It was a titanic struggle and then, quite suddenly, the conditions eased. They were through. The ship was a mess and repairs were needed but for Captain Mangor there were other dangers to consider.

"We were 98 days out of port and we were getting short of food," Kendall said. "We wanted to go north to get out of those latitudes. The Captain intended visiting the Falkland Islands for more food, but there were favourable winds and as we had managed to jury-rig our main mast and we had a windmill contraption pumping out the water, so he decided that we could sail on and make the best of it.

He wanted us to hang on until we got past the fever stricken ports of Brazil. Then it would be OK and we would go in somewhere further north. At one point two ships went by. The captain decided not to answer their calls because he did not want rumours to spread about the state of our ship. He refused to signal. We watched as one of the ships signalled the other: 'Can you see the name of this wreck?'."

The ports of Rio de Janeiro, Santos and Bahia were in the grip of a series of epidemics. The populations of these cities had grown so quickly that sanitation, housing and water supply had been unable to keep up. The result was outbreaks of yellow fever, malaria and smallpox in the shanty towns that ringed the cities. In 1891 Rio had suffered a terrible yellow fever outbreak, with a death toll of around 5,000 people. Hospitals had overflowed and every morning corpses were laid out on the streets to be collected. Any ships that arrived in the port ran the risk of contamination. It was said that every vessel arriving in Santos lost someone to the fever. Some ships lost everyone, others were left with too few men to set sail. It was impossible to find a new crew and with no-one to unload the ships, business ground to a standstill. A large number of ships were simply deserted in the harbour. They were quickly looted.

Matters were not helped by political upheavals in Brazil, following the 1889 insurrection that had deposed Emperor Pedro II. The leaders of the coup d'état fell quickly into conflict and a state of emergency was declared in the autumn of 1891. The country was on the brink of civil war. Nothing was done to help the cities.

The Rollo sailed within sight of Sugar Loaf mountain and the other hills that surround Rio de Janeiro. They then continued along the sandy coastline, where there were a series of lagoons separated from the sea by dazzling white sand bars, to Cape Frio. It was beautiful, but very quickly the ship sailed into calm waters. There was no wind. With food running out, Dennis the pig had been slaughtered and the crew was getting close to its limit.

"We were at our last gasp," remembered Kendall. "We had been living on biscuits and beans for a month."

Mangor decided that there was no choice but to risk a visit to the port of Salvador and while he went ashore to find supplies, the crew sat waiting, hoping that he would not return with any diseases.

He brought not only food but also an accordion that he had bought from a German sailor. He hoped that this would keep up spirits on the last leg of the trip.

"We resumed our voyage," Kendall recalled, "but we had many calms and head winds. We were in a hopeless state for sailing quickly, but after 197 days, we finally arrived in Falmouth, on the southern coast of Cornwall."

Mangor telegraphed the ship owners and received orders to proceed to London to unload the guano. It was arranged that the Rollo would be towed along the south coast. The crew was paid off. Mangor was given money to pay his debt to Kendall and with it came seven months of wages. Kendall had £81 (the equivalent of £6,500), in addition to four decent-sized pearls. The accordion was raffled by the captain and Kendall won that as well. He had money in his pocket. He had been around the world but for nearly two years had no word from home.

He found his home country in political upheaval. It was the end of June 1892 and Parliament had just been dissolved. The Marquis of Salisbury's Conservative government was fighting a General Election against the Liberals, led by the 82-year-old William Gladstone.

The talk was of Irish Home Rule.

Kendall headed for Kensington, keen to see his family and catch up on the latest news. It was very distressing for him to discover that not only had the family moved, but that this had happened after the death of his mother, at the age of only 38.

In Victorian times death was always closer at hand than it is today, but it was still a shock for Henry. He learned that his sisters had gone back to Liverpool. He took a train north and tracked them down, only to be admonished for his failure to send any form of communication. They all believed that he had drowned.

The big news in Liverpool was that his sister Beth had married a man called Dick Jones. His real name was Richard but as this was his father's name, he had to be called Dick. Henry soon began to get to know the Jones Family. They were an unusual lot, with a very curious history. Richard Jones was a customs officer, who 25 years earlier had married a girl called Ellen Wright. She had given birth to Dick but soon afterwards had died, leaving Richard a widower with a small child to care for. Ellen's sister Mary came to his rescue and in the years that followed she became devoted to her sister's baby.

Richard was a lonely soul and so desperate was he to find a new wife that he threatened to take Dick away from Mary, unless she agreed to marry him. The poor girl had a terrible choice to make: she either had to lock herself into a loveless marriage or give up the child that she had treated as her own. For Dick's sake she agreed to marry her sister's husband. Although they went on to have six more children it was never a happy marriage and Mary took to drink.

As each new child was born, she insisted that all be baptized with the surname Wright Jones. She believed that the family was connected to the Wrights of Osmaston, Derbyshire, one of the great industrial families of Britain. The Wrights had grown rich with iron production during the Industrial Revolution. They owned the Butterley Ironworks, near Ripley, and a grand country house in Osmaston itself. Mary had the eccentric belief that if the children all carried the Wright name they might one day inherit some of the money.

The oldest of the new children was a girl of 16 named Jane. She was known to all as Minnie. She was followed by Peter, Thomas and David, three brothers, each separated by two years. There was then a gap to the toddler Mary - although everyone called her May - and finally the baby Ernie.

Mary also told the children that they were also cousins of the Holt shipping family, explaining that Richard's mother had a sister who had married into the Holts.

For the 18-year-old adventurer Henry Kendall, the family member who stood out was Minnie. He was too filled with wanderlust to worry much about marriages and families, but the thought registered that when he did start to think along those lines, a girl like Minnie would be perfect.

Exchanging his accordion for a penny-farthing bicycle, Kendall and some of his old friends from Indefatigable days spent several weeks trying to kill themselves on this precarious contraption. They were 18 years old and - like all 18-year-olds - were utterly fearless.

Kendall recognized that he needed to go back to work fairly quickly in order to get back into the system. By doing that the break in his career between the Iolanthe and the Rollo would fade into history.

The incident with the Iolanthe had taken place in a remote and distant place and had involved a ship of little importance. It was an era when men switched around from ship to ship and no-one paid much attention to who had worked where and when. Henry had been young. The gold mining and the pearl diving had added to his experience, and to the stories he could tell. What he needed was a good solid job to re-establish his career. He decided to try the Inman Line, with which he had started his career on the City of Berlin. He explained that he had been in Australia and told them of his adventures on the Rollo.

He was taken on as an apprentice on the SS Philadelphia, the fastest steamship in the world at the time, running back and forth between Liverpool and Boston, Massachusetts. It was not the most exciting work, but it was the summer and the weather in the North Atlantic was not too bad.

It was a necessary evil.

Between the voyages Henry was able to spend more time at home, putting down some roots in Liverpool and getting to know his new clan. By the start of 1893, however, his desire to explore the world had returned. His problems on the Iolanthe were forgotten. His new goal was to sail as an apprentice on one of the windjammers.

The celebrated clippers of the mid-nineteenth century had been built for speed, but they had not been large enough to be profitable, unless they were transporting low-volume, high-profit goods such as tea, spices or mail.

These elegant multi-masted vessels had been designed to use every breath of wind. They were the ultimate in efficiency, but as steamship technology improved, so the companies that had continued with sail had to look for an advantage in other areas. They were forced to gamble on bigger sailing ships. It was a last valiant attempt to remain competitive in the face of the industrial efficiency of steam power.

The result was a fleet of windjammers, the mightiest of all sailing ships. These huge iron-hulled vessels - elegant three- and four-masters - weighed up to 3,000 tons. They had sails as far as the eye could see and boasted much larger cargo capacity than the clippers, yet could sail at the same kind of pace. They would become the final symbols of the romance of seafaring. In time the 1890s would be seen as a golden age of sail.

"We failed to notice it at the time," Kendall remarked, "but this was one of the most notable decades in the history of shipping."

Henry remained a confident and ambitious young man and he wanted to serve on the biggest and the best ships. The RW Leyland company's ships were the top of the range and thus he beat a path to their door. He wanted to be an apprentice on the Liverpool, a four-masted, iron-hulled, 3,330-ton ship, built in 1889 by Russell & Company in Glasgow. She could carry almost 6,000 tons of cargo on a single voyage, yet needed a crew of only 35. She was one of the greatest ships of the day.

There was much dispute at the time as to whether the Liverpool was faster than the Shenandoah, her American rival. Built in the Sewall shipyard in Bath, Maine in 1890, the Shenandoah had sailed from New York to San Francisco in just 124 days in her first year at sea. In 1892 she had cut that record to 111 days. She could carry only 4,800 tons of cargo - but she was fast.

The two ships had never gone head-to-head but when Kendall joined the Liverpool she was loading salt to be shipped out to Calcutta. Further up the river the Shenandoah was preparing to go to sea as well. It quickly became clear that matters would be arranged so that the two would depart at the same time so that the question could be settled. There was much excitement in the port.

Competition, so they say, improves the breed and while many think that all forms of racing are just games, there is no doubt that the rivalries between the shipping companies spurred them on to envisage bigger and better vessels, and to apply and develop new technologies. By doing so, the British stayed ahead of their rivals for much longer than anyone would have predicted.

The race with the Shenandoah was more than just fun. The great American ship represented a challenge that could not be ignored. Britannia ruled the waves and the sailors on the Liverpool intended to prove it.

In order to keep down the costs, ship owners hired their crews at the last possible moment before the ship sailed, relying on boarding masters in the ports to provide them with good men. Usually there was just a day or two between a sailor signing on and his departure. They used this time to spend their advances on wine, women and song. This meant that the average sailor was more than a little under the weather on his first morning at sea.

The captain of the Liverpool was Charles Whiting, as tough an old sailor as there was. He believed that discipline was the key to building a good crew and he and his officers would take advantage of the hangovers to bully the crews into shape. On this particular trip, however, Whiting found himself at a disadvantage as it emerged that he had unwittingly signed up a crew consisting largely of men who did not drink. This was a big advantage in the race with the Shenandoah.

The two ships departed Liverpool on the same tide and once out at sea the sails were unfurled and with good strong winds, the race was on. The crews of both ships were constantly at work to ensure that the vessels were using every inch of canvas. For the first two hours there was nothing between the two. They remained together but gradually, inch by inch, the Liverpool began to pull ahead. After 12 hours at sea, the Shenandoah had fallen 10 miles behind. By dawn the following day the American ship had disappeared over the horizon.

The point had been made - the Limeys would have plenty to brag about when they reached Calcutta.

CHAPTER ELEVEN

The victory over the Shenandoah may have meant a great deal to the crew of the Liverpool but from a commercial point of view, the most important part of the voyage was the race back from Calcutta to Dundee in Scotland, once the Bengal jute was ready to be shipped.

The Industrial Revolution had given Britain a dominant position in world trade. British manufactured goods were the best that one could buy. The Empire provided raw materials and the constant march of technology meant that the rival Great Powers had little chance of catching up.

Dundee was the best harbour on the eastern coast of Scotland and in medieval times had gained a reputation as a centre of the wool trade, exporting English wool and animal hides to Europe, in exchange for fine finished textiles, metal goods and wines. It did not take long for the canny Scots to realise that this did not make sense. They might not be able to grow grapes to produce fine wines, and other places might be better-suited for metal-working, but there was no reason at all why the Scots could not spin wool themselves. They could, they reasoned, weave and dye as well as anyone else.

Dundee quickly became a centre of the textile trade. After wool came cotton and then linen. High quality linen was a highly profitable product, but flax supplies in the region ran low and by 1800 the mills in Dundee were switching over to steam power and the farmers could not keep up. The mill owners turned to Scandinavia but it was difficult to compete with the Irish when the extra costs were added. The textile barons began to look for alternative products.

At the same time the East India Company had begun to produce huge quantities of jute on the fertile plains of Bengal.

Jute is one of the easiest and cheapest plants to grow. It requires a rich soil, heat and plenty of water. Bengal has all of these and the region produces large crops. The harvest begins in the midsummer but the process requires that the jute be immersed in water for several weeks in order to break down the fibres. These are then separated and dried.

The fibres boast extraordinary tensile strength but the problem with jute is that it is more difficult to spin than cotton. The textile barons of Dundee set out to find a solution and it was discovered that if treated with whale oil, jute could be spun on steam-driven machinery, in much the same way as cotton. Dundee had good supplies of whale oil, because of a well-developed whaling industry.

With the correct treatment jute could be transformed into thread that could then be woven into a tough material. This could be used for any number of purposes, ranging from sacking to curtains and carpets to chair coverings. It can be blended with other natural fibres to produce ropes and twines, and the finest jute strands could be spun into a material so fine that it could be mistaken for silk. Jute products did not fetch the same prices as fine linen, but sales volumes were higher and thus more money could be made.

Dundee rapidly developed into the centre of the jute trade with 50,000 people eventually working in the industry. In turn, the city started to build ships to bring the jute fibres home from India.

Once the drying process was completed in India, the fibre was packed into bales and transported to Calcutta to be shipped to Dundee. Each December the sailing ships of the age were queued up in Calcutta, waiting to race home. Speed dictated price and vast fortunes could be made or lost depending on who had the fastest ships. The textile mills of Scotland would be waiting for their raw materials and the ships that arrived first would make the most money. Slower ships would have more difficulty selling the cargo as the mills would by then be working at full capacity.

The crew of the Liverpool may have been clean-living when it came to alcohol, but as the voyage went on it became clear that the officers were not as feared as they would have been if they had been able to bully the crew on the first day out of port. The crew on the average sailing ship was always hungry, but they rarely dared to raid the stores, afraid of the retribution that would follow. Without the battering on the first day of the voyage, the crew of the Liverpool seemed to have less fear of the officers and it was not long before there was talk of robbing the stores. Only a few were willing to take part because there was a belief in some quarters that the Liverpool was a haunted ship, as a result of a murder and a suicide that had occurred on her first voyage.

The raid of the food stores had to take place in the dead of night, when the ship was at its quietest. All went to plan until the raiding party was creeping back to their quarters. Suddenly a ghostly white figure appeared in the darkness. The raiders panicked and ran in all directions, one or two of them striking out at the ghost before going into hiding. When they had time to think about it, they found it strange that the spirit had been a very solid thing. Curiosity got the better of them and the raiders returned to the deck to see the ghost. No-one was there. The ship was quiet again.

The next morning the First Officer seemed in very bad humour. He had slept badly, his cabin being close to the chain store and he had been kept awake by clanking noises as the ship moved with the waves. In the end he had decided that he needed to find a quieter spot and concluded that the covered wheelhouse at the stern would be suitable. He was asleep in a chair when he was awakened by strange noises outside. He emerged on the deck in his pyjamas and had been set upon by a number of frenetic shadowy figures, who had quickly vanished. Rather unnerved by the incident he decided that it would best to return to the safety of his cabin. The captain was informed of all that had happened during the night and was heard to remark that he would have been happier if the damned ghost had appeared before the food had been stolen!

The Liverpool dropped anchor at Sandheads, at the entrance to the River Hooghly, just 84 days after leaving the Mersey. The Hooghly is the western-most branch of the Ganges Delta. The delta, built up over centuries by silt from the river, stretches 220 miles to the east along the Bay of Bengal. It is the largest delta in the world and its flat plains are extremely fertile. Although large sections at the time were under cultivation, other areas remained as jungle and mangrove swamp, providing refuge for the celebrated Royal Bengal tiger.

The river is famously difficult to navigate. In the estuary there are treacherous sand bars and many a ship had run aground, despite the best efforts of the Bengal Pilot Service, which was long considered to be one of the best in the world.

Calcutta is 90 miles inland from the sea along the meandering Hoogly, and there would be many hours under tow before the Liverpool arrived opposite the Eden Gardens and dropped anchor. Unloading began and the crew was paid off, with only the officers and apprentices retained. From the ship Kendall could see the great Fort William, built in the later 18th century after the rising of the Nawab of Bengal had overpowered the original garrison. The prisoners taken had been left to die in a tiny guardroom in the old fort which became known to the world as "The Black Hole of Calcutta". The British responded and troops under the command of Robert Clive marched on Calcutta, defeating the Nawab at the Battle of Plessey and recapturing the city.

Plans were then laid for the construction of a much bigger fort, to the south of the original battlements. This vast walled construction was octagonal in shape and surrounded on all sides by a 30ft deep moat, which could be flooded from the river if necessary. The ground around it was cleared to provide a field of fire in all directions, although this quickly developed into a park, known as the Maidan, where the British soon built a racecourse, a cricket ground and other suitably imperial amenities, such as a riding path and a cathedral. As a result of the developments Calcutta became the capital of British India in 1772. The marshes around the city were drained and the city boomed with wealthy merchants building vast mansions with money they had made from jute and opium trading.

Kendall longed to explore the city, but Captain Whiting had other ideas. He had the youngsters working from dawn to dusk, cleaning and painting the ship, even in the hottest and most humid conditions. When eventually they were allowed ashore they had to be careful to avoid being shanghaied, as there was a constant demand for crews as ships came and went, and unscrupulous boarding masters had been known to kidnap sailors. Captains paid the agents for the number of men delivered to them, and so often crews were made up of seamen who had been rendered unconscious by drink, drugs or a simple bang on the head. By the time they came to their senses they were at sea, although in Calcutta there was at least a chance of escape as they might wake before they left the river. Amongst those dropped off at the mouth of the Hooghly were a clergyman, a corpse and, on one occasion, a woman, who was allowed to leave the ship after having "proved her womanhood" to the captain.

With so many ships waiting for jute, the port was crawling with sailors. The locals tried to provide entertainment to keep them out of trouble, but religious concerts and other such suitable Victorian amusements held very limited appeal. It was noted, however, that if buns and tea were served at an event, the number of apprentices attending increased dramatically. One place where the sailors were always welcomed was at the Priory of the Order of St Paul, in Garden Reach, to the south of Fort William. Father Hopkins made sure that no-one ever went hungry. Elsewhere, the good father's "opposition" proved to be a man called Ben Lyness, known as "Holy Joe", who provided tea and buns and weekly concerts for the youngsters. On one occasion Kendall was even convinced to appear on stage to sing. His renewed theatrical career was short-lived and ended amid a salvo of flying buns.

With as many as 300 apprentices in town there was endless potential for trouble. Egged on by a fellow apprentice called Lacey from the sailing ship Indore, Kendall decided one day that the Liverpool needed to have a pet. Captain Wilding showed no interest at all when Kendall asked for funding to pay for a small dog. The boys therefore decided that the only course of action was to "borrow" a local animal. They concluded, on their way to the Priory, that the best place to carry out their scheme was in the Kidderpur district, which lay between Fort William and Garden Reach. When they returned a few hours later, having been fed by Father Hopkins, they caught sight of a small white dog and Kendall immediately grabbed it and shoved it inside his jacket.

The theft was spotted by a local and he immediately began to raise the alarm. Before long, the two apprentices were being pursued by a small mob armed with sticks and stones. They raced to the Hastings Bridge, which crossed a small river called Tolly's Nala, separating Kidderpur from the Maidan district. The fugitives then sprinted to the river bank and jumped aboard a small boat which ferried them out to Lacey's ship, leaving the locals to remonstrate from the river bank.

Safely aboard the Indore, Kendall opened his jacket to show his pals his new pet, and discovered that he had stolen a small goat rather than a dog. There was much hilarity when word got round.

The jute finally began to arrive in Calcutta and soon all their time was spent loading bale after bale of the valuable fibre. On that trip the Liverpool successfully stowed 28,015 bales, around 6,000 tons of jute. Thus laden, she gathered a new crew and set off under tow down the Hooghly. The trip home would last just 102 days before the Liverpool arrived in the Firth of Tay, to be towed into the port of Dundee. Their only port of call was St Helena, the desolate island in the middle of the Atlantic where, years before, Napoleon had been sent in exile. They picked up a bag of potatoes and sailed on.

On the journey one of Kendall's crew was an Australian seaman called Frank Butler. He seemed a pleasant enough individual, but within a few years would become infamous in his homeland. Kendall heard that he had tired of life at sea and had decided to go into the gold prospecting business. It was not a success and in desperation, Butler devised a plan to lure rich investors into the wilderness with him and then killed them, taking their money and returning to civilisation to spend his ill-gotten gains. Often he used the identities of his victims to confuse anyone who was looking for them.

Unfortunately for the villain, in 1896 the friends of Captain Lee Weller, one of his victims, grew suspicious and Butler decided it was time to go back to sea. Using Weller's name he joined a sailing ship called the Swanhilda, bound for San Francisco. The Australian police were not far behind and sent a telegraph message around the world informing the authorities in San Francisco to watch out for the fugitive on the Swanhilda. Australian detectives were sent after Butler on the next fast mail ship. Disguising themselves as quarantine men, American marshals boarded the Swanhilda and arrested Butler. He was extradited to Sydney, tried and hanged.

When the Liverpool arrived in Dundee the crew was paid off. Captain Whiting had taken a shine to young Kendall and asked him to stay for the next voyage to Calcutta. Kendall agreed. The ship was towed back to Liverpool and once again began loading salt. As they had arrived in Calcutta too early the previous year, it was decided to sail a month later and so Kendall was allowed time off to visit his family, and his friends on the Indefatigable. He spent much of his time with Minnie Wright Jones, who was growing prettier with each passing year.

Towards the end of April 1894 the Liverpool put to sea again. The voyage was longer as conditions were not as good as they had been a year earlier and the ship did not reach the Hoogly until the middle of August. Once again the apprentices were allowed to run riot as the ships waited for the jute to arrive. In December, as loading was nearing completion, Kendall fell ill with a fever that was sufficiently serious for him to be transferred to the General Hospital, across the Maidan from Fort William. He was to stay there for several weeks. Captain Whiting left instructions that when Kendall was strong enough to be discharged from the hospital he should try to find a way to get to New York, as this was to be the Liverpool's next port of call, delivering jute to the mills at Greenpoint, on the East River, across from Manhattan.

The jute ships were by then clearing out of Calcutta for the winter, but when Kendall was released from hospital he found the Bangalore still loading and introduced himself to Captain Longdon, a tough old Rhode Island sailor, who agreed to take the young apprentice to New York. It was to be one of the fastest voyages on record, although the departure was delayed for several days because of bureaucracy. Officially the voyage lasted 83 days, but the actual time at sea was a remarkable 72 days. The speed of the journey meant that Henry arrived in New York ahead of the Liverpool. He was paid off by the Bangalore and, with nothing to do but wait, began to explore the city, crossing on the Greenpoint Ferry to the 23rd Street landing. Each day he called at the port to discover if there was any word of his ship. He had not been to New York since his first voyages six years earlier. The city was just beginning to sprout its first skyscrapers and Kendall marvelled at the new Manhattan Life Insurance Building, which rose 348 feet, surpassing the New York World newspaper building as the tallest building in the world.

It was a week before the Liverpool arrived and Captain Whiting was taken aback to discover that Kendall was already there. Henry soon rejoined his fellow apprentices and the bales of jute were unloaded. This took several weeks and then the ship sailed up the east coast to St John, New Brunswick, where it took on a cargo of Canadian timber to be carried to Liverpool.

It was July before the ship set sail from St John, across the Bay of Fundy towards the southern end of the Nova Scotia peninsula. As they rounded Cape Island and set course for southern Ireland, the First Officer called the apprentices down from the masts, where they had been working, and informed them that Kendall would henceforth be referred to as "Mr Kendall". It was Henry's first promotion. As a midshipman he was a junior officer.

They stopped off at Kinsale on the return journey to Liverpool but finally reached the Mersey at the beginning of August, after 16 months away from home. Captain Whiting was happy for Kendall to stay on with the Liverpool and was planning a voyage to Philadelphia, but his new midshipman had bigger ambitions.

CHAPTER TWELVE

The Victorian Age was coming to a close. Queen Victoria, the great constant, was 76 years of age and fast approaching her Diamond Jubilee, marking an impressive 60 years on the throne. William Ewart Gladstone, the dominant political figure for more than 40 years, had finally retired and a new generation of politicians was taking over. A general election that summer handed power to the Conservatives under Lord Salisbury.

Across Britain everyone was reading Arthur Conan Doyle's stories about Sherlock Holmes. The magic of moving pictures would soon arrive in Britain, and there was a new-fangled device called the automobile. It was an age of innovation and while the romance of sail was still attractive, Kendall yearned for a change of scenery. He had sailed the North Atlantic, had been to the Orient by way of Suez and around the Cape of Good Hope; he knew Australia and India; he had survived Cape Horn in a floating wreck and been a crewman in one of the mighty windjammers. His life had been one of great adventure. At 21, he was the perfect role model for the boys on the Indefatigable, but he wanted more adventure.

His next destination, he decided, was to be Africa.

A map of the Dark Continent in 1895 showed much of the eastern side coloured pink, an indication that this was part of the British Empire. The light blue of France was predominant in the west. Elsewhere there were a handful of other territories belonging to Portugal, Germany, Belgium, Spain and Italy. There were still a few regions marked "unexplored" but the Germans and the French, desperate to rival Britain, were sending explorers into these areas, in search of anything of value.

In the Colonial Office in London, the men who looked at the wall charts were worried that the Germans and the French would do anything to acquire more colonies. Even the Italians were causing problems. The French had taken control of Dahomey and Madagascar and were advancing in Chad, Mauretania and Upper Volta. The Belgians had conquered the eastern part of Congo and Italy had snatched Eritrea.

Britain's new Colonial Secretary Joseph Chamberlain was keen to ensure that not only would Britain maintain her empire, but that she should continue to expand it. If there was any excuse to send troops to create a protectorate, Chamberlain was willing to exploit it. The British had been trading on the West African coastline for centuries, competing with the Portuguese and the Dutch in the early years of the slave trade. Once that had been outlawed growth slowed, although there were still many raw material to be taken from Africa.

The African Steamship Company began to trade in the region in the 1840s, but by 1868 it had acquired the reputation for being a rather less than dynamic organization. John Dempster, the company's chief clerk, wanted the owners to be more ambitious, but the company did not have sufficient ships suitable for what needed to be done. Dempster was frustrated. So too were many of the merchants of Glasgow and Liverpool. They decided that the best way forward was to start a rival company and asked Dempster to become their agent in Liverpool. He drove a hard bargain and insisted on getting the help of ship designer Alexander Elder, the son of a celebrated Glasgow ship-builder. The result was the Elder Dempster company, which was given the right to run all operations for the new British and African Steam Ship Navigation Company. Within 10 years Elder and Dempster had bought the company from its founders - and had swallowed up the old African Steamship Company as well.

Elder and Dempster eventually wanted someone else to run the business for them and they turned to Alfred Jones, who had risen from humble beginnings in Wales to be the general manager of the African Steamship Company by the age of only 26. Frustrated by that company's slow progress he had quit the business and borrowed the money to start his own fleet. He soon realized that there was no future in sailing ships - even in Africa. He sold the firm and was examining ways to get into the steamship business when Elder and Dempster offered him a job.

Jones was as wily as Dempster had once been and agreed, but only on condition that he would be a partner in the firm. A deal was agreed and it was not long before Jones had persuaded both Elder and Dempster to retire and had taken full control of the business. He wanted a bigger and better company and dreamed of a fleet of 100 ships, expanding from the African trade to challenge the biggest shipping companies on more profitable routes.

When Henry Kendall joined Elder Dempster in 1895, the firm had scheduled services from Liverpool to the Gold Coast (now Ghana) and what was then known as the Niger Coast Protectorate (now Nigeria). The Elder Dempster ships carried not only passengers, but also cargo, specifically palm oil which was much in demand in Britain for the manufacture of soap, candles and for use as a lubricant for industrial machinery.

Kendall joined the SS Bathurst, one of the new ships that Jones had commissioned. She was only two years old and was smaller than the Liverpool, weighing in at 2,800 tons. She plied her trade on regular runs from Liverpool to Las Palmas on Grand Canary, and from there along the African coast, stopping at Bathurst in The Gambia, Freetown in Sierra Leone and Monrovia, Liberia. After that she would continue to Cape Coast Castle, Accra and finally to Lagos. Each voyage took around two months. Once goods were unloaded and a new cargo taken aboard, the ship would start back for Liverpool, following the same route.

During Kendall's first voyage on the Bathurst it became clear from talk at Cape Coast that trouble was brewing with King Prempeh of the Ashanti Kingdom.

This had its roots in the 1670s, when the tribal areas speaking the Akran language, were united by Osei Tutu. Kumasi was chosen as the Ashanti capital and the kingdom expanded with a series of treaties and wars. Inevitably, this ambitious nation came into conflict with the British, who had formed the Gold Coast in 1821 by seizing all private land along the coast. The first Anglo-Ashanti War had taken place in 1863 and a second followed in 1874. The Ashanti had little chance against such a powerful military empire, but that did not stop them fighting. King Prempeh was stirring up trouble in British-controlled areas and refusing to pay reparations resulting from the 1874 war. The Inspector-General of the Gold Coast Constabulary, Colonel Sir Francis Scott, was ordered to send a military expedition to Kumasi to restore order.

The biggest fear for the Colonial Office was that Prempeh would make a deal with the French or the Germans and give them more influence in a region that Britain wanted to dominate.

As soon as the SS Bathurst steamed back into Liverpool on November 18, 1895, she was ordered to prepare to depart immediately, this time carrying troops. Chamberlain wanted King Prempeh out of the way and was willing to give Scott a sizeable army to get the job done. The force that was gathering in Liverpool included not only Prince Henry of Battenberg, the 37-year-old husband of Queen Victoria's youngest daughter Beatrice, but also a rising military star called Major Robert Baden-Powell, who would become the founder of the Boy Scout movement at the end of his distinguished military career.

The Bathurst sailed on November 25 and was back at Cape Coast Castle by the middle of December, having wasted no time with stops on the way. The British troops were disembarked and began the 150-mile march across country to Kumasi. The heat was intense and conditions difficult, with thick jungle and swamps to be negotiated on the way. The wide path that began at Cape Coast soon petered out into a narrow track and it took the column five days to reach Prahsu, on the banks of the River Prah. A large base had already been established there and the troops rested for five days. They then pushed on towards the Adansi Hills and, to the north of that, Kumasi. Unfortunately, the stop at Prahsu turned out to be a major mistake. Many soldiers fell victim to malaria, including Prince Henry. He was rushed back to the coast and taken aboard the cruiser HMS Blonde. She immediately sailed for England, but the prince died before the ship reached Grand Canary.

Despite the losses from disease, Scott's expedition continued and in mid-January finally arrived in Kumasi. The Ashanti did not fight. Instead there were three days of negotiation before Prempeh announced his surrender. He and his leading advisors were taken to the coast and incarcerated in the castle at Elmina. He would eventually be deported to the Seychelles. The Gold Coast colony swallowed up the Ashanti lands.

While all of this was happening, Kendall and the crew of the Bathurst were waiting at Cape Coast, amusing themselves with trips to explore the numerous lagoons and tidal salt marshes that ran along the coast. It was lush country, with palms and banana trees. The white sand beaches were long and they encountered many fisherman, often working in dug-out canoes.

On several occasions they took small boats up the rivers into the dark rain forests that lay beyond the coastal grassland. The air was filled with insects and butterflies and they could hear monkeys calling and leaping from tree to tree. They caught occasional glimpses of crocodiles, lurking in the shallow waters.

When the expedition returned from Kumasi the Bathurst set off back to Britain. It had been an interesting visit but Kendall's wandering spirit had seen enough of West Africa. He set his sights on the western coast of South America, which was still very remote because work to create a canal through the isthmus of Panama had been stopped for more than five years.

The idea of a Panama Canal made perfect sense and had been discussed as early as the 16th century, when Spain was keen to find a way to speed up voyages to Peru and Ecuador. After the 100-mile Suez Canal was completed in 1869, the idea of building a 48-mile link through Panama seemed relatively simple and potentially profitable as it would not only cut the journey from New York to San Francisco from 14,000 miles to just 6,000, but it would also avoid the dangers of Cape Horn.

Ferdinand de Lesseps, the man who had built the Suez Canal, was such a hero in France that in 1880 he was able to raise money to secure a concession in Panama and to start work. His belief that the canal should be dug at sea level, and without any locks, meant that progress was slow and expensive. Disease killed 22,000 workers. The rocky ground proved to be much harder to break through than had been anticipated and in 1889 the company was declared bankrupt and dissolved. A series of corruption scandals followed, ending up with the convictions of a number of people, including de Lesseps and Gustave Eiffel, the celebrated engineer. It was not until these had all finished that the assets and land of the company were placed in the Compagnie Nouvelle du Canal de Panama, which was incorporated in 1894. Although the path of the canal had already been cleared and 20 miles of the canal excavated, progress was slow.

In this period the US began looking at building a canal through Nicaragua, but that idea was opposed by powerful railway barons and was scrapped. It was not until 1904 that the American government agreed to take over the French project - and another 10 years before the canal finally opened. Ships continued to travel around Cape Horn and Kendall the adventurer wanted to complete a passage from east to west, having previously gone from west to east, aboard the Rollo.

As Elder Dempster did not trade in South America, Kendall turned to the Lamport & Holt company, which specialized in the region. This had been founded 50 years earlier when George Holt, the older brother of Alfred Holt of the Blue Funnel Line, and William Lamport went into business together, aiming to run tramp steamers to ports in South America. They had gradually built up the business and eventually introduced scheduled services.

Kendall signed on as Fourth Officer on the SS Milton, a 2,679-ton steamer. Before he departed, he had a mission he had to fulfil. He proposed to Minnie Wright Jones. She accepted his offer of marriage and it was agreed that the wedding would take place as soon as Henry returned from his next voyage. There was little money for any fancy celebrations, but Minnie would organise the reading of the banns on three consecutive Sundays before the wedding, a legal requirement in those days. Lamport & Holt said that Kendall would be back in time for a wedding at the end of June.

Henry would be away for six months.

The Milton was under the command of the redoubtable Captain Graham, a towering figure who was intensely religious and spent half an hour each day on his knees praying, while the other officers were eating their breakfast.

The voyage took them north to Greenock where there was a cargo of sugar awaiting. The Scottish port, just down the Clyde from Glasgow, had been the centre of sugar refining for more than a century, processing sugar cane that arrived from the West Indies and exporting refined sugar to all corners of the British Empire.

From Greenock, they steamed down to the Cape Verde Islands, where they paused to take on coal. They continued until they reached the coast of Brazil, near Recife, and from there followed the coast southwards, passing Salvador, Rio de Janeiro, Santos and the River Plate. Captain Graham decided to take the Milton through the Straits of Magellan rather than round the Horn, much to Kendall's disappointment. In a steamship the route through the islands was much easier than with a sailing ship, but the narrow channels were still difficult to navigate.

When the Milton reached Cabo Virgenes, she steamed into the Straits of Magellan, to the Primera Angostura and Segunda Angostura narrows. Skirting Magdalena Island, the ship arrived at the Chilean port of Punta Arenas, which had enjoyed much growth since the Gold Rush of 1849, when clippers from Europe took thousands of miners to San Francisco. Twenty years later the first railroads had been built across the United States and the number of ships visiting the Argentine port declined as passengers chose what was seen as a safer route, taking ships to the eastern ports of the United States and then railways across the continent. Punta Arenas, however, remained a major port for shipping goods, notably Chilean wool. In order to get from there to the western part of the Straits of Magellan, the Milton had to go 50 miles due south to Cabo Froward and then skirt around to the west, in the shadow of the rocky Brunswick Peninsula. To the south there are a number of channels through to the Pacific Ocean, but these are highly dangerous as there are a multitude of islands and rocky outcrops. The main channel continues to the west, following an underwater fault line, and ships then navigate through narrows around the Cordova Peninsula and finally emerge in the Pacific. Although violent blizzards and strong winds made the region difficult for any ship, it was fascinating country for Kendall. There were few native inhabitants, most being nomadic and travelling from place to place by canoe. Despite the cold they wore little clothing and it was an established tradition to drop a sealed cask filled with food whenever a ship encountered locals. They had grown used to the custom and expected it. For the ships it was seen as a good investment lest one day they were wrecked and needed the help of the locals.

There was a lonely trip of 800 miles up the desolate coastline from there to Valdivia, the first major port on the coast of Chile. The ship continued to steamed north and the weather improved. From Valdivia onwards the Milton stopped off at all the major ports, the first being Talcahuano (Coronel), followed by Valparaiso, the port which served Santiago, Antofagasta, famed for its mining industry, and Valparaiso, from where Chilean wheat is shipped around the world. The following port of call was Arica, where an impressive hill towers over the harbour, but where the land is a desert.

Finally, Chile turned to Peru and the climate became more lush as the ship steamed on towards Lima. The voyage came to an end at Guayaquil in Ecuador. The city, known as "The Pearl of the Pacific", sits at the mouth of the Guayas River, and had been the centre of the world's cocoa trade since the Spaniards began exporting the beans to Europe in the 1740s. During the latter part of the nineteenth century, cacao exports increased tenfold and Guayaquil developed into the commercial and financial centre of the country. This created rivalry between the coastal region and the highlands, which had traditionally been the seat of power, and in 1895 the wealthy middle classes on the coast led a revolution that took power, opening the way for much greater commercial development.

The region was, however, prone to earthquakes and so the inhabitants had traditionally used wood for their building. This meant that Guayaquil suffered intermittent fires. There had been a major blaze a couple of months before the Milton arrived, but it was nothing compared to what would happen in October that year when 70% of the city was burned to the ground.

The Milton was loaded with cocoa beans and then began the long trip back to Britain, where the beans would be used for the booming chocolate manufacturing industry. The return trip was faster as there were fewer stops along the way and the Milton reached the River Mersey on June 29. The following day was a Tuesday, but Henry Kendall and Minnie Wright Jones had waited long enough. The families gathered that day at the rather grand St George's Church in Everton, which sits on the ridge, towering over the city of Liverpool.

In 1902 Kendall became the Second Officer on the SS Lake Champlain (above), which was one of the first vessels to be fitted with wireless equipment. Kendall would return to the ship in 1912 as her commander. For the captains on the North Atlantic runs, icebergs were part of life and even the most experienced were sometimes unable to avoid them. In 1908, Kendall was in command of the SS Monmouth when she ran into an iceberg in the Belle Isle Strait, between Newfoundland and Labrador. The ship suffered some damage to her bow, but was able to continue to Montreal for repairs. Below: An iceberg photographed by Kendall.

By 1910 Kendall was commander of the SS Montrose, a liner which ran from Antwerp in Belgium to the Canadian ports. It was one of only a few fitted with wireless and this became invaluable when Kendall began to ask questions about two of his passengers, the Reverend John Robinson and his son (seen right in a photograph taken by Kendall). Kendall guessed that the pair were in fact the celebrated murderer Dr Hawley Harvey Crippen and his mistress Ethel le Neve (below) and sent a telegram to Arthur Piers, the manager of the Canadian Pacific Steamship Service in Liverpool. Piers contacted Scotland Yard and Inspector Walter Dew rushed to Liverpool to board the Laurentic, a faster ship, which would arrive in Canada before the Montrose.

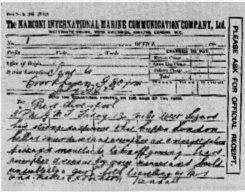

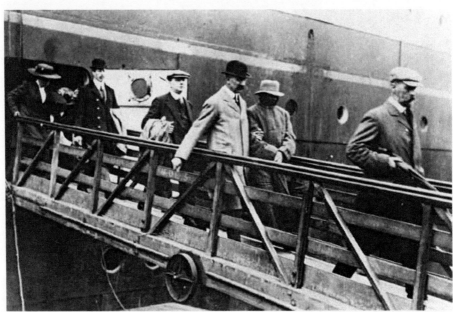

Inspector Dew boarded the Montrose disguised as a pilot when the ship stopped at Father Point, in the St Lawrence Estuary. Kendall introduced them and Dew arrested the fugitives, who were then taken into custody in Quebec City (above). Dew and Kendall (below) became friends and even took time off to travel to Niagara Falls together, to escape the media circus in Quebec City. It is said that Crippen cursed Kendall and there is no doubt that the sinking of the RMS Empress of Ireland in 1914 took place very close to where Crippen had been arrested. The elegant lighthouse at Father Point (left) had much significance in Kendall's life.

The Metropolitan Police had offered an award of £250 for information leading to the capture of Dr Crippen. The cheque was duly presented to Kendall, although he never cashed it. It was framed and mounted on the wall in a salon aboard the SS Montrose. Kendall went back to his normal work but two years later was posted to the Austrian port of Trieste, running immigrant ships from there to Canada.

Henry reckoned that he was the happiest man in England that day. He was 22 and his beautiful bride was 20. Minnie would be a good mother for his children. She was a strict teetotaller, as a result of her mother's tippling, and as Henry never drank they were well-suited. The couple settled in a house on Priory Road in Anfield, to the east of St George's. They would live in various houses in the area for the next 10 years before they finally had enough money to move out to a nicer northern suburb called Orrell Park, where they had a three-storey house with a garden. It was there that, for the first time, the Kendalls could afford to have a maid.

The Milton disappeared off to sea without Kendall and for the next few months Henry stayed at home. He wanted to be with his new bride, but he was also preparing for examinations to become a Second Officer. This involved not only practical seamanship, but also a considerable amount of theory as well. A candidate for this certificate had to provide evidence of his experience, his good conduct, his ability and his sobriety. Kendall had served his time and had impressed his captains. The Board of Trade was only too happy to grant him his first certificate.

More would follow in the years ahead.

CHAPTER THIRTEEN

Like most young wives, the newly-wed Minnie Kendall wanted to have her husband around. She had known that marrying an officer in the merchant navy was a guarantee that she would have to spend a great deal of time on her own, at least until children arrived. The problem with starting a family was that Kendall's salary would be insufficient to support them. They knew that as Henry moved up the ladder he would make more and so it was decided that he would concentrate all his efforts on securing whatever qualifications were needed in order to get higher-paying jobs.

The problem was that all the major steamship lines were only interested in hiring officers who had learned their trade in sailing ships. In order to progress, Henry would have to return to sail once again. This meant that he would be away at sea for long periods of time, rather than being able to come and go on a more regular basis, as was the case on the transatlantic steamer routes.

Having qualified for the Second Officer certificate, Kendall could move on to prepare for the examinations required to become a First Officer, but there was then a minimum period of two years before a First Officer could apply for a Master's certificate. This time had to be served on sailing ships.

Early in 1897 Minnie informed her husband that she was pregnant and, despite their desire to be together as much as possible, the pair knew that it was time for Henry to go back to sea. With a child on the way, he needed to concentrate on his career.

As they had to be separated anyway, Henry decided to find a

ship travelling to a part of the world that he did not know. His heart was set on a voyage to the west coast of the United States and he soon learned that the Lowden & Company firm had a vacancy for a young officer on the Mashona, a 2,300-ton four-masted barque that was bound for San Francisco, by way of Cape Horn. There was no doubt that Henry also felt the necessity to complete his education by going through the Drake Channel from east to west, as this was considered to be the tougher of the two passages. It was something that he wanted to be able to say that he had done. After his adventures with the Rollo, the voyage would probably be easier, because the Mashona was a much bigger ship and featured a steel hull.

What appealed to Kendall most of all was that the Mashona was commanded by Captain William Jones, a 56-year-old officer who had served with the company since the 1880s. Henry knew that an experienced captain was a good role model, from whom he could learn a great deal. The Mashona was towed out of the Mersey in March 1897, but the weather was bad and she could make little progress. She was driven back by the winds to such an extent that the lookout even sighted the Isle of Man at one point before the storm began to ease and the ship was able to began her voyage in earnest. It was a lesson that demonstrated why steamships would ultimately win the battle with sail for domination of the world's trade.

Once they had reached the Atlantic Captain Jones turned the ship to the west and with strong winds behind them they headed towards the Americas, aiming to pick up the North East Trade Winds.

The First Officer was a man of 60 and so Kendall and the Second Officer found themselves becoming close friends, as there was a big age gap between the pair and the two senior men. The younger men soon discovered that they shared a passion for boxing and would happily spar throughout an entire watch. It not only kept them very fit, but also showed the crewmen that the two were tough. When either of them gave an order, it was instantly obeyed and Captain Jones was happy to allow them to box, as the ship was more efficient as a result.

The voyage to Cape Horn took only 70 days and as they neared the area they hoped that the weather would be kind to them and allow them to get through to the Pacific without too much drama. No matter how much bravado the sailors may have when on shore, they were all afraid of rounding the Horn. It had been the graveyard of too many seamen not to inspire trepidation. As it turned out, the seas were against them. For 30 days they battled into the winds and mountainous seas, only to be blown back out into the Atlantic. Back they went, time and again. As the days slipped by the spirits of the crew sank. They were permanently wet, cold and miserable.

When finally they broke through Jones immediately turned the ship to the north and they headed into warmer and more pleasant latitudes. The mood improved. Soon they were moving along at speed, heading up towards the Equator. They used the north-easterly trade winds, which took them out into the Pacific Ocean, then turned to the east and rode the westerly winds back towards the coast of California. Jones's navigational skills were well-developed and they arrived not far from the Golden Gate, the straits that opened into San Francisco Bay. By the time they arrived it was September. They were met by a tug and towed to the downtown area, passing the Alcatraz Light before mooring finally at the Green Street Wharf, in the shadow of Telegraph Hill. They found a city in uproar.

The previous summer gold had been discovered in a place called Rabbit Creek, near the Klondike River, in the Yukon territory of north-western Canada. It was so remote a location that it was not until July 1897 that a ship sailed into San Francisco with the news, leading to reports that she carried more than a ton of gold. There was a new gold rush and it seemed that everyone wanted to be involved. Gold fever gripped the city. Thousands of people were pouring into the city from the east, looking for ships to take them north to Juneau and Skagway. From there they could trek overland to the gold fields. Few had any idea of the dangers that they would face in the Yukon and many were turned away by the authorities, who refused to allow anyone to begin the trek unless they had a sufficient supply of provisions for the Yukon Trail. Many of those who were turned away returned to San Francisco, keen to find ways to raise the money they needed.

Even before the gold rush, San Francisco had been a wild town. A few years earlier, Rudyard Kipling had visited and concluded that it was "a mad city - inhabited by perfectly insane people", although he did register the fact that the women were "of a remarkable beauty".

Although the voyage had taken them 182 days, during which not one of the crew had set foot on dry land, Captain Jones kept their shore time to a minimum, worried that if he let the crew leave the ship, most of them would never return. And so they stayed on the Mashona while the unloading was completed. They could see a strange entertainment pavilion and observatory called the German Castle on the top of Telegraph Hill, but they could see also that it was deserted and gradually falling down. It was only once the loading was completed that Captain Jones allowed Kendall and his friend the Second Officer leave to visit the city. Henry quickly concluded that the district known as the Barbary Coast was a neighbourhood "alive with gaudy wickedness". The chance to go ashore was short-lived. Almost immediately they were ordered to go to Mission Bay to await orders. The locals would row to the ship in small boats, offering the sailors food, books and other comforts, but Captain Jones would not let his crew ashore. He was relieved when word came that he could set sail for Astoria, a port at the mouth of the Willamette River in Oregon. Their mission was go from there to Portland to load wheat.

When they arrived in port and began unloading, the Mashona fell victim to the boarding masters. They needed crewmen for other ships that were ready to sail and began to lure away the sailors with promises of wine, women and gold. The captains did what they could to keep their men, but one by one they began to disappear, either lured to other ships that were willing to pay exorbitant prices for a crew, or because they wanted to go to the Yukon and look for gold. The Mashona lost two of her eight apprentices to gold fever.

In the end, after two months loading, Captain Jones was forced to pay the boarding masters for new men. They set sail in December, bound for Cape Horn and Le Havre, on the northern coast of France, where customers were waiting for the wheat. The voyage took 147 days. On arrival Captain Jones paid off the entire crew and Kendall caught a ferry back to England, taking a train to Liverpool. In his absence Minnie had given birth to a baby boy and for the next three months Henry stayed at home with his wife and child. He studied for the examinations to become a First Officer and soon had another certificate to add to his collection. Having been frustrated in his desire to see San Francisco, he signed up as an officer with the W Leyland shipping firm, which was preparing a steel-hulled three-master called the Ditton for a voyage to California.

The Ditton was unusual as she featured cabins above the level of the deck, a rare thing in sailing ships. These would provide shelter in the rough seas around the Cape.

It was under the command of Captain Henry Stap, a 69-year-old veteran from Yorkshire, who had previously made a name for himself as the master of Isambard Kingdom Brunel's SS Great Britain. This was to be Stap's last voyage, and he had decided to take along one of his daughters to give her the opportunity to travel a little before he retired from seafaring. They were to load coal in North Shields and from there sail to San Francisco in August 1898. It was to be a difficult voyage. The weather around the Cape was worse than ever and it took 187 days before the Ditton arrived at the Golden Gate. They were unloading the coal when the city was hit by a powerful earthquake, centred on Mare Island, in the northern part of the bay. This caused widespread damage, including several fallen buildings, bridges that were rendered impassable, and roads that were damaged by crevices.

All around the bay, chimneys fell. There were serious fires in the Vallejo district. The people of San Francisco had grown used to the rumblings of the San Andreas Fault, and life was quickly back to normal. Little did they know that within a few years the city would be destroyed by a massive earthquake, and by the fires that would follow, burning out of control for four days. By the end of the nightmare, 500 blocks of the downtown area would be completely destroyed and the world that Kendall and his colleagues so enjoyed would be gone forever.

Captain Stap received orders as soon as the cargo had been unloaded and the ship cleaned. He was to sail the Ditton down the coast of California, across to the Galapagos Islands and then on to the Chilean port of Tocopilla, where it was to load nitrates to be taken to Hamburg in Germany. At the time Chile had what amounted to a monopoly on nitrates, which were very valuable as they could be used in the manufacture of both fertilizer and explosives. These had been created because there was so little rain in the Atacama Desert that the soluble nitrates were never washed away. As demand increased and other sources ran out, Chile boomed. There was even a war between Chile and its neighbours, Peru and Bolivia, for control of the nitrate business. In the end the government granted licences to foreign companies to exploit the nitrate reserves and cashed in by introducing a tax on the exports. Much of the trade ended up in the hands of British trading companies, but Tocopilla remained a small port with only limited room for ships to dock. There were few workers available in this remote spot and so the crews had to do the loading themselves, which involved carrying bag after bag of nitrate onto the ship. It was a time-consuming business and so the Ditton waited for two months before finally being able to load. As each ship finished the laborious process the waiting crews cheered the departing vessels.

There was not much to do in the town. There was plenty of silver at reasonable prices, and no shortage of bars and whorehouses, but otherwise it was small port on the edge of an empty desert.

As time went on, Captain Stap became more and more impatient to get home and begin his retirement. Finally their turn to load came and, once that was achieved, they set sail for the Cape. But there was another surprise in store for Stap and his crew. When they arrived at Cape Horn they found a strange and unusual phenomenon. For most of the time, the winds around Cape Horn blow from the west, making it easier to pass from the Pacific into the Atlantic. It is still not easy, but it is generally agreed that going east to west was more difficult. On this occasion, however, the winds had reversed direction and easterly gales meant that it took the Ditton another month to get through the Drake Passage. From there it should have been an easy run to Europe, but things took a downward turn when the Third Officer lost control and went mad. They had to lock him up in a cabin for his own safety.

The voyage to Hamburg took 156 days. When they arrived there was bad news for Kendall. He telegraphed Minnie to say he would be home soon and learned the devastating news that the baby Evelyn had died. He hurried back to Liverpool. Henry would remain with Minnie for Christmas and together they celebrated - as best they could in the circumstances - the arrival of a new century.

He then turned his attention to studying for his Board of Trade certificate of competency as a Master Mariner. He was still only 26, but the new qualification meant that there were many more opportunities available. Having a Master's certificate put him on the map of the big steam ship companies, which meant that he could have a more organized lifestyle. At the same time, he knew it was probably the end of his career on sailing ships, for there was little future in these elegant and romantic vessels.

He applied for a number of different positions with various steamship companies and quickly found himself being appointed the Second Officer on a tramp steamer called the Aphrodite. She had run aground on the coast of Spain, and was laid up in dry dock, undergoing major repairs. This was a good position as it meant that Henry could spend more time at home with Minnie.

The Captain and the First Officer of the Aphrodite were away on leave, but Kendall felt that there was still much that could be done by the crew. On steamships, the old system of hiring crews for individual voyages had disappeared. Crewmen on the steamers had contracts and Kendall found that the crew he had inherited did not share his work ethic. He tried to make them work harder, but the result was that the crew defied his orders and walked out. Kendall, the hard nut from the world of sailing ships, was not about to back down. He called the police and had the entire crew arrested. As many of them came from India, they were deported. Kendall was worried that the owners of the ship would be angry, but it turned out that they were delighted as they had been saved the cost of keeping a crew that was doing no work for three months.

A few weeks later Henry received word that another of his applications had been accepted, and he was offered the position of Fourth Officer on the Beaver Line's SS Lake Superior. This was a far better opportunity as the Beaver Line was an important company in the North Atlantic trade. He made the necessary arrangements with the owners of the Aphrodite and moved on. They did not stand in his way.

Originally named the Canada Steamship Company, the Beaver Line had acquired its nickname because the company flag featured a beaver. The ships were all named after Canadian lakes and ran back and forth across the Atlantic. They were not the glamorous ocean liners that would come later, but rather immigrant ships that made their money transporting thousands of poor Europeans who wanted to start new lives in the United States and Canada. In the 1890s the flood of immigrants had increased the competition in the Atlantic shipping trade to such an extent that the Beaver Line had run into financial difficulties. Alfred Jones of the Elder Dempster line saw the opportunity to expand his empire beyond the African steamship trade and bought the Beaver company, establishing a weekly service between Liverpool and Quebec, although during the winter months when the St Lawrence was closed because of ice, the ships ran into Halifax in Nova Scotia. From the Canadian ports the immigrants would head west by train.

The SS Lake Superior was not a modern ship. She was 16 years old and had survived a brush with an iceberg in 1894. At almost 5,000 tons, she was the biggest ship on which Kendall had served, and she boasted 1,270 berths, the majority of them in Third Class.

It was the start of Kendall's career as an officer on the North Atlantic liners. Glamorous, it was not, but at last he was able to spend more time at home, and feel that his career was moving in the right direction.

The days of sail were over.

CHAPTER FOURTEEN

Henry's plans for a more ordered life were disrupted by the Boers in South Africa. Descendants of early immigrants from the Netherlands and the German states, the Boers had established two independent republics in the 1850s. The Zuid-Afrikaansche Republiek and the Orange Free State were in competition with the British dependencies of Cape Colony and Natal. The Afrikaners wanted the British out of South Africa and decided to settle the affair once and for all by invading the British areas, besieging of the garrisons at Mafeking, Kimberley and Ladysmith.

If they had hoped for a weak British response, the Boers were in for a surprise. There was a massive reaction from London, where the government of Lord Salisbury, and particularly the combative Secretary of the Colonies Joseph Chamberlain, were not about to accept any attack on the British Empire. Chamberlain saw the attack as an opportunity for the British to turn the tables and take complete control of South Africa. Half a million soldiers were mobilized and the government requisitioned ships to transport the troops to South Africa.

Kendall might have been expecting that the Lake Superior would be one of the ships involved, but instead she sailed from Liverpool with a large number of immigrants, returning from New Brunswick laden with cattle for the slaughterhouses of Wallasey.

It was more than 10 years since Henry had first crossed the North Atlantic as a cabin boy on the City of Berlin. He remembered the howling gales, freezing fogs and icebergs, and recalled that he had not enjoyed them. But the first voyage on the Lake Superior would be a very significant moment in his life, as he discovered himself drawn into the challenges that the North Atlantic routes presented. This interest quickly became a fascination. Every voyage was different and the challenges, while perhaps not as dramatic as battling around Cape Horn, were just as interesting.

By steamship from Liverpool, there were two major routes by which the Canadian ports could be reached. The most efficient took the liners to the south of Ireland, where they would often call at Queenstown, in order to pick up goods or passengers. From there the ships steamed due west. In the winter months, the route edged gently to the south, in order to allow ships to pass to the south of the rugged island of Newfoundland. In the summer months the ships kept the westerly course in order to arrive at the northern tip of Newfoundland, where they could pass through the Belle Isle Strait into the Gulf of St Lawrence.

At any time of year the Belle Isle Strait was a dangerous place to be. The great liners that were being built in that era may have seemed huge and unsinkable, but icebergs were often bigger. An iceberg normally weighs in excess of 200,000 tons. They can rise to terrifying heights above the water. The biggest on record in the North Atlantic was 500 ft tall, but they came in all shapes and sizes. The one thing they all have in common is that, because of the difference in density between fresh water, from which icebergs are made, and the salt water in which they float, only 10% of the ice is ever out of the water. The tip of an iceberg is simply an indication of a much bigger danger that lurks beneath the water.

It is estimated that as many as 10,000 icebergs a year break away from the glaciers of western Greenland and are carried north, by the Labrador Current. This then swings to the west and then turns south, taking the icebergs along the desolate coast of Labrador, towards the warmer waters of Newfoundland. It is here that the icebergs meet the North Atlantic shipping lanes. By that point there are perhaps only 400 still large enough to be dangerous to ships. When these survivors reach the south-eastern tip of Newfoundland, in the area known as the Grand Banks, they encounter the warmer waters of the Gulf Stream and quickly disappear.

The problem with icebergs was that in an era before radar and sonar, they were impossible to track. They could move at considerable speeds, depending on the currents in the water and the winds around them. Once an iceberg had gathered momentum, it took a very long time for it to slow down, even after the winds had disappeared.

For the captains of the North Atlantic liners, the biggest fear was a collision with an iceberg. The most dangerous were those that sat low in the water, with just a few feet visible. They were very difficult to spot, particularly when visibility was reduced by fog. The waters around Newfoundland are among the foggiest in the world, particularly in the spring and summer months when warm air from the south meets the cold waters of the Labrador Current. In some areas there is fog for more than 200 days a year.

The Belle Island Strait is where all these dangers coincide. It is a narrow channel with rocky shorelines, there are icebergs and fog. In the summer months many ships pass through each day, bound for the estuary of the St Lawrence, and on to Quebec, where the river narrows. Some can go further up river to Montreal. In the autumn the temperatures drop and the ice shelf that runs along the coast of Labrador expands southward. Belle Isle Strait is closed for the winter months and the ships must take the southerly route around Newfoundland, and then across the southern entrance to the Gulf of St Lawrence to the Nova Scotia peninsula. They can connect with the Canadian railway system either in Halifax, or in the Bay of Fundy, where the port of St John, in the province of New Brunswick, offers faster rail access to Montreal and Quebec.

St John had developed into a major port thanks to a spectacular harbour and railways that brought raw materials for the British Empire. This growth began with timber, but as the railways improved, St John became the destination for cattle from the vast prairies of central Canada. The development of Canada, the United States and indeed Argentina, meant that farmers were soon producing much more beef than was needed. The animals were driven to the railheads and transported to slaughterhouses and canneries on the outskirts of the major cities. Tinned beef was good business, but delivering fresh meat was also a lucrative trade and many animals were taken to St John, loaded on ships and transported to Europe. Outbreaks of disease meant that the Europeans did not want the herds to mix with the local livestock and so vast slaughterhouses were established in the major ports, fenced off and carefully regulated to make sure that none of the foreign animals came into contact with native cows. The largest such facility in Britain was at Wallasey, on the Cheshire side of the River Mersey. Thousands of head of cattle would arrive from the Americas and would be slaughtered there and the meat transported around the country, while it was still fresh.

This continued to be big business until improvements in refrigeration enabled the industry to relocate to the big cities in the United States and Canada, where meat-packing became big business, alongside the canning trade.

Putting around 1,000 cattle on a ship was not an easy business. Loading was highly dangerous, although unloading was probably worse, as the animals were frantic to escape after 10 days of being locked in the hold of the ship. Many a cattle man was gored in the process.

Once the cattle had been unloaded, the ship moved across the river to Liverpool, loaded with immigrants and finished goods from Manchester, and sailed back to Canada.

"In every man's life there occurs a big crisis when the future trends of his career are determined," said Kendall. "That first voyage in the Lake Superior was the moment that I made my decision."

He wanted to be in the North Atlantic, to make it his territory.

After a number of voyages on the Lake Superior, the ship was laid up for a refit. Kendall and the ship's Third Officer were ordered ashore to help organize the vast movement of men and horses, bound for the Boer War. Elder Dempster had five ships waiting to be loaded and despatched: the Montrose, Monteagle, Monterey, Lake Erie and Montcalm. When they were ready the troops would be marched to the docks, behind brass bands. The streets were filled with patriotic, flag-waving crowds, cheering the soldiers on their way. The Lord Mayor of Liverpool would make a suitable speech and the soldiers would file aboard the great ships.

"I remember one day seeing the South of Ireland Imperial Yeomanry boarding one of the ships," Kendall recalled. "I remarked to an army officer nearby that they seemed like a fine body of men. He replied that he did not know, but he had heard that if they could not storm a Boer town, they would certainly be able to steal it."

With so many ships being taken by the government, Elder Dempster needed to look elsewhere for vessels to continue its normal trading activities. A series of purchases and leases were organized and the fleet grew. One of these new ships was the SS Wassau, a 3,500-ton ship, which had previously belonged the Union-Castle Line, under the name of SS Trojan. Kendall was appointed First Officer on this ship and returned to the North Atlantic runs.

On the first voyage, an elderly cattle man died as the ship was returning from New Brunswick. It was a couple of days before the body was found in his cabin and by then the corpse was beginning to smell rather less than fresh. The captain ordered a burial at sea and two seamen were instructed to prepare the body, sewing it into a canvas bag. They were not happy with the task given them, and informed the officers that they would not carry out the job unless the captain gave them a bottle of rum. Such insubordination was frowned upon, but the captain knew that he had a problem. He could punish the offenders, but he would then have fewer crew available and still have a body that needed to be got rid of. He quietly agreed to let the sailors have some rum.

At the appointed hour, the officers formed up to await the arrival of the body. The seas were running high, and they all wanted to get the ceremony over and done with. But nothing happened. After several minutes waiting, the irritated captain told Kendall to find out what was going on. Henry discovered the two sailors refusing to finish the task, unless they were given a second bottle of rum. The captain was furious at this news, but accepted that he had little choice. A new hour was set for the funeral, and the process was repeated. Once again there was no corpse. Mad with rage, the captain told Kendall to sort it out. Once again the young officer rushed to find the two missing sailors. To his astonishment they were lying on the floor of the cabin, singing songs. More worryingly, the corpse had disappeared.

Kendall could get no sense from either man about what had happened to the body. It was only when he encountered a fireman who had been up on deck for a breath of fresh air, that he learned that the two sailors had been carrying the body along the deck, with the ship rolling with the waves, when they decided that it was simply too difficult a task. They threw the corpse overboard with a cry of "Go to the devil, you smelly old man!" It was hardly a Christian burial, but there was not much that could be done, except to punish the offenders.

On the second voyage out to Canada the ship ran into a huge storm to the south of Ireland. The steering gear collapsed under the strain and one of the masts was snapped clean. The captain ordered the crew to take the ship into Queenstown, and from there telegraphed Liverpool with the news of the problems. It was decided that the passengers would be put aboard another liner going west and the Wassau would be brought back to Liverpool under tow. She would soon be sold on to another company.

While Kendall was serving on the Wassau, Queen Victoria, the sovereign for 63 years, died. The Victorian Era came to an end, and with it went some of the security of the age. The world was changing fast. The new King Edward VII, who was by then 59 years of age, seemed a less solid individual than the old queen. He was famous for his romantic dalliances with the likes of Lillie Langtry and Alice Keppel.

Kendall moved on and was appointed an officer on the SS Lusitania. This was a much smaller vessel than the celebrated ship that would later bear the same name. She was a 3,900 ton iron vessel, built in 1871 for the Pacific Steam Navigation Company. For many years she had plied her trade between Britain and Australia. Re-engined and updated in 1886, she was acquired at the start of 1900 by the Beaver Line, to replace the ships being used in the Boer War. After a few months she seemed to be excess to requirements and was sold back to her original owner, but seven months later Canadian Pacific bought her again and she began work on the Liverpool-Halifax-St John route, sailing the southern route to Canada, avoiding the dangers of the Belle Isle Strait.

At the end of June 1900 the Lusitania, en route to Canada, ran into some of the celebrated Newfoundland fog. Normally this would not be a problem as the ships would proceed slowly, sounding regular warnings. Navigation was impossible without the stars for guidance, but the course was calculated to allow the ship to pass comfortably to the south of Cape Race.

Unfortunately, something went wrong.

Kendall was woken when he was thrown from his bunk as the Lusitania hit the rocks at the foot of the cliffs, on the coast of the Avalon Peninsular, about 45 miles to the south of St John's, Newfoundland. Ten miles north of Cape Race.

There were some lurid accounts of what happened that night, after the impact. Some of the immigrants on board panicked and trampled women and children as they fought to get the lifeboats free. The crew fought back and several passengers were subdued with fists. There was even talk of knife-play. The crew won control and the lifeboats were lowered and correctly loaded. These were then able to make for a sandy inlet nearby. Although a couple of the lifeboats overturned in the surf, none of the passengers was drowned. The officers stayed on the ship, hoping to be able to salvage the vessel, but it soon became clear that the crashing of the waves was threatening to break the wreck in half. The captain ordered the officers to abandon ship, and they joined the miserable group of survivors gathered on the shore. The rain was driving down and many of the passengers were freezing in their nightclothes. The officers took control and decided that the best course of action was to march everyone to the nearest settlement, to keep them warm by walking, and hope that the locals would be able to help.

The village of Renews was awakened by a horde of bedraggled and freezing survivors, many of whom spoke not a word of English. The fishermen and their families did what they could, but it was not until the early afternoon that the SS Glencoe arrived from St John's to pick up the passengers. They were ferried out to the Glencoe in the dories that the fishermen used. Once aboard they were finally able to get warm clothes and a hot meal.

Kendall and the other officers organized the evacuation. When it was nearly completed, he spotted an old woman sitting on a box on the beach, refusing to move. The wind was blowing strongly and she was not responding to commands. Kendall decided that the best course of action was not to try to explain the situation, but simply to pick her up and carry her to the dory. She immediately began to fight, kick and scream, but Kendall soldiered on into the surf intent on putting her on the small boat. A wave broke over them and they fell, but Kendall and another officer were able to grab the woman before she was swept out to sea.

They took her back to land and, having coughed up a great deal of water, she finally spoke - in English - explaining that she was the wife of one of the fishermen and had no desire at all to be sent off with a bunch of immigrants on a ship to St John's.

Kendall apologized profusely for his mistake, but they all saw the humour of the moment.

Once the loading was completed the Glencoe sailed up the coast to St John's. The passengers and crewmen were put aboard other ships to complete their journeys. The officers had to remain in Canada to take part in the Court of Inquiry.

They returned to the site of the shipwreck to see whether salvage was possible and found that the locals were delighted. One inhabitant, carrying home items washed up on the shore, remarked to Kendall that it was "the best wreck in years".

CHAPTER FIFTEEN

It may seen strange for an officer to be promoted after a shipwreck, but when Alfred Jones, the boss of Elder Dempster, heard the reports of how the officers on the SS Lusitania had behaved, they were rewarded. Jones sent word to Canada that they would each be get two additional months of pay, in recognition of what they had done. For Kendall and his fellow officers the additional money was not perhaps the windfall it might have seemed, as they were forced to use all of the money replacing the kit that had been lost.

While they were waiting in St John's, the officers of the Lusitania decided to express their discontent at the way in which the local newspaper had reported the shipwreck. They went to the office of the local newspaper to complain and were met by the editor. A lively argument soon began about what had been written: the officers claiming that the reports had been hugely exaggerated; the editor declaring his innocence. It seemed an odd stand-off, until someone finally asked whether they were in the offices of the Telegraph. The editor laughed and explained that he was in charge of a newspaper called The Telegram, and that if there was a problem with The Telegraph, they would have to cross the street, and visit the offices of that sensational rag!

The Court of Inquiry that followed exonerated the officers of the Lusitania, blaming the wreck on stronger than expected currents and the impenetrable fog. The court commended the crew for having saved all of those on board the vessel.

They headed home as Second Class passengers on an Allan

Line ship, which took them to Glasgow and from there they returned to Liverpool by train. When Kendall arrived at the offices of Elder Dempster he was informed that he had been promoted and should report to the SS Lake Simcoe, the biggest and best ship in the company's fleet. The wreck had definitely done him more good than harm.

The Lake Simcoe was a 4,700-ton liner, built in Bremen in 1884 by the Norddeutscher Lloyd company. Originally known as the Ems, she had just been acquired by Elder Dempster to replace the ships that had been requisitioned for government service in the Boer War. The ship could carry around 1,400 passengers, most of them in Third Class. Her career with Elder Dempster did not begin well, with the ship breaking down on its first voyage and creeping into Quebec behind schedule, after running repairs had been made. In the months that followed, however, the vessel provided Kendall with a few interesting stories.

The life of an officer on an Atlantic liner was such that they would meet a constant stream of interesting characters. Very few normal people travelled abroad and while there were thousands of immigrants, crossing the ocean in the cramped conditions in Third Class, there was little contact between them and the officers. They were a cheerful group, looking ahead to getting a new start in life and dreaming of building better lives for themselves in America and Canada. They would amuse themselves with music and dancing on the decks, but higher up in the ship, in the luxury sections, the passengers were fewer in number. The ability to travel in such style was still a privilege enjoyed by just a few. There were the wealthy, a few businessmen, imperial administrators, government officials and military types. This meant that the ship's officers spent their time with a fascinating assortment of characters. The passengers liked to hear the tales of adventure that the mariners had encountered, and there was never an officer on a liner who did not have a thousand good stories to tell.

Some of them were even true.

The Lake Simcoe had room for about 100 First Class passengers and this group enjoyed close contact with the officers. They dined together every day.

Prince Ranjit of Baluchistan made quite an impact when he arrived in Liverpool from London, accompanied by 25 advisors and servants, including two dancing girls. He seemed to be a pleasant individual and there was clearly no shortage of money.

Indian rulers were the subject of much confusion, even in the highly organized world of Britain's India Office, from where the British ran the country. Large parts of India were under direct British rule, but there were several hundred "princely states" which operated independently. Each had accepted British rule by treaty, but were run by the locals. These featured a bewildering array of Maharajas, Badshahs, Rajas, Nawabs, Nizams, Mirs, Walis and other more exotic royal titles. The British translated all such titles as "Prince", in order to avoid any suggestion that the rulers might have the same status as the British monarch. Baluchistan, in modern Pakistan, was divided into four such princely states.

When Prince Ranjit appeared in London, it was said that he was the son of one of the Rajas, but there was suspicion as it was felt rather unusual for any royal person, even an Indian, to appear with no prior warning. Discreet enquiries were made and word got round that not only was the prince real, but he was also extraordinarily wealthy. London accepted his presence with suitable deference. Once the party had sailed for Montreal, however, other stories began to emerge, suggesting that London's high society had been duped.

There was no hint of Prince Ranjit being an imposter when he was aboard the Lake Simcoe and, on arrival in Montreal, the Prince and his party were despatched by special carriages to the Hotel Windsor. Soon afterwards they caught the Adirondack Express to New York's Grand Central Station, departing just before word arrived from the India Office in London, informing the Canadian authorities that there was no Prince Ranjit.

When the party reached New York the Prince informed his entourage that he would like a little privacy and told them that they should go ahead to the hotel and he would meet them later. He and one of the dancing girls took a taxi. This was later traced and it was discovered that they had been taken to a subway station in uptown Manhattan and disappeared.

The New York Times found the story fascinating and within

days had managed to trace the missing potentate, who turned out to be Ranjit T Smile, who had previously worked as a curry cook at a Fifth Avenue restaurant, known as Sherry's, where he was known to the world as "Joe". Questioned by the newspaper, his wife explained that he had been baptized "Prince" and had travelled to India to claim his inheritance, after the death of his father, a wealthy merchant. When he arrived in London and reserved 23 rooms at a hotel near Charing Cross station, using the name Prince Ranjit, as he was entitled to do, people had jumped to the wrong conclusions. The dancing girl was really his niece and the whole party had been travelling to New York in order to set up a restaurant with the money he had inherited.

This unlikely story was followed by the suggestion that one of the Prince's advisors, an American lawyer, had orchestrated an elaborate hoax in order to spend a vast sum of money which had been acquired illegally in the crash of 1893. At the time, it was said, he had been acting as a trustee of a very considerable fortune and had withdrawn the money from the bank on the day before the crash. The establishment had been bankrupted and the trustee omitted to mention the withdrawal to the real owner of the money, who assumed the fortune lost. The problem was that the lawyer could not spend his ill-gotten gains without arousing suspicion, even after the death of his client, and so came up with a plan to use the prince as a cover to travel the world and have a good time, disguising himself as a mere advisor. The story quickly faded from the newspapers, the authorities apparently accepting the story of the curry cook who went on a spending spree.

Soon afterwards, Kendall encountered another interesting couple, known as the Goolds.

Vere Thomas St Ledger Goold was the son of an Irish baron, and had become famous in 1879 when he was crowned as Ireland's first tennis champion. That year he played in the final at Wimbledon, being beaten to the championship by the Reverend John Hartley. Goold remained a star name in tennis circles until the mid 1880s, but then retired from the sport and in 1891 married a well-known dressmaker called Violette Girodin, who had a boutique in London. The couple emigrated to Canada intending to make their fortune and for several years ran a shop in Montreal. After this failed they travelled home on the Lake Simcoe. They would go on to open a business in Liverpool, but when that too failed, they took the unusual decision to head for Monte Carlo, Goold apparently being convinced that they would make a fortune at the gaming tables of the celebrated casino.

This did not happen and in August 1907 they left Monte Carlo for Marseilles, where they left a large trunk in the left luggage office at the railway station. A railway employee became suspicious and the police were called and the remains of a Swedish woman called Emma Liven were found. She had disappeared after going to visit the couple to ask them to repay money that they had borrowed. The Goolds were put on trial. Violette was sentenced to death and Vere to life imprisonment on Devil's Island. They appealed and her sentence was commuted, but within a few months of their arrival in French Guiana she had died of typhoid fever. He committed suicide soon afterwards.

Surrounded by such colourful characters, Kendall settled into life on the North Atlantic steamer runs. The focus of his life had now changed. His ambition was to become the captain of one of the great Atlantic liners.

He soon transferred from the Lake Simcoe to the SS Garth Castle, another ship that had joined the Elder Dempster fleet from the Union-Castle Line. After a couple of voyages, the Garth Castle was laid up for an overhaul and Kendall returned home, in order to study for his Extra Master certificate. This was the highest qualification available for any mariner, and would allow him to command any ship, anywhere in the world. It was suggested that it would also be a good idea to join the Royal Naval Reserve, as this was considered to be a useful qualification by many of the shipping companies. This meant that Henry had to attend a course at HMS Eagle, an old wooden ship moored on the Mersey, which dated back to the Napoleonic era.

Part of the training was a shooting test, which meant visiting a rifle range in Cheshire. Henry was ordered to fire at a target placed 300 yards away. As he was settling down, preparing to shoot, a naval officer rushed up and congratulated him and informed him that all was well and that he had passed the test. He tried to explain that he had not fired a shot but the officer did not seem to care. He had done what was necessary and the fact that another candidate had been shooting at the wrong target was deemed unimportant.

Thus he became a Sub-Lieutenant in the Royal Naval Reserve. Soon afterwards he passed the examinations to acquire his Extra Master certificate. His formal education was finally complete. There were no more qualifications necessary. It was just a question of gaining experience, and impressing the management.

His next appointment was as Second Officer on the SS Lake Champlain. She was a new ship but in her two years had already enjoyed a colourful career. She had first acted as a troopship during the Boer War, but then in May 1901, had found fame as the first British merchant ship to be fitted with a permanent wireless system.

Guglielmo Marconi was then 27 years of age, but he had been experimenting with his ideas about radio waves for more than seven years. Born into a wealthy Italian family, he had not needed to work but had become fascinated by wireless telegraphy while conducting amateur experiments at his home. Marconi was never a scientist. His early experiments were trial and error, rather than pure science and they would remain so for years, until others were able to explain it. He never claimed to know what was happening, but based his work solely on the results he achieved. These were spectacular.

As early as 1897 he had successfully sent a message from the town of La Spezia to an Italian warship, operating 10 miles off the coast. Two years later, as a means of publicising his work, he equipped two US ships to send reports on the America's Cup yacht races to New York City. This was not a great success, but experiments with German and Belgium ships created interest from Britain in Marconi's inventions.

Legend has it that Alfred Jones of Elder Dempster was less than keen to try out one of Marconi's magic boxes, and it was only when his Marine Superintendent FH Smith shocked Jones by declaring that he would pay for it himself, that the shipping magnate began to take an interest. Thus Marconi was allowed to establish the first radio cabin on a British ship. This was little more than a large wooden cupboard, tacked on to the back of the superstructure at the rear of the Lake Champlain, sheltered from the wind and the seas on three sides. As the Lake Champlain steamed from Liverpool to Halifax, Marconi's operators were able to make contact with stations he had established at Holyhead and Rosslare. When Kendall joined the ship, the experiments had been going on for a year but Marconi's focus had moved on to sending messages across the Atlantic. He first claimed to have achieved this in December 1901, but there was no independent confirmation of the messages and he spent 1902 going back and forth across the Atlantic preparing his transmitting stations in Newfoundland and Cornwall. Kendall soon made Marconi's acquaintance and was an early convert to the use of wireless communication at sea.

The life of an officer in the merchant navy was never dull, even if one sailed the same routes over and over again. There was always some kind of drama and Kendall and his colleagues had to be resourceful to solve the problems thrown at them.

On one voyage the Lake Champlain was entrusted with a shipment of animals, en route to a zoo in British Columbia. They were all stowed away before the ship sailed, but shortly after their departure, at around two o'clock in the morning, Kendall was awakened by a crew member, who explained that there was a leopard roaming around the ship. Henry threw on his uniform, relieved that the drama was occurring at night, when most of the passengers were safely asleep. When he reached the deck he discovered that there was further good news. The leopard had decided to explore and had gone into a bathroom. The door had closed behind him as there was quite a swell that evening. The danger was at least contained. There was the option of shooting the leopard, but that would cause problems for the company, and Kendall concluded that it was best to attempt to capture the animal and get him back to his cage. He ordered the sailors to raid the medical stores and find a bottle of chloroform. When this arrived, he carefully opened the door of the bathroom a fraction and threw the bottle into the room. It would obviously take a few minutes for this remedy to take effect and Kendall decided that he would go to the sick bay to see what other drugs were available, as he was not totally convinced that the chloroform would do all that was needed.

When he returned, armed with a syringe, he found several of the sailors lying on the deck, having been overcome by the effects of the chloroform. The fumes were beginning to clear and Kendall was able to ascertain that the leopard was unconscious. He found more crew members and together they carried the leopard from the bathroom back to its cage, making sure that the locks were properly secured, and then transferred the sleeping sailors to their beds. Finally, Kendall turned in for a little more sleep. In the morning no-one was aware of the drama that had occurred in the course of the night.

During the summer of 1902 moves were afoot that would have a profound effect on Kendall's career. In the United States John Pierpoint Morgan, the celebrated banker and railway baron, decided to try to improve the profits of his empire by gaining more control over shipping companies. He hoped to be able to fix prices in the Atlantic shipping business and by doing so generate more business by offering cheaper and more efficient transportation, combining shipping lines with his railroads.

In the Panic of 1893, Morgan had helped the US Treasury to avoid collapse and had won some very powerful friends, notably with the Republican Party, to which he donated heavily. He was thus able to gain tacit support for his plans from the government which, although publicly opposed to trusts, was happy to see American influence in the shipping trade increase. Morgan put together the International Mercantile Marine Company, which featured 14 different steamship companies from various nations. The British Government was alarmed and began encouraging other companies to avoid joining the cartel. To do this it offered the shipping firms generous subsidies, in exchange for agreements to provide ships in times of crisis and commitments to limit foreign ownership and not allow foreigners to be directors.

Cunard, P&O and the Royal Mail Steam Packet Company all took advantage of these incentives.

The Canadian government, working in league with the British, offered the Canadian Pacific Railway a lucrative mail contract if it entered the Atlantic shipping trade. Canadian Pacific, which had been running liners between Vancouver and Hong Kong from 1887 onwards, jumped at the chance, as it was keen to remain competitive with the Morgan empire. The firm was happy to accept all incentives on offer.

It was the beginning of a long-running series of fights between the US-backed trust and the government-supported independents in Britain and Canada. The price wars that followed were ruinous, although the Canadian Pacific was able to avoid much of the effect of these by selling immigrants complete packages, including not only the costs of the voyage and the railway journey into Canada, but also the land on which they would build their new lives.

In order to fulfil the requirements stipulated in the mail contracts, the Canadian Pacific needed a fleet of fast liners to go from the Canadian ports in the east to the new European destinations. The company soon concluded that it was best to buy an existing fleet. The obvious choice was the Beaver Line. Alfred Jones of Elder Dempster was happy to sell the business. The deal netted Elder Dempster $7.5 million ($600 million at modern prices) and the Canadian Pacific acquired a total of 15 liners.

These were the Lake Champlain and her sister ship the Lake Erie, the smaller Lakes Manitoba and Michigan, plus the Milwaukee, Monmouth, Montcalm, Monteagle, Monterey, Montezuma, Montfort, Montreal, Montrose, Mount Royal and Mount Temple.

With the Canadian Pacific purchase Elder Dempster withdrew from the North Atlantic trade.

Henry Kendall found himself with new bosses.

CHAPTER SIXTEEN

The new owners promoted Kendall to the position of First Officer on the SS Lake Champlain, under Captain William Stewart, a man who had spent 30 years working on North Atlantic liners. The Lake Champlain would be the very first ship to sail the Atlantic under a Canadian Pacific flag and, in the course of the next few years, Stewart and Kendall would complete more than 80 crossings together, dodging the fog and the icebergs, and finding their way through the ice fields of Belle Isle and the St Lawrence each spring and sailing to Halifax and St John, New Brunswick, in the winter months. Stewart was considered such an expert that he would appear as a witness during the Court of Inquiry into the sinking of the RMS Titanic in 1912.

One of the first problems that Canadian Pacific needed to overcome was with the longshoremen of Montreal. The unions were by then powerful and tried to force the company's hand. One of the Canadian Pacific ships docked in Montreal and as there were no longshoremen to do the work, the crew was set to work unloading the cargo. This resulted in around 300 strikers invading the docks and attacking the crew, in order to stop the work. The captain was not amused by this and prepared himself rather better for the following day. The ship carried a couple of old brass cannons, largely for decoration, but the captain decided that these could still be fired and ordered them to be loaded with bags of corn. He also arranged for the ship's hoses to be made ready.

Early in the morning the dock workers appeared, a crowd of around 400 of them milling around on the dock. The gangways on to the ship had been secured, so that the strikers could not board the vessel. They were left to shout abuse and threats at those onboard. The captain allowed this for a while and then gave the order to fire the cannons and turn on the water pumps. The crowd, pelted by stinging pieces of corn and soaked with jets of water, scattered rapidly. Once the dock had been cleared the crew began unloading again.

Once the problems had been solved, the Canadian Pacific began expanding the operations of the old Beaver Line. In order to extend its immigrant business to continental Europe, it arranged for four of its ships to stop off at Antwerp, in Belgium, on their way from London to Canada. The Montezuma, Montreal, Montrose and Mount Temple were picked to ply this route, and for the next 10 years that service ferried thousands of Europeans across the Atlantic.

That year Henry and Minnie had a new child, named William Easterbrook Wright Kendall, although he was known to all as Billy. Minnie's mother insisted that the name Wright continue to be used, in the hope that one day the family might come into money.

It was easier not to argue.

Henry continued to meet interesting people on his voyages, the most famous being the celebrated explorer and mountaineer Edward Whymper. He was a real character and went everywhere dressed in mountaineering garb. He had shot to fame in 1865 when he led an expedition to the top of the Matterhorn, which had long been the most feared of all mountains in the Alps. On the descent, however, one of the party slipped and dragged three others over a precipice. The rope connecting them with the rest of the party broke, and the four men fell more than 4,000 feet to their deaths. It was rumoured that the three survivors had cut the rope to save themselves. Whymper was outraged at the stories and explained that the rope had snapped after he had looped it around a rock, in the hope that it would save the whole party from being dragged over the edge. Kendall was enthralled by the tale and, happy to have an audience, Whymper told him that there was rarely a day that passed when he did not once again see his colleagues being dragged over the precipice, one after another, with their arms outstretched towards him. By the early 1900s he had taken to climbing in the Canadian Rockies and had made arrangements with the Canadian Pacific to transport him free, if he promoted the Rockies as an exciting destination. In 1901 he even had a mountain named after him.

Unfortunately, he also developed a taste for drink and on one occasion, when the Lake Champlain was transporting cattle, Whymper arrived at the ship rather worse for wear. As it was too early for the cabins to be ready, Kendall invited Whymper to his own cabin so that he could rest. They talked for a while and then the explorer fell asleep. Kendall left him on the couch and went back to his duties. He was rather surprised to find Whymper missing when he returned in the morning. Even more strangely, Whymper had disappeared completely from the ship.

On a later voyage they met again and Kendall asked him what had happened. Whymper explained that when he awoke he was rather confused and disorientated. He was stumbling about when suddenly the head of a large steer appeared through the open porthole, just above his head and bellowed an unwelcome greeting. This unnerved the great hero to such an extent that he fled the ship in a panic.

By the time he had regained his composure he was so embarrassed that he decided to go home by a different route.

The idea of what constituted a hero was also changing. The explorers and adventurers of the previous age were being replaced by men who were pushing the boundaries of science: doing things that had previously been unthinkable.

At the end of 1903 the first news came of the exploits of the Wright Brothers at Kittyhawk, North Carolina. The first powered flight lasted just 12 seconds, but there were several other flights that same day, the longest lasting nearly a minute. Mankind was learning how to leave the ground and take to the air. The Germans had already launched the successful Zeppelin LZ1 airship, although it would be 10 years before the first commercial flights were introduced, and nearly 20 before an airship crossed the Atlantic for the first time.

At the time the idea that flying might one day replace the big ocean liners seemed fanciful, but Kendall was nonetheless enthralled by the madmen who were trying to break free from the earth.

A year after the first flights at Kittyhawk, Wilbur Wright had managed to fly two and three-quarter miles at Dayton, Ohio, and by the end of 1905 the Wright Flyer III was able to fly for 24 miles non-stop. The brothers then ran out of money and were forced to stop their development for the next three years. Although others took up the challenge, they were a long way behind the Wrights and by the end of 1908 the longest flight on record was still only 77 miles. The quest for new boundaries was constant.

In the 1890s the Canadian Pacific had built three liners for the Pacific trade, known as the Empresses of India, China and Japan. These 6,000-ton vessels rushed the mails from Canada to various destinations around the Pacific, their timings organized to meet railway trains that would hurry across the American continent, delivering mail at speeds that had been unimaginable a few years earlier. By the end of 1904 the Canadian Pacific decided that it wanted bigger, better and more luxurious ships. The aim was to guarantee that the company kept its lucrative mail contracts, but there was the hope that the new liners would attract more high-paying customers. The company placed orders for two new ships to be built at the Fairfield Shipbuilding yards on the River Clyde, near Glasgow. These would be 14,000 ton floating palaces, designed to sail the Atlantic in just six days, departing every fortnight. They were to be called the Empress of Britain and the Empress of Ireland.

As work began on the construction of the Empresses in March 1905, Henry and Minnie rejoiced in the birth of a daughter. She was christened Lily Maud Wright Kendall.

The two new Empresses were completed in 1906 and entered service soon afterwards. As hoped, their speed resulted in the company winning half of the mail contracts on offer from the government, although one stipulation of the deal was that the Canadian Pacific should work closely with the rival Allan Line. The government wanted the two companies to merge operations, and the new mail contracts nudged the two towards one another.

In 1906 Captain Stewart retired and the Canadian Pacific Steamship Service reorganized its officers. Kendall was named as First Officer of the Empress of Ireland, under Captain John Forster. Henry knew that this would be the last step before being given command of his own ship. He was 33 and everyone in the company knew that he was going places.

He spent a year on the Empress, which gave him a complete

understanding of the ship and helped him to hone his social skills with the VIP passengers. His earlier ships might have carried some interesting people, but the Empresses moved things to a very different level. Rather than dealing with the likes of Prince Ranjit, Kendall found himself entertaining Japan's Prince Fushimi Sadanaru; the Governor-General of Canada Earl Grey; Viscount Lascelles, who would later marry King George V's daughter Princess Mary; and international celebrities such as Marconi and Rudyard Kipling.

It was during the voyage taking Grey to Canada that a Hungarian immigrant died and Kendall was asked to prepare a funeral at sea. He arranged for the sailors to prepare the body as usual and to have a Union Jack placed over the corpse during the brief service. When everything was ready and the ceremony had begun, Kendall noticed that it was not the Union Jack that had been used, but rather Earl Grey's personal flag, which was a Union Jack with a crest in the centre. Fearing this was a major lapse of protocol, Kendall began quietly berating the seaman responsible.

The ceremony passed off without incident, watched by the Governor-General. When it was over Captain Forster requested Kendall drop by to see him. Forster asked for an explanation and Kendall told him the full story.

"When we have the next funeral on this ship," the captain said, "will you kindly moderate your damned language!"

Early in 1908 Kendall received word that he had long been hoping for. He was being put in command of the SS Milwaukee. He was finally going to become "Captain Kendall". The bad news was that this appointment would be for just nine days, the task being to transfer the ship from Liverpool to London.

The Milwaukee boasted one of the strangest stories in maritime history. Built for Elder Dempster in the celebrated Swan Hunter shipyard at Wallsend, near Newcastle, in 1896, she was the largest British ship since the Great Eastern in 1858. Weighing in at 7,355 tons, she was specifically designed to operate on the Liverpool-New Orleans route.

The Milwaukee had been commissioned for little more than a year when she ran aground at Cruden Bay, near Peterhead, in Scotland. Salvage crews were sent to see what could be done and found that the bow of the ship was lodged firmly on the rocks, which had ripped through the bottom of the hull. They concluded that there was no way that she could be refloated. This was frustrating as much of the ship was completely undamaged, including a very costly set of engines. Alfred Jones called in his engineers and they began to investigate what could be done. They came up with the radical suggestion of blasting the ship in half with dynamite, leaving 180 of the original 470 ft vessel on the rocks.

A month after the wreck, a salvage crew closed the watertight bulkheads, blew the ship in half and refloated the stern. This was towed to the Albert Edward Dock on Tyneside, where a completely new forward section was grafted on to the original stern. Just seven months after the shipwreck, the Milwaukee was back on the North Atlantic runs, although her crews would often joke that she was the world's longest ship, as her bow was in Scotland when her stern was in Canada.

When the Boer War came, the Milwaukee was requisitioned by the Royal Navy, for use as a troop ship. In April 1900 she carried the Boer General Piet Cronje and 500 other prisoners to the island of St Helena, where nearly 5,000 Boers were being held. The Milwaukee then returned to civilian activities, coming under the Canadian Pacific flag in 1903.

Kendall's nine-day command passed without incident and on arrival in London, he received orders to travel by train to Avonmouth, near Bristol, where the SS Monmouth was awaiting his arrival. A much smaller ship than the Milwaukee, she had been built for the Beaver Line by the Harland and Wolff shipyard in Belfast in 1900. The 4,000 ton vessel had begun her career on the Montreal run before being transferred to the New Orleans route. She made six voyages as a troop ship during the Boer War, but then returned to normal activities on the Liverpool-New Orleans run. Kendall's orders were to switch the ship to the Avonmouth-Montreal schedule, a route he was well-qualified to sail.

Later that summer, after a couple of runs across the Atlantic, he found himself heading towards the Belle Isle Strait, aware that somewhere not far behind was HMS Indomitable, a brand new battle cruiser, hurrying to Quebec to take the Prince of Wales (later to become King George V) to the 300th anniversary of the founding of the city. The weather was fine until after they passed the Belle Isle lighthouse, at around midnight on July 30. In the course of the day they had spotted no fewer than 55 icebergs and so Kendall was very cautious. When the fog rolled in, he slowed the ship to a stop. He was worried that the warships, travelling at 25 knots, would founder on the icebergs, taking the heir to the throne with them. There was also a danger that they might collide with the Monmouth. Kendall and his crew heard the howl of sirens on the port side, but there was no wireless to warn the Royal Navy ships and so they blew Morse Code messages on their whistles, hoping they would be heard.

The liner captains knew that when it came to hitting icebergs, they important factors were the speed and angle of impact. The faster the ship was travelling, the more likely it was that there would be serious damage. The loss of the RMS Titanic in April 1912, with more than 1,500 fatalities, brought home the dangers, but even during the Titanic inquiry, Kendall's old commander, the retired Captain William Stewart, summed up the approach of the crews when he was asked if he would slow his ship if he knew there was ice ahead, on a clear night, with no moon and a calm sea.

"No," he said emphatically. "Not as long as it was clear."

Stewart added that he would maintain the same speed until he saw the icebergs.

"Then I should do what I thought proper."

Without proper visibility, however, going too quickly was considered reckless. In the fog there was always an element of luck involved. Finding icebergs in the middle of the summer was not unusual in the area, but much depended on the weather in a particular year. There was little logic in the number of incidents. In 1899, for example, there had been six ships that hit icebergs, including the Beaver Line's SS Montrose. In 1902 and 1904 there had been none at all, but in 1903 there were three. The Montrose (again) and Kendall's old ship the Lake Champlain would hit icebergs in 1909. Some ships did sink as a result of these collisions, but these tended to be the smaller wooden schooners which were less able to continue if damaged.

"At 01.20 the weather cleared slightly and I put the ship slow ahead," Kendall reported. "At 02.26 the lookout man reported an iceberg ahead and the engines were immediately put full astern."

Unfortunately, the warning had come too late for the Monmouth. A ship takes a finite amount of time to stop moving or to begin to turn and if there is an obstacle which is not seen soon enough, there is nothing that can be done. For a captain there is nothing worse than the moments before an impact, when they know there can be no escape, they must watch the drama unfold and hope that the damage will be limited.

"The iceberg was lying low in the water and stretched right across our bow," Kendall reported. "It was not prudent for me to turn to port or to starboard for this would have caused the berg to pierce the side of the ship. As a result the bow of the ship took the whole blow and we slid gradually onto and then off the iceberg."

The ship was stopped and Kendall immediately went to inspect the damage.

"The peak tank was the only part that had suffered," he said. "Seven frames and three plates on the starboard and three plates and four frames on the port were set in. None of the plates appeared to be fractured but she was making water at a rate of five inches per hour. All the damage was below the water as there was nothing visible from the outside."

Despite the damage, Kendall decided to remain stationary. It was nearly four o'clock in the morning before the fog finally lifted. Around them were no fewer than 16 icebergs. In the distance, five and half miles to port, they could see Cape Norman. They moved up to full speed until 05.45 when the fog returned. The remainder of the journey was completed at varying speeds depending on the visibility.

The Monmouth underwent temporary repairs in Montreal before heading back to Avonmouth, but there would be further drama on the way home when they encountered HMS Argo, broken down and burning distress signals, off the southern coast of Ireland. Taking the Argo in tow, the Monmouth steamed into Queenstown, where Captain Boyle Townshend Somerville expressed his gratitude to Kendall and his men.

Somerville was a well-known mariner and would go on to become a Vice Admiral before retiring to the family home at Skibbereen, in County Cork. He then became the author of many popular books, recording his adventures while surveying New Guinea and the Solomons. In 1936 he was murdered, at the age of 72, by the Irish Republican Army for having given references to young men who wanted to join the Royal Navy.

When they returned to Avonmouth, Kendall's worries about the iceberg incident disappeared. The management of Canadian Pacific accepted that this was one of the risks involved in running liners in and out of the St Lawrence.

Henry would spend the whole of 1909 in command of the Monmouth, running back and forth to Canada. There might be new excitements in the world, with flying machines and other great inventions, but there was still a need for strong nerves when the liners were running in and out of the icebergs.

CHAPTER SEVENTEEN

By 1908 the automobile had ceased to be a novelty, although the horseless carriages was still the preserve of the wealthy. Motoring was no longer considered a sport and the huge cars of the early years were replaced by smaller, more practical machines. The automobile was suddenly capable of impressive feats. In February that year a car race was held from New York to Paris, with the competitors going west across the United States, taking ships to eastern Russia and then driving overland to the French capital. National pride was at stake, and by the end of the event there were protests aplenty. There was uproar when the stewards ruled that a German entry had missed parts of the route and that victory should be awarded to an American machine called the Thomas Flyer.

That same year Henry Ford revolutionized the industry by revealing his low-cost, mass-production Model T. This remarkable little car was cheap, reliable and easy to maintain. It opened the way for normal people to become automobile owners. In the years that followed Ford sold an astonishing 15 million Model Ts.

The year 1908 also saw William Durant establish a new automobile company called General Motors, which would one day topple Ford as the world's biggest car manufacturer.

Aviation continued to move forwards, although it was still considered an activity for eccentrics and madmen. Large cash prizes captured the imagination of the public and stimulated aeronautical development.

In the summer of 1909 there was great excitement as the

British and French fought over a £1,000 prize (£80,000 at modern prices) for the first man to fly the English Channel. The Wright Brothers had flown the distance as early as 1905, but Europe was still lagging behind the Americans. It was not until four years later that they caught up. The fight to fly the Channel was between England's Hubert Latham and France's Louis Blériot.

On July 19 Latham made his attempt, flying a French-built Antoinette. He ended up in the water, when his engine let him down. Six days later Bleriot took off from a field close to Calais and flew to Dover to claim the prize.

Within a matter of weeks French-based Englishman Henry Farman had made the first flight of more than 100 miles.

It was an age in which progress was suddenly expected. Ships were becoming bigger and faster. In 1875 the City of Berlin had been the largest ship in the world at 5,526 tons. Ten years later Cunard's Lucania weighed in at 12,952, and by 1905 Germany's Hamburg Amerikanische Packetfahrt AG (Hapag) had built the 22,225-ton SS Amerika. Two years later Cunard responded with the 31,550-ton Lusitania, but it was dwarfed within four years by the White Star Line's Olympic, at 45,234 tons. A year later the Titanic, Olympic's sister ship, arrived and before the outbreak of the Great War Hapag pushed the record to over 50,000 tons with the launches of the Imperator and the Vaterland.

For Canadian Pacific such wild extremes seemed pointless. The existing fleet was sufficiently large and sufficiently fast. And while the ships might not be as glamorous as the new generation of giants, they earned good money. There was no shortage of immigrants deserting Europe and heading to America and Canada, in search of wealth and freedom that they did not have at home.

Kendall was still a long way from getting his hands on the newest machinery, but in April 1910 he was promoted from the Monmouth to become the Master of the SS Montrose, a 6,278-ton liner with accommodation for more than 1,900 passengers.

Built for Elder Dempster by the Raylton Dixon yard at Middlesbrough in 1897, the Montrose was neither glamorous nor modern. She had started her career on the Avonmouth-Montreal run, but was then requisitioned by the British government for service in the Boer War. Like the Monmouth, she had been used to transport Boer prisoners, disembarking a thousand of them in Bermuda, where they remained until the war came to an end. From Bermuda the Montrose returned to Britain and was in the process of being refitted when the Beaver Line was taken over by Canadian Pacific. The following year she was put on to the new London-Antwerp-Quebec route. She had been designed for the immigrant trade and featured berths for 1,800 in Third Class, but just a handful of cabins for First and Second Class passengers. The Montrose had only one real point of interest. She was one of only 60 ships in the world to be fitted with wireless equipment.

After the initial impact surrounding the wireless, the spread of radio communication slowed. Marconi was never an engineer and did not understand how best to improve his inventions. They remained rudimentary for much longer than might have been expected, but in the summer of 1910 the SS Montrose would put the wireless firmly into the international spotlight.

That year Kendall was often in London and on Derby Day, he went to Epsom racecourse in Surrey to watch the Derby. He met an old tipster and taking his advice, ended up backing five winners in six races, the big race being won that day by the American horse Lemburg. Soon afterwards Kendall decided that he would look up Charles Coburn, an old friend from his childhood days in Liverpool. Coburn was 20 years older than Henry, but had been appearing in music halls when Kendall was a contortionist. He had enjoyed much success with songs such as "Two Lovely Black Eyes" in 1886 and "The Man Who Broke the Bank at Monte Carlo" in 1890.

"We strolled into a cafe to have a cup of tea and a talk over old times," Kendall recalled. "Coburn was rather upset and I asked what was wrong. He explained that his wife's best friend, a woman called Belle Elmore, had gone missing. She was supposed to have left her husband and run off to America, but he thought it very unlikely, that she would do that without her telling any of her friends. He added that Belle's husband had wasted no time at all in starting a relationship with his secretary, who was already living in his house. She had even been seen wearing Belle's furs and jewellery.

"The man was called Dr Hawley Harvey Crippen," Kendall

said. "The name meant nothing to me. I suggested to Coburn that he talk to Scotland Yard. He replied that he had already done so and had even met Chief Inspector Frank Froest, the head of the Criminal Investigation Department of the Metropolitan Police. Coburn was told that hundreds of people disappeared every year and that most turned up again. Furthermore, making public accusations that might prove to be false was a dangerous business, as it might lead to legal action."

Coburn did not give up and arranged a meeting with Paul Martinetti, who was one of the last people to have seen Belle at the end of January, when he and his wife Clara went to dinner at the Crippens in Hilldrop Crescent, in the London suburb of Camden. Two days later she was due to attend the weekly meeting of the Music Hall Ladies Guild, of which she was the Honorary Treasurer. Instead the Guild received a letter saying that she had been summoned to the United States because of a sick relative and that she was resigning her position, as she would be gone for several months. The letter was not in her handwriting and various members of the Guild thought it odd that Belle would disappear without a word. At the end of February Crippen appeared at a ball at the Criterion, organized by the Music Hall Ladies Benevolent Fund. He was accompanied by a woman called Ethel Le Neve, who worked as his secretary. Although no-one knew it at the time, she had known Crippen since she was 18, when fresh from a secretarial course at Pitmans, she had begun working in his office. It was five years before the two became lovers, although it later emerged that Ethel had become pregnant by Crippen but had lost the baby.

Ethel's presence at the ball created a scandal, not least because she was seen to be wearing jewellery that had belonged to Belle. No-one had heard from Belle and Crippen had been very vague when asked about her. In the middle of March, with the secret out in the open, the 27-year-old Ethel moved in with the 47-year-old Crippen, ostensibly as the doctor's housekeeper. A few days later Crippen informed Clara Martinetti that he had heard from America that Belle had been taken ill. On March 24 Clara received a telegram from Crippen stating that Belle had died. It had been sent from Victoria Station.

It later transpired that Crippen had sent the message while on his way to Dieppe with Ethel, where the two spent the Easter holiday, registered under the name Mr and Mrs Crippen. When they returned to London Crippen put an announcement in a theatrical newspaper announcing Belle's death. This was more than her friends could accept and soon afterwards Louise Smythson, a member of the Guild, went to the police to report what she believed to be suspicious behaviour. There was no evidence of any foul play and the police explained that there was nothing that could be done.

Isabel Ginnett, a former president of the Guild who had returned to America and lived on a farm in New Jersey, training performing horses, was convinced that the story about Belle going to Los Angeles was not true. She began making enquiries in the United States and found that there was no trace of Belle at all, and so decided to try to locate her family in Brooklyn to see if they knew of her whereabouts. She would find that Crippen had written letters to her father and sisters, telling a different story to what was being said in London. He had informed Belle's step-sister Louise Mills that she had gone to California to "secure important property for ourselves", as one of his relatives was dying. Belle, he said, had died of pleurisy.

In June John Nash, the husband of another Guild member, visited the United States and met with Ginnett. He was soon convinced that Crippen was not telling the truth. He returned to London and met Crippen on May 28. The questions he asked were not answered to his satisfaction and he and his wife went to the police on May 30. Chief Inspector Walter Dew listened to the Nashes, but remained sceptical.

A few days later Dew and Detective Sergeant Arthur Mitchell visited Hilldrop Crescent and met Ethel. She took them to Crippen's office in Albion House on New Oxford Street, where they interviewed him. Crippen immediately admitted that he had not been telling the truth about his wife's death and said that as far as he was aware she was still alive. He suggested that she might be found with an American called Bruce Miller, with whom Belle had an affair some years earlier. He also admitted his relationship with Ethel. He explained that he had made up the story of Belle's death in order to disguise the fact that his marriage had failed and because he wanted to be with Ethel.

Dew later admitted that he felt rather sorry for Crippen. The three men went out for lunch together and then took a statement from the doctor. That afternoon they went to Hilldrop Crescent and looked around the house. The only thing that struck Dew as odd was that Belle had left all her dresses and jewellery behind.

The following day was a Saturday and Dew had a chance to think about the affair. He decided to visit Crippen again on the Monday to ask a couple more questions. When he went to Albion House he discovered that Crippen and Ethel had not been seen since the Saturday. No-one knew where they were. Dew and Mitchell went back to Hilldrop Crescent and renewed their search.

On the morning of July 13 the newspapers were filled with the news that the Hon Charles Rolls, the son of politician Baron Llangattock, who was both a partner with Frederick Royce in an automobile company and a noted aviator, had been killed at Bournemouth the previous day when the tail of his Wright Flyer broke off in flight. He was the first Briton to be killed in an aviation accident. This was big news as only six weeks earlier he had become the first pilot to make a non-stop double crossing of the English Channel, dropping a message for the Aero Club de France as he flew over Calais.

That morning Dew and Mitchell dug up parts of the garden at Hilldrop Crescent, looking for Belle's body. Dew then decided to take a look at the floor in the coal cellar. He dislodged several bricks and was sent reeling into the garden by an awful smell of decomposing flesh. Belle Elmore had not gone to America.

This was no ordinary murder. The newspapers reported with much sensation that Belle's flesh had been cut from the bone. There was no head, but her internal organs had been removed as one and deposited in the hole. The gruesome details were such that Dr Crippen would soon acquire a status similar to that of the celebrated Jack the Ripper, who had murdered and carved up prostitutes in London 20 years earlier.

There was a connection in that early in his career Inspector Dew had worked on the Ripper investigation.

There were important clues found in the hole, including hair samples, a curler and the remains of a pyjama jacket in which some of the flesh had been wrapped. The detectives quickly found a matching pair of pyjama trousers in the cupboards upstairs. Forensic science was rudimentary at the time but one of the pieces of skin was found to include a scar, which several witnesses later confirmed, matched one that Belle had on her lower abdomen. The evidence seemed overwhelming and "wanted" posters were distributed, featuring Crippen and Ethel. The public response allowed Dew and Mitchell to begin piecing together the movement of the two fugitives, but they remained several steps ahead of the police.

One key point was that before his departure on Saturday, Crippen had asked an office boy at Albion House to purchase a suit for a teenage boy. Ethel had gone to see her sister and had told her that she was going away. Dew concluded that Ethel had then gone to Albion and disguised herself as a boy, in the hope of confusing pursuers. The couple was traced to Charing Cross station from where they took a train to Margate, where Crippen made the mistake of posting a letter to a London department store. A deckchair attendant reported that he believed he had seen the couple on the beach at Ramsgate on the Sunday, and another witness claimed to have seen them boarding a ferry called the SS Kingfisher on the Monday, heading for Boulogne amid the throng of summer holidaymakers. This last report was erroneous as they were later traced to Ostend, probably on the Sunday. From there, they took a train to Bruges, Ghent and Brussels. On arrival in the Belgian capital that evening, they checked into the Hotel des Ardennes, conveniently located next to the Gare du Nord. The register was signed in the name of John Philo Robinson, a 55-year-old merchant from Quebec, and his 16-year-old son John. They told the hotel that they had arrived from Vienna. Philo was Crippen's grandfather's name.

On the Monday Crippen visited the Canadian Pacific office and purchased vouchers that could be exchanged for steamer tickets. They spent a week in the Hotel des Ardennes but then departed, telling the management that they were leaving Brussels, but actually moved to a different hotel in the city, where they remained until July 20. Very early that morning, they checked out of the hotel and caught the train to Antwerp, a journey of just 15 miles. They were at the port by eight. Crippen exchanged the coupons for Canadian Pacific tickets, but did so less than three hours before the SS Montrose sailed. This meant that the names of John Philo Robinson and his son did not appear on the ship's manifest. They were also able to avoid being recognized by the policemen, who were watching the gangways of the Montrose, looking for a man and a woman. There were only 266 passengers on the ship, but no-one paid much attention to the Robinsons.

Because of his discussions with Coburn earlier in the summer, Henry Kendall had followed the case with much interest, initially in London and then in Antwerp after the ship transferred there. The Montrose spent five days in the port and each evening Kendall dropped in at the Grand Hotel Weber for a drink and to collect his copy of the Continental Daily Mail, which arrived from Paris in the afternoon.

On Wednesday, July 20, there was no time for a visit to the Grand Hotel Weber. Kendall busied with the final preparations before the Montrose sailed in the late morning. When all was ready, the ship cast off and slipped quietly out into the River Scheldt. No-one aboard had any idea of the real identity of John Philo Robinson and his quiet son John. As they stood on the deck on the Montrose, breathing the fresh sea air, Crippen and Ethel hoped that they had done enough to escape. They looked forward to a new life together in Toronto.

Hiding behind a lifeboat, they held hands.

CHAPTER EIGHTEEN

"As we were passing a place called Fort Bath, on the Dutch side of the river, I left the pilot to do his work and went to my cabin to fetch a cigar," Kendall remembered. "I happened to look out of the porthole and saw what appeared to be two men, standing behind a lifeboat. Only their legs were visible but it struck me as odd that they were clearly holding hands. I reached certain obvious conclusions. At one point one of the men emerged from behind the boat and looked around, as if to check to see if anyone was looking. He was a small man with rather protruding eyes."

Kendall was curious and decided to take a stroll on the deck and see more of this decidedly odd couple. He walked past the lifeboat and after a few paces turned around, as if he had forgotten something and needed to return to the bridge. As he did so, he could look behind the lifeboat. The two men were no longer holding hands, and were in the process of emerging from the secluded spot. Kendall bid them a cheery "Good day", as if nothing was amiss, and there followed a discussion about the countryside to starboard, where the low sand islands had been joined together by man-made dams to create a peninsula. It was flat as a board, the skyline marked only by an occasional windmill.

While they were talking Kendall took careful note of the pair. He spotted that the older man had marks on the bridge of his nose, which suggested that he normally wore glasses. He had the beginnings of what was called "a royale" beard, a chin beard favoured by the French military at the time. And he spoke with a slight American accent. The boy said nothing unless spoken to, but had a very bad cough. Robinson explained that his son had a weak chest and that they were going to California for his health.

Kendall excused himself and went back to the cabin and through the porthole observed the pair a little longer. It had struck him during the conversation that the pair might perhaps be Hawley Harvey Crippen and Ethel Le Neve. He wanted to find the copy of the Continental Daily Mail in order to re-read the descriptions given by the police. After consulting the newspaper, he felt that he was probably jumping to conclusions. The heights were not right as Le Neve was reported to be two or three inches taller than Crippen. Robinson was an inch taller than his son. There were possible explanations for this, given that women at the time generally wore high heels and the style was for big hats. This might have created the impression that Ethel was taller than Crippen.

Kendall decided that he would try to discover more. He returned to the deck and asked the pair if they had reserved their places in the dining room for lunch. They had not and so Kendall invited them to join him at the Captain's table. It seemed a generous gesture. He then hurried to see the purser to discover more about the Robinson booking, on the premise that they would be his guests for lunch. This revealed that the coupons had been purchased in Brussels. The newspaper suggested that this was where Crippen and Le Neve might have been. The booking also revealed that Robinson had paid extra to ensure that the two of them were left alone in a four-berth cabin.

The bell went for lunch. Kendall watched the entrance of the dining room until the Robinsons had entered, and then hurried to their cabin to have a quick look around. Most of their belongings were locked in a large trunk, but he found two hats: one from a shop on the Boulevard du Nord, a well-known street in Brussels; the other, without any markings, had been packed with newspaper in order to fit on a smaller head. It was obviously new and a makeshift solution. The only real clue was a piece of material that was being used as a face-flannel, which Kendall concluded had come from a sleeve of a female under-bodice. That struck him as rather suspicious for a man and his son.

So as not to arouse suspicion, he then took his place at the lunch table and watched the Robinsons closely in the course of the conversations. Robinson was seated next to Kendall and his son on his other side, making it difficult for anyone other than him to converse with "the boy". In the course of the lunch Kendall became more and more convinced that John Robinson Jr was a girl in her twenties, rather than a 16-year-old boy. The way in which young John used his cutlery and the dainty way in which "he" handled fruit seemed out of place. Kendall needed more evidence before taking any action. Denouncing the wrong person would have been a disastrous move.

After lunch he tried a new trick and walked behind the pair on the deck, calling out "Mr Robinson" three times before he finally got a reaction, although the American apologized and said that he had not been able to hear because of the wind. They then discussed the immigration forms that needed to be filled out and Kendall offered to help them. His aim was to get a sample of Robinson's handwriting, as there was an example of it in the newspaper, which would enable a comparison. Once the forms were done, Kendall left the pair to their own devices. It was a warm day and they settled on the deck just outside Kendall's cabin. He was able to observe them through the porthole.

Taking his copy of the Continental Daily Mail, he used chalk to carefully alter the picture of Crippen, removing the moustache and spectacles. The resulting image looked disquietingly like Robinson. The picture of Ethel was more difficult, because it featured a large amount of hair. Kendall took a piece of card and having measured the girl's face cut a circular hole in it and placed it over the newspaper picture.

There, staring up at him, was John Robinson Jr.

He looked out of the porthole again and, at that moment, a gust of wind blew the back the boy's jacket up and Kendall saw that the trousers had been altered in order to fit the contours of the boy's slim waist. The two sides had been hurriedly secured with a safety pin.

Kendall was by then close to being convinced that he had stumbled upon Crippen and Le Neve and mused that if they had booked in steerage, travelling as man and wife, or had boarded at different times to avoid the detectives on the gangway, they would probably never have been found. With Ethel in disguise, however, they needed a Second Class cabin to ensure privacy. The ship carried only 20 Second Class passengers and the Robinsons were the only two who spoke English.

That evening after dinner Kendall and Robinson were in discussion, standing at the entrance of one of the Second Class lounges, when a French lady passenger sat down right in front of them, reading a copy of Le Matin.

"Facing us was the headline: 'Crimes de Londres' and 'Dr Crippen' in large letters," Kendall said. "I could see from the corner of my eye that Robinson was slightly agitated, but I did not for a moment suggest moving, in case he smelled a rat. Fortunately the lady turned the page and our conversation carried on in the usual way."

Back in London, Inspector Dew was still trying to piece together the story of Hawley Harvey Crippen, Belle Elmore and Ethel Le Neve.

Crippen had been born in Coldwater, Michigan, an unremarkable town near Kalamazoo, in the gentle hills between Chicago and Detroit. He had studied medicine at the University of Michigan, before going on to the Homoeopathic Hospital College in Cleveland. He later served an internship at Hahnemann Hospital in Manhattan, a homeopathic hospital where he worked as an eye and ear specialist.

He was briefly in England but did not have the qualifications to practice as a doctor in the UK and so returned to the United States and spent three years working in Detroit before marrying a nurse called Charlotte Bell at the end of 1887. The couple decided to move to California and settled in San Diego. In 1889 Charlotte gave birth to a son called Otto, but she died a year later and the baby was sent to live with his grandparents in San Jose.

Crippen went east again, and in 1892 met a 17-year-old actress called Cora Turner. Her real name was Kunigunde Mackamotski, the daughter of a Polish father and a German mother. Her father had died when she was a baby and her mother had remarried a Brooklyn man called Fritz Mersinger. Kunigunde grew up in Brooklyn, using the name Cora Mersinger, surrounded by an increasing number of step-brothers and sisters. When she decided that she wanted to go on the stage, she changed her name to Turner, in order to sound more American.

She was never exactly pretty, but had great presence and she was soon living in her own apartment, as the mistress of a stove manufacturer called Lincoln. He paid for her singing lessons. When Crippen came along she decided that he was a better bet and, after a whirlwind romance, the couple were married in Jersey City, at the end of 1892. Cora continued to sing, while Crippen began selling patent medicines for the Munyon company. This brought in plenty of money and Crippen showered his wife with expensive gifts.

In 1900 Munyon decided to send Crippen to London. Cora saw this as an opportunity to launch her singing career, which had not been a success in the United States. She adopted the name Belle Elmore and began working in music hall. Sadly, her voice was not good enough for stardom.

In 1902 Munyon recalled Crippen to the US for several months. Cora decided to stay in London and had a romance with a singer called Bruce Miller. When Crippen returned and Miller went back to America, Cora decided to stay with her husband, but the marriage was no longer a happy one. She was completely dominant, and her lifestyle was such that he needed to make more and more money to fund her excesses. He tried a variety of different business ventures before rejoining Munyon.

When he returned to his old firm he met Ethel. By then Belle had failed as a singer, but had carved herself a niche with the Music Hall Ladies Guild, through which she could mix with successful stars, and enjoy a little reflected glory. Crippen stayed in the background, paying her bills. Towards the end of 1909 Cora threatened to leave Crippen and take £600 in savings (around £47,000 at modern prices) with her.

Dew's investigations revealed that Crippen has pawned some of his wife's jewellery the day after the dinner with the Martinettis. He had collected £115 (£9,200 at modern prices).

He also discovered that, early in January, Crippen has ordered five grains of the highly-poisonous hyoscin hydrobromide at Lewis &

Burrows in New Oxford Street. He had noted down that the poison was to be used for "homeopathic preparations". This was not unusual as the drug was often used to ease pain, although one had to be careful not to use too much. Forensic tests would later show that the remains found under the floor in the cellar at Hilldrop Crescent had traces of the poison.

Dew had a hunch that Crippen would try to escape to the United States and sent word to the US authorities that they should conduct systematic searches of all passengers disembarking from steamships that had arrived from English or French ports. This added to the media coverage generated by the manhunt for Crippen.

A ship at sea was immune to all of this. The wireless system was there, but it was not used to send and receive anything other than shipping information. It was still rudimentary. Kendall was fairly confident that he had identified Crippen and Le Neve, and so took one of the stewards into his confidence, ordering that all newspapers on the ship be collected up to avoid problems if other passengers reached similar conclusions. As captain, he had the right to arrest the fugitives whenever he wanted to, but he knew that such a course of action would mean the use of manpower to hold them prisoner and he felt that as the pair appeared to be unaware of his suspicions, it was quite safe to let them go on as they were.

Kendall also knew that he had to be very careful before blowing the whistle, because an incorrect identification would have serious implications. He had to be absolutely sure before taking any action, and he was troubled by the question of the heights and the suggestion in the newspapers that Crippen had false teeth. Although this was corrected by the police in later statements, Kendall was relying solely on the edition of the newspaper that he had available to him.

He began to look for more clues and carefully steered the conversations that followed to subjects that would give hints as to Robinson's background. The newspaper had listed various places where Crippen had lived and, having visited San Francisco himself, Kendall was able to talk about the city. During one conversation he made a deliberate mistake about the location of a certain building. Robinson corrected him. Kendall responded and asked how Robinson could be so sure, and he replied that he was quite certain because he had lived there when he was 18. The newspaper did not mention dates, but said that Crippen had moved around a great deal in his youth.

At another point they were discussing the water available on the ship, and whether they preferred fresh water that was carried in the tanks of the ship or distilled water. Robinson volunteered that he used distilled water when he was mixing medicines.

In an effort to solve the question of the false teeth, Kendall decided to tell jokes and soon had Robinson roaring with laughter, which enabled him to discover that Robinson's teeth were very definitely not false. The police were wrong about that.

It was Friday, July 22, and the Montrose was heading out into the Atlantic Ocean. Kendall knew that if he did not act, the wireless on the Montrose would not have the range to reach the English mainland. Although it could receive messages from as far away as 600 miles, the transmitters were weak and messages tended not to get through beyond about 150 miles.

Once clear of the mainland, any messages would have to be sent from ship to ship, and that was unreliable as only 60 ships in the world were fitted with wireless equipment, and there was no guarantee that one would be in range. The other option was to wait until they were in range of the Canadian coastal wireless stations, but Kendall felt that this would probably be too late for the English police to organise an arrest.

It was time to make a decision.

Kendall called wireless operator Llewellyn Jones and explained the situation. They then drafted a message to be sent to Arthur Piers, the Canadian Pacific Steamship manager in Liverpool. It read: "Have strong suspicions that Crippen London cellar murderer and accomplice are amongst saloon passengers. Moustache taken off, growing beard. Accomplice dressed as boy, voice, manners and build undoubtedly a girl. Both travelling as Mr and Master Robinson. Kendall."

As Jones tapped away with his Morse Code key, history was in the making. No criminal had ever been apprehended using wireless transmissions. For the radio operator and the captain the significance of the moment did not really register. They were simply trying to do the right thing. For 48 hours they heard nothing but on the Sunday evening Jones intercepted a message from a London newspaper to a journalist on board the White Star Line's SS Laurentic asking what Inspector Dew was doing, and whether the passengers were excited by the chase. This was the first indication that his message had been taken seriously.

On the Monday the newspapers of the world were filled with stories of how Dr Crippen had been spotted on a ship and how Inspector Dew of Scotland Yard had immediately taken an express train to Liverpool and boarded the Laurentic, a faster ship than the Montrose. The Inspector would be arriving in Canada before Crippen and would set a trap for the murderer. Dew was travelling under the name of Dewhurst, but the press seemed to know all about it.

It was a story that had everything: there was crime and sex and the very strange situation of the whole world being able to watch a suspect who was totally unaware that he had been unmasked.

It was great theatre.

In the early hours of Monday morning, Kendall sent a message to his friend Captain James Gillies, the master of the Canadian Pacific liner SS Montezuma, which had steamed into range of the Montrose wireless. He asked for a message to be forwarded to London, as soon as the Montezuma could broadcast to the mainland.

"With reference to wireless I sent regarding Crippen, I feel more fully convinced that it is him," Kendall wrote. "All descriptions corresponding fully with information from papers and police report received in London. Is very reticent, also accomplice, although they are the only two English passengers. They have no luggage except a small cheap grip bought on continent. Is still letting beard grow, but shaves upper lip. Managed to examine his soft grey felt hat while at lunch. Name inside Jackson Boulevard du Nord. Grey felt hat of accomplice no lining. Is packed inside of band to make it fit. Both wearing brown suits and white canvas shoes. Crippen speaks with American accent. Have also heard him speaking French when alone with French passenger. Noticed accomplice using safety pins to hold up pants. According to conversation I had with him he has travelled all over the States. Up to present has no suspicion of being watched.

On board keeping everything quiet. Kendall."

On the Tuesday Kendall followed up with a message sent via the SS Royal Edward, in case the report that had been sent to the Montezuma did not get through. Jones was constantly listening to the wireless, hoping to pick up hints of what was happening from intercepted radio traffic, but aboard the Montrose they had no idea at all of how big the story was becoming.

CHAPTER NINETEEN

Marconi's revolutionary, but rudimentary wireless system created dramatic blue sparks where an electric charge jumped from one wire to another. This created the radio waves necessary but also made a dramatic crackling noise. It was obvious when the apparatus was being used so Kendall and Jones decided that it was best to keep transmissions to a minimum.

Nonetheless Robinson was curious as to why there were so many messages being transmitted and one day even asked Jones what he was sending. The Welshman kept his cool and replied that the messages related to ice warnings for other ships. Robinson seemed satisfied and a couple of days later remarked to Kendall, as they listened to the crackling noise, that wireless was "a wonderful invention".

Using another recent invention, Kendall snapped a photograph of the pair through his porthole, as they strolled on the deck.

Kendall continued to watch the two fugitives as closely as he could. They dined together each day and Kendall happily lent the Robinsons books to help them pass the time. This way he was able to keep an eye on them and judge their mood. One day he witnessed John Jr faint from what he guessed was the strain of the deception. Kendall understood the feeling as he found that he was constantly alert and unable to sleep much. He became convinced that Robinson had a gun in his possession.

It was not until Friday, July 29, that the Montrose steamed into range of the wireless station at Belle Isle. Llewellyn was suddenly inundated with a multitude of messages that had been sent to the wireless station to be passed on when the Montrose arrived. Most were from the press. Some messages were addressed to Dr Crippen. One even invited him to conduct a service on the Sunday after landing in Quebec, as some newspaper reports had mentioned erroneously that he was travelling, disguised as a clergyman. Others asked Crippen to answer the accusations that he had murdered his wife.

The most important message came the following day from Inspector Dew. The Laurentic was ahead of the Montrose and was approaching Father Point, a major pilot station on the St Lawrence estuary, where the river pilots embarked to navigate the liners to Quebec, 150 miles to west. They would then return on other ships, being dropped off before the liners headed out into the Gulf of St Lawrence.

Dew's message was short and to the point.

"Will board you Father Point," he wrote. "Please keep any information till I arrive there. Strictly confidential. Dew. Scotland Yard."

Kendall replied that the Montrose would arrive at Father Point as about six o'clock in the morning on Sunday, July 31.

"Would advise you to come off in small boat with pilot," Kendall wrote. "Disguised as one if possible. Pilot steamer with reporters, if any, could go ahead and board later."

As plans were made, life on the Montrose went on as before. On the Saturday morning Kendall was sitting in his cabin when there was a knock on the door.

"Looking round, I saw Crippen with a book in his hand," he said. "I invited him in and he held a book out towards me and looked me straight in the face. 'I have brought this for you to read,' he said. 'It is a book that will just suit you. It's a detective story.' I did not turn a hair, but casually said: 'Who is it by? Conan Doyle?' He said it was by Edgar Wallace. 'It is called Four Just Men,' he added, explaining that it was about a group of vigilantes who murder people in the name of justice."

Kendall did not react. He sensed that this was some kind of a test; that Crippen was looking for a reaction, to see whether the captain had seen through the disguise.

It was a challenge.

"For days I had been living the life of a hunter," Kendall said. "Each hour was making me harder and more callous, and it would have taken more than his trick to have upset me. I turned to him and asked if he was finished with the book and whether he had anything else to read. 'Only Pickwick Papers,' he said. 'And the young fellow is reading that'.

"I opened my book case and took out a book: 'Have you read this?' I asked. 'It's called the Murder of Delicia. It is by Marie Corelli. It is the story of a man who murders his wife'."

Kendall looked directly at Crippen as he spoke and wondered, in the same instant, whether he should simply arrest him there and then. Crippen blushed slightly and, perhaps sensing this, turned away and stared towards the porthole. He put his hand to his mouth and began squeezing his lower lip, and muttered that he had not read the book. Kendall explained that the title was a little misleading, because the man did not actually murder his wife, but carried on is such a fashion that she died of a broken heart. Crippen took the book, thanked Kendall and departed.

For a moment Kendall sat motionless, wondering how Crippen would analyze the exchange they had just had. The murderer had been taken aback that his attempt to trap the captain had failed. The response had been a message, and yet had been so outrageous that it might be construed as a simple innocent conversation. Would Crippen conclude that the captain had guessed his identity? Kendall could not judge, but felt that it would leave Crippen disconcerted.

The Laurentic was by that time arriving at Father Point. There were rules and regulations that forbade passengers to land, without going through the necessary quarantine and customs formalities and even in exciting moments such as this, the bureaucrats had to be obeyed. Captain Jean-Baptiste Bélanger of the pilot steamer Eureka was given permission to pick up Inspector Dew, but only on the understanding that the detective and the ship be inspected by two doctors. A cargo hatch in the ship was opened and Dew, wearing a long green Ulster coat and a black Derby hat, stepped aboard the Eureka. His presence on the Laurentic had not been widely known amongst the passengers until wireless messages started to arrive and word had got out. He stuck to the identity of Mr Dewhurst doggedly.

When the Eureka arrived at the dock at Father Point there were no fewer than 32 journalists from newspapers across the world, all keen to talk to the English detective. The village had never seen such excitement. Dew was met by a number of Canadian detectives and together they went to a local boarding house where Dew was to stay that evening. Soon afterwards they hurried to the wireless station, in order to send messages to Kendall on the Montrose.

When Dew arrived there he found a message from Kendall waiting for him. "Received wire," it said. "Will pick you up at Father Point. He is ignorant of suspicions. Have made no arrest. Is cunning so be prepared. At present appears uneasy. Compliments. Kendall."

At his trial Crippen claimed that the quartermaster of the Montrose had been very friendly with him in the course of the voyage and had told him that the captain had recognized him and that he would be arrested when they landed in Quebec. The quartermaster, he said, had offered to hide him in the cargo and make a loud splash at some point during the night so that it would appear that Mr Robinson had gone overboard. His plan was to slip away later and then join Ethel in Toronto when the hue and cry had died down. There is no evidence to suggest that this story was true and all four men of the rank of quartermaster on the Montrose were indignant at the suggestion. They were so upset, in fact, that when they heard news of the claim, they all told the Montreal Daily Star that this was not true.

Kendall was worried that Crippen had sensed the danger and might jump off the ship and drown. He expressed these fears in a cable to Dew, and the detective responded that the fugitive should be "kept under discreet observation to prevent self-destruction". It was by then nine o'clock in the evening. In nine hours the Montrose would arrive at Father Point to pick up the pilots. The game would be up.

A series of messages passed between the two men in the dark hours until all arrangements had been made. Both was acutely aware that a false arrest would be a terrible embarrassment for all concerned. Dew, who had been criticized for not arresting Crippen before his escape, was hoping that Kendall's identification was correct. A failure would be a huge setback for Scotland Yard.

In 1914 Kendall was promoted to the position of Captain of the RMS Empress of Ireland (below), a ship on which he had served for a year as Chief Officer in 1907. He was one of the youngest captains on North Atlantic liners and the future looked promising. But on the ship's third voyage, disaster struck – with heavy loss of life.

ANGLO-AMERICAN

WESTERN UNION · DIRECT UNITED STATES

CABLEGRAM

No. | Service Instructions. | Time Received. | Receiving Office.

9 12 | Via Anglo. | 12 25 |

Handed in at | No. of Words:

Radio Cable Lady
Evelyn via Fatherpoint | 18

No inquiry respecting this Message can be attended to without the production of this paper.

To Jones 8 Oban road
Anfield Liverpool
Henry saved found
hanging on piece of
wreckage after ship
had foundered

Kendall's family learned that he had survived the sinking of the Empress of Ireland in a dramatic telegram from Canada (left). More than one thousand others were not as fortunate (below left). The Storstad (above) tore a huge hold in the side of the liner, which sank in just 14 minutes. Kendall gave evidence to the Court of Inquiry (below). He was cleared of blame for the accident but, for the rest of his life, he found the subject too painful to talk about.

Soon after the Empress of Ireland sank World War I broke out. Kendall served on HMS Calgarian (above), a converted liner, which was used as a troopship, until it was torpedoed in March 1918. During that period the ship was called to help out when a munitions ship blew up in Halifax, Nova Scotia (right). It was the biggest conventional explosion in history and the destruction in Halifax was unprecedented (below).

Kendall was a man of many contrasts. A proud sailor (above), he had an unexpected sense of fun (left). He enjoyed family life and in 1961 he was photographed with his daughter Lily, his grandson Michael and great-granddaughter Rachel. He died at the age of 91 in 1965.

On the Montrose Kendall was less worried. He was by then convinced that Robinson was Dr Crippen.

"My watch was unceasing," Kendall remembered. "Every hair on my head was on duty. My anxiety was to reach Father Point as soon as possible, but that night dense fog came in and every sound on the ship was weird. I knew that by daylight, we should be at Father Point. Dew would be there to meet me, assisted by Canadian detectives. I knew they would come on a small boat instead of the pilot steamer. I had told Crippen to get up early to see this place, for it was beautiful, and also mentioned that we would be picking up half a dozen pilots returning to Quebec. This was done to put him off the scent if he saw so many people in uniform boarding the ship."

That last night was dreary and anxious, the sound of the fog whistle every two minutes adding to the monotony as the hours dragged uneasily on.

"I paced that narrow bridge," Kendall said. "Every now and then I would see the dark form of Crippen creeping about the deck. He too was restless and uneasy. He was making his plans. The sea was smooth and we were able to push our vessel along at the utmost speed, the Chief Engineer Mr Vine down below all night getting every ounce of power out of the engines. Sleep was out of the question."

At four o'clock in the morning dawn began to break. They were then skirting the coast, five miles off the shore.

"At about seven o'clock we heard the distant moan of the fog signal at Father Point," Kendall said. "It sounded weird, but it was a welcome sound. The fog was still thick and I longed for it to remain like that until the drama all was over, as Crippen would be not be able to see the pilot boat and perhaps spot Inspector Dew and do something drastic. Within five miles of Father Point the wind died away and suddenly a westerly wind blew up. Within a few moments the fog had lifted. It was like raising the screen at a theatre and revealing the beauty behind. The sun shone brightly and the small boat with Dew and his colleagues onboard was about half a mile away on the port side. I could also see the pilot steamer Eureka, which seemed to have about 40 people on board, the world's press, about a mile ahead. Everything was as planned. The ship came to a stop. I watched from the bridge. Crippen was pacing the deck uneasily, while the Chief

Officer went to the stern to receive the visitors. I did not want them to be seen. They were taken to my cabin. I left the bridge and within a few moments I was shaking hands with Inspector Dew of Scotland Yard and two Canadian detectives called McCarthy and Dennis, who would officially make the arrest. Dew wanted to know where Crippen was to be found and I looked through my porthole along the saloon deck and pointed him out.

"My God, Captain, that's not him!" Dew said.

Kendall would have none of it.

"I replied that it was certainly him and that if Dew did not arrest him, then I would!" Kendall said. "Someone was sent to ask Crippen to come to my cabin. Dew and the others were all dressed as pilots, but I advised them to be careful as I believed Crippen had a revolver."

Crippen came into the cabin and Kendall introduced him to Dew, using the name Robinson.

"Dew turned around," Kendall said. "He extended his hand and, in a strong tone, said: 'Good Morning Doctor Crippen'. Crippen was stunned. He did not recognise Dew. The Inspector removed the pilot's cap he was wearing and said: 'I am Inspector Dew from Scotland Yard. I've come here to have you arrested under the name of the King for the murder and mutilation of your wife Cora Crippen on or about Feb 1. Whatever you say will be used as evidence for or against you.'

"Crippen's quivered. He was struck dumb, was inclined to sit and turning around with Dew still holding his hand he sat and sank back on the settee. He then gasped out: 'Thank God. It is all over. The suspense was too great. I couldn't stand it any longer.' He was immediately put into handcuffs and left in the charge of one of the Canadians."

Dew, Kendall and the other Canadian detective went below to arrest Ethel Le Neve.

"The warrant for the murder of Belle Elmore was read out to her and she was then left in charge of the Canadian detective," Kendall remembered. "We then returned to my cabin and organized that Crippen be moved to another cabin which had been prepared for him. He was searched and told to wear pyjamas. His clothing was searched and we found five valuable diamond rings sewn into the material. In his pockets were notes written by him to Miss Le Neve about contemplating suicide. How he had ruined her life."

There was no doubt, however, that Crippen had had no idea that any arrest would take place at Father Point. He had been caught unawares.

"He had felt that the danger would come at Quebec," Kendall recalled. "It seems that his intentions were to hide himself somewhere in the vessel and leave the notes to Ethel to make believe that he had jumped overboard and committed suicide."

With the fugitives safely locked away the signal was given for the journalists to be allowed to board the ship. It was the first indication for Kendall about the scale of the story.

"They came aboard like pirates," he remembered.

There were many questions to be answered and it was several hours before all were satisfied. It was then that Kendall got another surprise.

Dew turned to him and said: "You get a reward of £250 (£20,000 at today's prices) for this. It is as good as in your hand."

It was early afternoon before Kendall was in a position to order the Montrose on her way. There were still 12 hours of steaming ahead before their arrival in Quebec. Crippen asked for something to read and Kendall supplied "Letters from a Self-Made Merchant to his Son" by George Lorimer, a book of fictional letters of advice from a father to his son. Perhaps, Kendall thought, there would be something in it for Crippen to learn.

The ship arrived in Quebec at three o'clock the following morning. Despite the hour, and the fact that it was a very hot night, Kendall found that there were crowds of people lining the quay, hoping to catch a glimpse of the evil Dr Crippen, the redoubtable Inspector Dew and Kendall, the hero of the hour.

It was not until breakfast time that the prisoners were taken from the ship and driven to the Quebec City Prison on the Plains of Abraham, in the old city up above the port.

"I felt that one of the biggest crises in my life has passed," Kendall wrote. "Victory had come at the end of nearly a fortnight's constant worry. Every nerve in me was stretched to the utmost. The most desirable thing in all the world just then was a good sleep."

Kendall slept for most of the day. As the captain was sleeping, Crippen was taken before Judge Charles Panet Angers and admitted his real identity. He offered no objection to being extradited to England. Ethel was too upset to appear, but was charged with being an accessory after the fact.

In the days that followed Kendall stayed in hiding, as the press continued to hound him for more details of the adventure. At the same time Dew became increasingly frustrated with the Canadian authorities and, eventually, the two men decided to escape and take a train 300 miles to Niagara Falls. For Kendall it was a chance to "fill our imaginations with nobler things than a sordid tragedy".

Crippen and Le Neve stayed in jail. They accepted no visitors. Finally, when all the legal details had been sorted out, the pair were woken early one morning and departed with Dew by automobile. This took them by a circuitous route to the small village of Sillery on the St Lawrence River, where it had been pre-arranged that they would be met by a tugboat, called the Queen. They boarded the tug and set sail just as the first journalists arrived to see Dew, smiling in victory having escaped them.

Unfortunately the victory was to be short-lived. The pressmen worked out that the tug would be meeting up with the SS Megantic, which was travelling down river from Montreal. They knew that Queen would have to wait several hours in the river and rushed back to Quebec to hire another tug. This was loaded with photographers and arrived on the scene just as the Megantic and the Queen were due to rendezvous. This was followed by a merry dance was the tug tried to get close enough in to photograph the prisoners being transferred. In the end it became dangerous and Dew was forced to give up. The Queen went alongside the Megantic and pictures were taken. Crippen boarded the liner with his hat pulled own over his head and his coat collar as high as possible. Le Neve followed, wearing a blue suit with a veil. The remainder of the party, consisting of two wardresses, who were there to oversee Ethel, Dew and Detective Mitchell, who had travelled from London to accompany the prisoners on the journey home, followed them aboard.

They were lodged in a suite of cabins with guards in the

corridors. The two prisoners were allowed only a short time on deck each day. When the Megantic arrived in Liverpool the prisoners began to understand the unprecedented nature of the case. Everyone had been following the adventures of Crippen, Dew, Le Neve and Kendall. At the quayside hundreds jeered the prisoners. There were more people waiting for them at London's Euston Station. There were crowds too outside Bow Street Magistrates Court where the pair were remanded in custody. Crippen would get no peace until the door of his cell slammed behind him in Brixton Prison.

Kendall returned to England a hero. He enjoyed every moment of it. On October 5 he received the reward cheque that Dew had mentioned. Typically, he did not cash it. Instead it was framed and mounted on the wall in one of the salons on the SS Montrose.

CHAPTER TWENTY

Outside the Old Bailey a huge crowd gathered on the morning of Tuesday, October 18. Inside the celebrated Court Number One the trial of Dr Crippen began, Lord Chief Justice Alverstone presiding. The court heard witnesses for the prosecution. The following day, Inspector Dew took the stand and a long statement made by Crippen was read out. Forensic evidence was presented that afternoon, and this continued into the third day with pathologist Bernard Spilsbury giving his evidence. On day four Crippen was cross-examined and then both sides moved to the summing up. In the end it took the jury just 27 minutes to reach a decision: Crippen was guilty. Lord Alverstone withdrew for a few minutes. He returned wearing the square black cap that judges put on when passing a death sentence.

"Harvey Hawley Crippen," he announced. "You have been convicted, upon evidence which could leave no doubt on the minds of any reasonable men, that you cruelly poisoned your wife, that you concealed your crime, you mutilated her body, and disposed piecemeal of her remains; you possessed yourself of her property and used it for your own purposes. It was further established that as soon as suspicion was aroused you fled from justice and took every measure to conceal your flight. On the ghastly and wicked nature of the crime I will not dwell. I implore you to make your peace with Almighty God. I have now to pass upon you the sentence of the court, which is that you be taken from hence to a lawful prison, and from thence to a place of execution, and that you be there hanged by the neck until you are dead.

"And may the Lord have mercy on your soul."

Crippen was taken from the Old Bailey to Pentonville Prison, not far from the house in Hilldrop Crescent.

Ethel's trial as an accessory after the fact was very short. Within a matter of minutes she had been set free, the court accepting that she had not been aware of the fact that Crippen had murdered his wife.

Ethel remained devoted to Crippen. In the weeks that followed she was a regular visitor to see him in Pentonville. His appeal on November 5 was rejected and there remained only the smallest hope of a reprieve from the Home Secretary, a 35-year-old rising star called Winston Churchill. Not only did Churchill reject any thought of a reprieve, he also ordered that Crippen be kept under close watch to avoid suicide. Churchill wanted justice to be seen to be done. Crippen tried to slash his wrists, using the glass in his spectacles, but the watchers were able to stop him before he could even draw blood.

On November 19 Crippen was told that he would hang four days later. He remained calm and friendly, making it hard for many to believe that this was the cold-blooded murderer that he was supposed to be. There was some sympathy amongst those who encountered him for Belle Elmore had clearly not been an easy woman, and Crippen was clearly much in love with Le Neve, and vice versa. In his last letter to Ethel, written a few days before his death, he described them as "two children in the great unkind world, who clung to one another and gave each other courage".

There were crowds outside Pentonville when the executioners arrived. Crippen received a final telegram from Le Neve, saying: "My living thoughts and prayers are with you. God bless you darling."

It was signed "Wifey".

Crippen spent some time with the Roman Catholic Prison Chaplain Thomas Carey and then, after a breakfast which he barely touched, he waited for the execution party to arrive. It took just a minute to take him from the cell to the gallows. He was smiling all the way. His arms and legs were secured and a white hood placed over his head. The trap-door was opened and Hawley Harvey Crippen was gone. In accordance with the regulations, the body was left hanging for an hour and was then taken for a post-mortem examination in the prison mortuary. The corpse was buried in the grounds of the prison. The bell that usually rang when an execution had taken place remained silent on this occasion. The governor decided that it would not be a pleasant sound for the others who sat awaiting execution. The crowds outside the prison slowly dispersed.

The name Crippen lived on. The sensational nature of the murder and the chase that followed turned Crippen into one of the most famous of all British criminals, and even 100 years after the event, the name still creates headlines.

The newspapers reported that Ethel sailed to the United States on the same day as the execution, boarding a ship at Queenstown and travelling under the name Miss Allen. It may have been so, but there were many other rumours of her whereabouts.

The legal actions were not over. Before his death Crippen had made a full will in favour of Ethel. Under the normal rules Belle's property would have been inherited by Crippen, as she had died without making a will. He wanted everything to pass on to Ethel. This was challenged by Belle's family and Sir Samuel Evans ruled that "a murderer cannot benefit from the person he murdered", thus establishing an important legal precedent in Britain.

Ethel ended up in Toronto, where Crippen had planned for them to go. She worked as a typist using the name Ethel Harvey, one of Crippen's names and stayed for six years, before returning home to look after her sister Nina, who was dying. After that, using the name Ethel Nelson, she went to work at Hampton's furniture store in Trafalgar Square. While there she met Stanley Smith, the firm's accountant, and eventually became Mrs Ethel Smith. The coupled settled in Croydon and had two children, Bob and Nina. After her husband's died, Ethel led a quiet life. In the end her brother Sidney complained that an article about her in the Sunday Despatch, written by the novelist Ursula Bloom, was unfair. He agreed to pass on letters from Bloom to Ethel. The two women met finally in the summer of 1954. Ethel refused to talk of the past, but Bloom was convinced that she was still in love with Crippen. Ethel lived on until August 1967.

The effects of the Crippen Affair were wide-ranging. Edgar Wallace sold millions of copies of "The Four Just Men" as a result of the publicity resulting from the Crippen case. It made him famous, but not rich, for he had sold all his rights to the book for just £89 (£7,100 at modern prices). There were many plays and several films about the Crippen case, and even the great thriller maker Alfred Hitchcock said that he took much inspiration from the story.

The use of wireless in the Crippen Case was of huge significance for Marconi. His wireless systems had captured the imagination of the world and in the six months after Crippen's arrest the number of ships with wireless installed increased from 60 to 600. Eighteen months later wireless played a significant role in saving hundreds of people when the RMS Titanic hit an iceberg and sank. The 1914 Merchant Shipping (Convention) Act which followed the accident ruled that all ships carrying more than 50 people must have a radio onboard if they wanted to enter British ports.

Henry Kendall was an international celebrity for a while. He received some extraordinary mail, including threats, offers of marriage, letters asking him to track down missing people, and even an incredible offer to give up his job as a sea captain and appear in a 20-week run in American theatres. For this he would be paid the princely sum of £4,000 (£320,000 at modern prices). He was offered £100 just for a cast of his face, so that a wax model could be made from it. Kendall enjoyed the attention but went back to work as captain of the Montrose.

According to newspapers at the time, which are not to be trusted at all, Dr Crippen felt that Kendall had betrayed him. He had thought the captain friendly but discovered that Kendall had been playing a rather different game during their time together on the SS Montrose. Some of the newspapers even reported that Crippen put a curse on Kendall. If he did, Henry was not worried by it.

A few months later Kendall was taken off the Montrose and put in charge of the SS Lake Erie, as her captain was unwell. He took a train north to Glasgow to take command of the ship and spent the next three months working on the Glasgow-Boston route. His fame did not go away. During one visit to Boston the manager of the local theatre came to wharf to invite the officers to see a production of a play entitled "Caught by Wireless". This was the story of the Crippen case. During the interval the theatre manager marched on to the stage and announced that the great Captain Kendall was among them that evening. Somewhat embarrassed by this adulation, Kendall and his fellow officers, slipped away before the end of the show, ending their day in a quiet restaurant, with a dinner of oysters.

When the captain of the Lake Erie recovered, Kendall was returned to the SS Montrose. At the time she had been requisitioned by the British government to take troops to Bermuda, where the 2nd Battalion of the Duke of Cornwall's Light Infantry was being replaced as the garrison by a battalion from the Bedfordshire Regiment.

The Governor came to visit and stayed for lunch. Lieutenant-General Sir Walter Kitchener was a distinguished soldier and colonial administrator, but did not seem much given to diplomacy. After lunch Kendall mentioned that he had seen the Governor's brother Field Marshal Viscount Kitchener - the man who had led the British Army to victory in Egypt in 1898 - in London during the celebrations which marked the coronation of King George V in May 1910.

"You mean that idiotic brother of mine from Egypt?" Kitchener said.

Taken aback, Kendall nodded.

"Why do you call him that?" he asked.

"Well, why shouldn't I?" came the reply. "He always refers to me as that damned fool of a brother in Bermuda."

When they returned to Southampton the Montrose was laid up, being rebuilt. Now a famous ship, the Canadian Pacific decided to take advantage and made her more spacious and more luxurious. Kendall was then given command of his old ship the SS Lake Champlain, on which he had served as First Officer between 1903 and 1907. As the first British ship to be fitted with wireless, it was apt that Kendall, a man closely associated with wireless technology, should be captain. The Lake Champlain was little changed although in 1909 she had hit an iceberg and undergone major repairs.

There was a shock for the Canadian Pacific soon afterwards when the Empress of China was wrecked on a reef in Tokyo Bay. No lives were lost and all the mail was saved, so the company did not suffer too much damage to its reputation as a result. In April 1912, however, the whole industry was rocked to the core when the RMS Titanic went down after hitting an iceberg in the North Atlantic. The loss of life was unprecedented and, for the first time, there were questions about the safety of the big liners. These huge ships had seemed somehow invulnerable but after the Titanic, passengers thought twice about taking voyages. The families of the crew realized that the next time there was a disaster, it could be their husband, father, brother or son, who did not return. In August that year that point was driven home to the Kendalls when Henry took the Lake Champlain to assist the CPR liner SS Corsican, after she hit an iceberg in the Belle Isle Strait. On that occasion the damage was not significant, but the danger had been highlighted.

Minnie had long ago grown used to the fear that Henry might one day disappear, but she found solace in the fact that great liners were far safer than the sailing ships on which he had sailed during the early years of their marriage. It was more worrying for the children. The Kendall family home in Orrell Park was the perfect place for the young family, but life there was spoiled after her mother died and her father moved in with them. With him came Minnie's brother Dave, her younger sister May and the teenaged Ernie. Having so many relatives around all the time proved to be too much for Minnie, who already had two children to look after, and she announced one day that she would be moving to Bournemouth, on the south coast of England, because of her asthma. It was not quite the truth, but it worked. Her father moved in with Minnie's half-brother Richard in Eccles.

Once rid of the family members, Minnie moved to a new house in Crosby, further out of Liverpool towards Blundellsands. Within a few years they had moved on to Blundellsands itself, where Billy and Lily were able to run down to the seashore from the house, to watch their father's liners depart on their transatlantic runs. They waved frantically in the hope that their father would see them.

In 1912 Minnie was pregnant again and this time produced a son. They christened the baby Henry George Wright Kendall, after his father, although little Henry was soon known only as 'Harry".

World events continued to shape their lives. The British Empire remained the dominant force around the globe, but other Great Powers were strengthening their positions. Austria, under the rule of the Hapsburg Family, was keen to remain a powerful force in Europe, even after the Germans and Italians had began to assert themselves. The Emperor Franz-Josef, who had taken control of Austria in 1848, at the age of only 18, had been an ambitious ruler and encouraged expansion. He had done his best to strengthen Austrian influence in the Balkans. As part of his plan, the Vienna to Trieste Railway was opened in 1857. This was a marvel of engineering with a celebrated section climbing up to and over the Semmering Pass. Once the railway was completed, the port of Trieste began to develop quickly. The opening of the Suez Canal in 1869 helped and the Austrian Lloyd shipping company, which was headquartered in Trieste, soon opened new routes to Bombay, Colombo, Hong Kong and Singapore.

A second transalpine railway opened in 1906 and Trieste boomed. There even developed an Austrian Riviera around the port. The investment in Trieste was aimed at taking away much of the immigrant trade from the rival German empire, and to increase Austrian influence in Asia. The Atlantic Shipping Trust refused to agree to an Austrian restriction on carrying passengers from Trieste, if they were of an age that made them liable for Austrian military service. The government in Vienna turned to the Canadian Pacific, which was happy to score a major victory against the Trust. In 1912 the company entered into an alliance with the Austrian Imperial Railway to provide a steam ship service between Trieste and the ports of Canada. The Lake Champlain and the Lake Erie were put onto the new route and Kendall's friend James Gillies was appointed the Canadian Pacific Marine Superintendant in Trieste. To please the Austrians, the company agreed to renamed the Lake Champlain as the SS Ruthenia and the Lake Erie as the SS Tyrolia.

The link between Trieste and Canada created much interest in Austria and on the day of the Ruthenia's first departure from the port, the Archduke Franz Ferdinand of Austria, the heir to the Imperial throne, sailed over from the castle at Miramar with his wife Sophie von Chotkavato, to inspect the Ruthenia. At the end of the visit he asked Kendall if he might fire off some fireworks when the Ruthenia sailed past Miramar. He was keen to entertain his children Sophie (11), Maximilian (10) and Ernst (8).

Several hours later, as they steamed up close to the imperial castle, a magnificent white building, perched above the sea, they fired two rockets high into the air. These exploded in dramatic fashion and many more followed. The passengers and crew could see the royal party watching the action from the roof of the castle. When the display was over the ship swung round to the south and steamed away. A few hours later Kendall received a message from "His Imperial and Royal Apostolic Majesty Emperor Franz Joseph", the Austrian emperor, thanking the ship for its "enthusiastic ovation" and wishing them well on their first voyage. Another telegram came from the Archduke.

The Ruthenia and the Tyrolia each made six westbound voyages in the course of the next 18 months, calling at Naples and Gibraltar en route to New Brunswick and then returning via Liverpool and Gibraltar. Together they carried 25,000 passengers to Canada.

Towards the end of 1913, however, there was intrigue in Vienna and it was suddenly announced that the Canadian Pacific concession was being revoked. The company's agent in Vienna was arrested on the charge of having knowingly transported men of military age from Austria and a parliamentary investigation was initiated. In the end Canadian Pacific would win back the right to sail from Trieste, but the interlude was over for Kendall. The ships switched back to the old London-Antwerp-New Brunswick route for the winter months and, as soon as the St Lawrence opened in April 1914, they began sailing up the river to Quebec and Montreal.

On arrival in Quebec, Kendall received orders to hand over the Ruthenia to Captain Gilles, who had departed Trieste when the troubles began with the Austrians. Henry was to go to St John, New Brunswick, to take command of the Empress of Ireland.

It was not without a little nostalgia that Kendall turned his back on the Ruthenia. They had travelled many miles together. Although he did not know it at the time, within a few months his old ship would be requisitioned by the government and converted, along with her sister ship Tyrolia into a dummy battleship, known as the HMS King George V. She would have fake turrets made of wood and canvas. The aim was to confuse the Germans about the size and location of the British Fleet. Gillies would serve with distinction during the Gallipoli Campaign of 1915, and would end the war as a

Commander of the Order of the British Empire.

Perhaps later he would mull over their different fates, but as he headed to St John, he was at the pinnacle of what had been a glittering career.

CHAPTER TWENTY ONE

The railway journey from Quebec to St John was a scenic one, particularly in the spring. He took the Quebec Central Railway as far as Megantic, where a change was necessary to switch to the Canadian Pacific's International Railway of Maine, which winds through the picturesque wooded hills and lakes of central Maine, before crossing back into the Canadian province of New Brunswick.

Kendall spent the journey not pondering the likelihood of war, but rather enjoying the thought that he would soon not only be the captain of the Empress of Ireland, but would also be able to meet up with many old friends, with whom he had served, a few years earlier. The Empress was an important job, but he was not overawed. This was what he had been trained to do. It was his destiny. He had only just turned 40 but the idea of being responsible for 420 crew and more than 1,000 passengers was not a burden. He looked forward to seeing Mansfield Steede, the man who had been Second Officer when Kendall had been with the Empress. He was now the First Officer and a man with much experience, not only as a skipper on the African runs, but also as a Marine Superintendant in the Gambia. There were many other friendly faces to look forward to.

When the train pulled into St John, Kendall hurried to his new ship. They would sail the following day for Liverpool. The voyage passed off without drama and the Empress headed back to Canada, bound for Quebec on the first of its summer runs through the Belle Isle Strait. The ice was not bad that year. In Quebec they spent their time getting ready for the return voyage. Preparations were completed by two o'clock in the afternoon on Thursday, May 28. Kendall was there to greet the new passengers.

The Empress was ready to depart.

Twelve hours later Henry's worst nightmare had become a reality. He was in the freezing water of the St Lawrence, fighting to stay alive. The ship was gone and the river was lit up with a ghoulish light, created by chemical flares which were fitted to each of Empress's lifebuoys, which reacted to water. Several hundred people were with him in the water. The only sounds were splashes and desperate cries for help, but there was no-one to answer. Those with life belts stayed afloat; those without found wreckage to cling to, or quickly slipped beneath the waters when their energy was exhausted.

Henry was lucky. When he came to the surface after being thrown from the ship, a piece of wreckage rose up beside him. He grabbed it and clung. After only a few minutes one of the lifeboats passed near him and he was hauled from the river.

"I took command of the lifeboat," he recalled. "We continued the search for survivors. When the boat was full, we rowed to the other ship, which had returned, and unloaded our unhappy cargo. With a few volunteers I went back to try to find more survivors. We spent three hours rowing back and forth."

Kendall and his volunteers pulled 73 people from the water, although a number of them died of injuries or from exposure when they were aboard the Storstad. Most were rescued in the first half an hour after the Empress sank.

There had only been time for one SOS message to be sent before the Empress lost all power, but the pilot boat Eureka, still captained by Jean-Baptiste Bélanger, the man who had played an important role in the arrest of Dr Crippen four years earlier, was in the scene within 45 minutes of the alert. It was able to pick up only 32 survivors, most of whom were found clinging to wreckage or to bodies that were kept afloat with lifebelts. The Eureka carried out a search but found only one woman alive, she had been swimming without a lifebelt, but died from exhaustion and exposure soon after being taken aboard.

The mail tender Lady Evelyn was slower to reach the scene, as she had to get up steam. By the time she arrived there were only bodies left in the water. The Empress's physician Dr James Grant, who had escaped from the ship by squeezing through a porthole on the port side as the ship lay on her side, worked non-stop aboard the Storstad, treating the injured and, at the same time, fighting off hysterical survivors. One man was so out of control that he had to be flattened with a punch from the doctor, who was trying to concentrate on the injured Chief Engineer William Sampson.

At first light people on the shore could see the collier, the two small steamers and nine lifeboats.

"There was nothing left to be rescued," Kendall recalled. "We returned to the other ship with its mangled bows, and I climbed to the bridge."

There he came face to face with Captain Thomas Anderson.

"You have sunk my ship," Henry declared. "You were going full speed ahead in that fog".

The two men exchanged a few words, but as an argument was the only likely result, Kendall withdrew to the chart room. Mrs Anderson, the wife of the Storstad's captain, found him there, asking: "Why did they not let me drown?" over and over. Dr Grant was sent to see him and Kendall told him that his only regret was that he had survived. Grant forced him to drink brandy, ignoring the fact that Kendall was a teetotaller, and then the bruised, exhausted and mentally-drained captain fell into a deep sleep.

In the days after the disaster, there is no question that Kendall had trouble coping with what had happened. A Canadian Pacific official told The New York Times a couple of days later that the captain was "all unstrung and cannot tell a coherent or continuous story. The awful scenes which he witnessed are still too strongly impressed on his mind".

The official added that he was convinced that Kendall intended to go down with the Empress. When the ships headed into Rimouski wharf and landed the survivors and the bodies of the victims, Kendall did what a captain was supposed to do, but he was going through the motions, unable to cope with the enormity of the disaster.

There were more than 200 bodies, some of them badly mutilated, either as a result of the initial impact, or because of flying machinery. A roll call was held on the wharf to establish the names of the living. There were more than 400, although it was difficult to ascertain an exact number as some of the injured had been rushed to hospital as soon as they landed. The 800 residents of Rimouski did what they could for the survivors. All the available doctors were working at the pier and citizens soon began to arrive with food and clothing for the freezing survivors.

Major Henri-Romuald Fiset, the mayor of the town, declared that the railway station would be taken over to house the survivors, but he soon realized that the town could not cope with the scale of the disaster. He telegraphed for help. The Canadian Pacific responded by sending a train, filled with medical staff. By the afternoon it was at Rimouski's Intercolonial Station being loaded with survivors. There were 396 people put aboard, leaving 37 injured behind in the hospitals.

The train took the survivors to the town of Levis on the southern side of the river, opposite Quebec City. A fleet of ambulances took the passengers to the ferry and they arrived in the city, in the early evening. Preparations had been made to house them aboard the SS Alsatian, which was berthed in the docks. The First Class passengers were taken to the Chateau Frontenac.

The newspaper reports the following morning were lurid, with stories of the many dramas that had occurred in the fateful 14 minutes. It was seen as odd that so few women and children had survived, while more than 200 crew members had been saved. Reports about the movements of the ships were contradictory with Captain Anderson was quoted as saying that the Storstad was going full ahead in an effort to fill the breach his ship had made in the Empress, while there were also quotes from him saying that the ship was going full astern trying to avoid the impact. There were suggestions from crew members of both ships that the other had not done enough to save the people in the water.

The one thing that remained constant was that all reports agreed that there had not been time to do anything. Back home in Liverpool, the sinking of the Empress created widows and orphans throughout the city, but for the Kendall and Wright-Jones families there was a telegram bearing good news.

"Henry saved," it said. "Found hanging on piece of wreckage

after ship had foundered."

On the Saturday an inquest was opened in the schoolhouse at Rimouski. Doctor Joseph Pinault was the coroner. Kendall was asked the cause of the accident and said that it was caused by "the Storstad running into the side of the Empress, which was stopped". He also said that the Norwegian ship had not responded to his pleas to keep the engines at full ahead after the impact, to keep the hole in the side of the Empress from filling with water.

"If he did not hear," Kendall said, "he should have done it anyway, as a seaman should have known that."

He was also critical of the Storstad for not having done enough to rescue survivors.

"About four boats were launched as the ship sank," he said, "the people who were saved were saved by these boats and by the wreckage. The Storstad had three or four of her boats and pulled around and took people off the wreckage, but they did not get many. I passed a couple of their boats and they only had three persons in them. I saw no reason why the collier did not keep much closer than she did. If she had been there would have been many lives saved."

Kendall also said that if the Storstad had stayed with the Empress the two ships might have reached the shore and the majority of the passengers would have been saved.

Evidence was heard from the radio operator William James and from Captain Bélanger, but the inquest was then adjourned as there was no-one present from the Storstad, which had sailed up to Montreal to unload its cargo.

One hundred and eighty-eight bodies had not been identified. These were placed in coffins and loaded aboard the Lady Grey, which steamed up to Quebec with the British warship HMS Essex in attendance. The bells of city tolled solemnly as the little tender arrived on Sunday morning. A huge crowd watched in horror as sailors carried coffin after coffin into a shed that had been transformed into a temporary morgue. What was most upsetting were the small coffins for the children. A third of the bodies were never identified and were buried in Quebec. On the Sunday the White Star liner Megantic, heading in towards Quebec City, stopped at the site of the collision. Prayers were said and hymns sung.

For Kendall the days that followed were a blur. The crew of the Storstad reacted to the stories in the newspapers and attacked Kendall and the crew of the Empress, claiming that the ship had not been stationary, but had actually been moving forward at a great pace. Captain Anderson changed his story and said that he had ordered the engines to full ahead, but this action proved to be hopeless as the Empress was going so fast that the Storstad was left behind. He said that the Empress had simply kept going and thought that it had not been seriously damaged. After the impact he had inspected his ship and did not realize the gravity of the situation until he heard the cries of the people in the water. As soon as he understood what had happened, the lifeboats were launched and the crew worked flat out to save as many people as they could. Mrs Anderson was widely quoted in the newspapers and revealed, amongst other things, that Anderson had not been on the bridge until just seconds before the impact. She said that she had joined him on the bridge soon afterwards, and had been astonished that the Empress had kept going.

"When I heard the crying," she said, "I was nearly mad. I wanted to jump overboard it was so terrible. I put my hands to my face and walked away. It was not 10 minutes before every lifeboat was out with our crew in them."

The bitterness between the two ships was not helped when a couple of days later crew members of the Storstad were arrested using travel cheques that had belonged to an Empress passenger.

The Canadian Pacific sent officials to meet the Storstad when she arrived in Montreal. The ship was seized by a marshal, although one of the crew immediately tore down the notification letter that had been nailed to the ship. Canadian Pacific claimed $2m in damages. There were complications as the Storstad, whilst owned by a Norwegian shipping company, had been leased to the Dominion Coal Company's Black Diamond line. While all this was going on the SS Alsatian sailed for Liverpool on June 4, taking many of the survivors with it.

The following day, Minnie Kendall left her children in Liverpool and boarded the SS Calgarian, bound for Quebec, to support her husband during the difficult days of the court of inquiry.

The process opened on June 16, with Lord Mersey presiding.

He had led the inquiry into the sinking of the Titanic two years earlier, and was agreed by all to be the leading light in maritime law of the era. There would be 11 days of sessions, during which Kendall answered more than 850 questions during four separate appearances. There were 60 other witnesses from the crews of both ships. What emerged was that their two stories did not correspond at all. They were completely irreconcilable.

It was, however, significant that Jacob Saxe, the Third Mate of the Storstad, admitted that he had turned the ship hard to starboard, on the orders of Second Officer Alfred Toftenes, who he believed gave the order because he was worried about getting too close to the shore on the port side. Saxe said that Toftenes thought throughout that the Empress was between the Storstad and the shore. These revelations came to light only after Saxe had answered 500 other questions.

Charles S. Haight of the New York Bar, representing the owners of the Storstad, argued that the steering of the Empress was erratic and brought forward several witnesses to argue the case, among them several members of the crew of a Norwegian steamer called the Alden. It was then revealed that the crews of the Storstad and the Alden had met up in Montreal after the accident and thus the evidence was considerably undermined.

Butler Aspinall, representing the Canadian Pacific, said that the blame lay entirely with the Storstad.

Lord Mersey adjourned the Inquiry on Saturday, June 27.

The following day the Archduke Franz Ferdinand and his wife Sophie arrived by train in Sarajevo, the chief city in Bosnia-Herzegovina, a province that had been under Austro-Hungarian control since 1878, despite the fact that independent Serbia strongly opposed the occupation.

Serbian military intelligence, working with the Black Hand nationalist group, had learned of the planned trip and sent seven assassins to try to kill the heir to the Austrian Empire. As the six-car procession carrying the Archduke made its way from the station to City Hall, it passed Sarajevo's main police station. One of the terrorists burst from the crowd and threw a hand grenade at the Archduke's car. The driver, Franz Urban, saw what was happening and accelerated. The bomb landed on the road behind the Archduke's car and exploded just as the following car ran over it. Franz Ferdinand's aides Erich Edler von Merizzi and Count Alexander Boos-Waldeck were both injured, along with a number of spectators.

Urban left the scene immediately, driving the rest of the route at high speed, a move which meant that the other assassins were not able to continue the attack.

When they arrived at City Hall the Archduke expressed his anger at the attack and demanded to go to the hospital, to see his injured men. He was warned that this was not a good idea, but he insisted and so the convoy set off again towards Sarajevo Hospital, following the same route, but travelling in the opposite direction. The fastest way to the hospital was along the quayside, but in the confusion resulting from the Archduke's insistence on the visit, no-one had told Urban to go that way and so he followed the streets he had used previously. When he turned off the quayside, the officials immediately ordered him to stop and to reverse back to the route they wanted him to take. He was backing the car slowly towards the quay when it drew level with Gavrilo Princip, one of the assassins. After the earlier incident he had seen the Archduke's car flash by at speed and, believing the assassination to be a failure, had popped in to a cafe on the corner to have a sandwich. He emerged just as the Archduke's car returned.

Presented with a perfect opportunity, the 19-year-old stepped forward, pulled out his revolver and fired into the car, hitting the Duchess Sophie in the chest and Franz Ferdinand in the neck. There was pandemonium. Urban, realising that his passengers were seriously wounded, drove immediately from the scene, heading for the Governor's residence at Konak, where he hoped there would be doctors.

It was, however, too late to save the royal couple.

There was shock across Europe, but in Vienna members of the Austrian administration saw the killings as an opportunity to invade Serbia, which had long been trying to destabilize the Austro-Hungarian influence in the region. The murder of the heir to the imperial throne was the excuse they needed. The Austrians knew that Serbia was allied to Russia and that the alliance between Austria and Germany committed both to fight if Russia declared war on them. Kaiser Wilhelm II of Germany gave his strong support to the Austrians, but in Vienna there was a strong belief that the Russians would not react with force. It was a fatal misjudgment.

A Franco-Russian alliance committed the French to supporting Russia if it went to war with Germany or Austria, and Britain was bound to help France if she found herself at war with Germany.

In the weeks that followed Europe slid into war.

CHAPTER TWENTY TWO

Lord Mersey delivered his findings on the sinking of the Empress of Ireland in Quebec on July 16. The Storstad was ruled to be wholly responsible for the accident, having changed course in the fog. Kendall's decision to stop the Empress was questioned because it meant the ship could not react, but it was accepted that the action had been taken as a precaution and was not the cause of the collision.

A separate inquiry, conducted later at the Norwegian Consulate General in Montreal, exonerated the Storstad and blamed Kendall for not following the accepted convention of passing port-to-port, ignoring the fact that passing starboard-to-starboard is acceptable if it judged that there is an obstruction making it impossible to pass port-to-port.

Kendall was outraged at the Norwegian findings.

"There had been all manner of slurs on my character which I chose to ignore," Kendall remembered. "I didn't go to hear the findings. I was ill, at the end of my tether. The company ordered me back to Europe, but the court preferred my view of the incident to that of the Norwegians. I was completely exonerated. Canadian Pacific expressed every confidence in me. But it meant little to me. I was no longer the man who had caught Crippen, I had become the man who had sunk the Empress. The scene of my greatest triumph, a few years before, had become my nightmare. Some said Crippen had put curse on the captain who had caught him. Perhaps he did, I don't know."

Of the 1,477 people estimated to have been on board the

Empress of Ireland that night, a total of 1,012 lost their lives. This included 175 members of the crew of 417. The official figures suggest that 840 of the 1,057 passengers died. The majority of these were in the Third Class accommodation. They had almost no chance of survival. The high percentage of crew that survived was explained by the fact that many were still working at the hour of the collision and that they knew the ship better than the passengers, who had only been aboard for just a few hours.

Of the seven deck officers on board only two survived: Kendall and his First Officer Edward Jones.

The number of passengers drowned was actually higher than the 807 who went down with the RMS Titanic, but as the crew of the Titanic consisted of 903, of whom 690 drowned, the White Star liner remained the worst shipping disaster of the era.

The Canadians considered trying to refloat the Empress, as she was lying in only 130ft of water. Divers soon reported that it would be impossible to salvage the ship, as the damage was simply too great. Eventually they blasted a hole in the side of the hull in order to retrieve the mail and the ship's safe, in which was stored $150,000 of silver.

The Storstad was eventually handed over to Canadian Pacific as part of the settlement. It was sold for $175,000.

Captain Anderson remained the master of the ship until she was torpedoed off the southern coast of Ireland three years later.

When Henry and Minnie arrived back in Blundellsands, he was given some time at home. He needed a rest. It was not long, however, before the Canadian Pacific decided that it would be best to get him back to work. A man who has just been the captain of a much-publicized wreck is not the best candidate to be the master of another big liner. Even if he was found to be blameless, there was still a stigma that might drive away business. First and foremost Canadian Pacific was a business.

The answer was to promote Kendall to a new position as Marine Superintendant in Antwerp. This gave the message that the company supported him, but did not have to worry about passengers being scared away. It was a desk job.

Or so they thought.

When Kendall arrived in Belgium at the end of July 1914, the world around him seemed to be falling apart. Austria declared war on Serbia on July 28 and immediately launched an invasion. Two days later Russia mobilized against the Austrians. On July 31 Russia's ally France mobilized it armies. Austria's ally Germany demanded that the French stand down but their ultimatum was ignored and, on August 4, Germany launched its long-planned attack on France. The German armies drove through neutral Belgium, bypassing the French fortresses on the Maginot Line. Their target was Paris. Britain came to the defence of her ally France and declared war on Germany.

It was clear that the Belgians could offer little resistance to the invaders. Liege fell on August 16 and two German armies under Alexander von Kluck and Karl von Bulow advanced towards Brussels. This was taken on August 20. The Belgian government fell back to the heavily-fortified port of Antwerp.

In the city a large crowd gathered each day outside City Hall to discover the latest news of the fighting. The government began calling up all able-bodied men, while in the port German ships were dynamited, while the British ships began leaving.

As Marine Superintendant Kendall was responsible for all the Canadian Pacific ships in the port. It was obviously not desirable to leave any ships behind, but the situation was complicated because the Montrose had no crew, no coal and no supplies. The Montreal, on the other hand, had all that she needed to sail, but some of her machinery had been removed. She could not move under her own steam.

The British Consul General Sir Cecil Hertslet was besieged by around 600 British refugees, all of them looking for a way to escape the advancing German armies. They were terrified by stories of atrocities that the Germans had been accused of committing across Belgium. These were later detailed in a number of different reports that were extensively used for propaganda purposes, but there is no doubt that some of the awful claims were true and that Germany's use of a terror campaign against Belgian civilians was designed to stop all resistance amongst civilians.

After discussions with Hertslet and Montrose's chief engineer Mr Vine, Kendall formulated a plan for the Montrose to tow the Montreal out of the port. The former was placed alongside the latter and in 24 hours the coal and all the basic stores needed were transferred from one ship to the other. The Montrose then raised steam and the refugees were embarked. The Montrose steamed into the lock at the dock's entrance with the Montreal astern in the charge of two tug boats.

The operation was nearly completed when the Belgian Minister of the Marine Paul Segers telephoned to say that the British ships must not leave. Kendall ignored the instruction and edged the Montrose a few feet forward so that the lock gates could not be closed on her. This meant that there was nothing to stop the two ships from heading out into the River Scheldt.

Navigation in the Scheldt was not easy, but the tugs stayed with them until they reached Flushing. It was by then evening and the two ships headed out across the English Channel as darkness descended around them.

"It was a dark night," Kendall remembered, "but before long the British torpedo boats found us and were soon buzzing around, wondering what we were doing there. Once our credentials had been established they acted as our escorts, dropping phosphorus flares to help us on our way. From the Tongue Lightship to the Nore we sailed without a pilot and being well-acquainted with the system of buoys, I carried on and placed the Montreal at anchor off the Nore and proceeded to Gravesend to land my British, American and Canadian refugees. The old Montrose had turned into a Fairy Godmother."

Vine and Kendall went on to Tower Hill where they offered their services to the Royal Naval Reserve. The reaction they received was extraordinary. They were told that only a few officers would be needed as the war would be over in a few months. They left their addresses and departed for Liverpool to see their families. A few days later a letter arrived appointing Kendall as a Commander in the Royal Naval Reserve.

Back in Belgium, the Germans had decided to bypass Antwerp and surged towards Paris until the Battle of the Marne stopped their progress in the early part of September. Once the lines had been established the Germans turned to Antwerp, which had become a dangerous threat to the flank and the city fell in October. As the battles in France descended into trench warfare, attention turned to the sea. Just days after the war broke out, Germany despatched 10 U-boats from Heligoland to attack Royal Naval warships in the North Sea.

In September several ships were sunk and the British realized that they were extremely vulnerable to such attacks. There were also fears of mines which sank the battleship HMS Audacious in the Irish Sea in October. Winston Churchill, then the First Lord of the Admiralty, ordered that ships be requisitioned to be sunk at the entrances of the harbours of Scapa Flow and Dover to protect the ports from torpedo attack.

The Montrose was chosen to be one of the block ships. She was bought from the Canadian Pacific and her holds were filled with concrete. Steel masts were erected on her decks, with torpedo nets strung between them. When all was ready, she sailed to Dover where she was to be sunk the following morning.

"There were only two watchmen on board," Kendall said. "At about midnight a violent south-westerly gale blew up and my old ship snapped her moorings and sailed through Dover harbour, without touching another vessel, and drifted out through the eastern entrance and into the Straits of Dover. The two watchmen on board burned distress signals and tugs were sent out from Folkestone to try to get her back. When they found her she was beyond saving but thanks to some superb seamanship the two men aboard were rescued.

"There was however a strange coincidence for the last man to leave the ship was a William Crippen."

The Montrose found her own resting place, running aground on the dreaded Goodwin Sands. It was not until 1963 that her masts finally collapsed beneath the waters.

By the time the Montrose went to her watery grave, Kendall had been appointed second-in-command on the HMS Calgarian, under Captain Thomas Webster Kemp. The converted Allan Line streamer, on which Minnie Kendall had travelled to Quebec a few months earlier, had been fitted with six inch guns and was classified as an armed auxiliary cruiser. Despite weighing 17,500 tons, she could sail at 20 knots. Once fully converted for military use, she had been assigned to the 9th Cruiser Squadron, operating off the coast of Portugal. When war broke out there were 36 German and Austro-

Hungarian ships trapped in Portuguese waters, mainly in the River Tagus in Lisbon. The 9th Cruiser Squadron's orders were to stop them from escaping into the Atlantic.

Kendall found that Kemp was a mariner of the old school, who believed in strict discipline. This made him unpopular with his crews, particularly when he was captain of the HMS London, a Formidable Class battleship, in 1913. After newspaper reports of his unpopularity, Winston Churchill decided to replace Kemp, who was told quietly that his Royal Naval career was over. He sued the newspaper in question and won considerable damages, but he remained a frustrated and angry man. The war, however, revived his career. Britain needed all the trained naval officers she could muster and Kemp found himself in command of the Calgarian. His celebrated temper and difficult personality resulted in a flare-up with Kendall even before the Calgarian had reached the Bishop Rock lighthouse, off the Scilly Isles. Both men were used to being in command and both were used to getting their own way. Working together was not going to be easy. After the argument the two made peace, but Kendall said that he would request a transfer when they arrived at Gibraltar.

Kemp was taken aback by this and asked Kendall not to do that as he knew that he would be blamed by Churchill. The two men agreed to patch up their differences and in the years that followed developed both respect and a close friendship.

The squadron was under the command of Admiral John de Robeck, of the HMS Vindictive, an outdated Arrogant Class cruiser, launched in 1897 and the last of her class still on active service when the war broke out. The flotilla consisted of three Royal Navy ships and five auxiliary cruisers. It proved to be very effective, but gradually the danger from the German ships in Portugal subsided and the Calgarian was despatched to the Canary Islands, with orders to patrol the mid-Atlantic, protecting the trade routes and watching out for German surface raiders. The ships in Lisbon remained in port until February 1916 by which time the British losses to German submarines had become so severe that the ships in Portugal was considered so valuable that Portugal seized them and turned them over to the British for use as transports. This resulted in Germany declaring war on the Portuguese.

For many years before the outbreak of the war the German navy had been making plans about how to best attack Britain. The strategy devised was simple. The island would be cut off from her empire and starved into submission. To achieve this goal, the Germans had built a strong navy, but also a large number of liners and merchant ships that could be rapidly converted into fighting ships. This had resulted from Kaiser Wilhelm's inspection of the Teutonic at the Naval Review in 1889 when Kendall had been a cadet.

Such was the level of planning that some of the German liners even had pre-prepared rendezvous points in the event of war. They would meet supply ships, bringing stores and guns, and would become commerce raiders. These ships proved to be a serious problem in the first two years of the war, before the submarines developed to such an extent that there was no longer a need for surface raiders. The existence of the German raiders meant that the British had to use many of its ships to track them down.

In the early months of the war, it was ships of the German Imperial Navy that created problems, with the cruisers Koenigsberg and Emden operating in the Indian Ocean and the Karlsruhe in the Atlantic. As these were hunted down and destroyed, the British suffered a disastrous defeat at the Battle of Coronel, where Britain's West Indies Squadron was routed by Germany's Admiral Maximilian Graf von Spee. Spee's fleet then attacked the Falkland Islands, unaware that the British had sent HMS Inflexible and HMS Invincible to protect the islands. In the ensuing battle four German ships were lost.

At the end of 1914 the Calgarian steamed into Gibraltar for supplies and discovered the HMS Invincible in port. She was under the command of Rear Admiral Frederick Sturdee, who happened to be one of Kemp's oldest friends. He was invited aboard the Calgarian and Kemp called for cocktails, only to be informed by the steward that there was no means to make a drink.

"Well in that case," said Sturdee, "You should be sunk!"

They enjoyed a spirited evening nonetheless and Kendall learned much from Sturdee, notably the value of radio silence.

By the spring of 1915 the Calgarian had been switched to patrolling the US coastline. There were at least 50 German ships stuck in US ports, including nine large liners in New York. Early in March 1915 there were rumours that these ships were planning to break out into the Atlantic. This alarmed the Admiralty, not only because of the trouble it would cause in the Atlantic, but also because it might encourage other German ships to break out of other ports.

The Calgarian was sent to patrol the entrance to New York Harbour. This proved to be a bad mistake as in her absence German raiders Kronprinz Wilhelm and Prinz Eitel Friedrich both managed to slip into Newport News. The Kronprinz Wilhelm had sunk 15 ships in the six months since the start of the war, while the Prinz Eitel Friedrich had begun the war in Asia and had been converted into an auxiliary cruiser in Tsingtao, before beginning a voyage in the Indian and South Atlantic Oceans, during which she sank 11 ships. Both the raiders were interned by the Americans, but the British were still worried that they might break out again.

The Calgarian intercepted a German ship flying a US flag. The ship was captured and an armed prize crew was placed aboard and instructed to sail the vessel into Halifax, Nova Scotia. The German crew did not make life easy and secretly dumped their coal into the sea, but the voyage was completed and the crew interned. The Calgarian was ordered back to Chesapeake Bay to make sure that the German raiders did not re-emerge.

It was monotonous work but Kemp kept the crew alert with constant gunnery practice. This meant that the ship was highly efficient, but used up its ammunition rather more quickly than had been planned.

A month later, in May 1915, a German submarine sank the RMS Lusitania off the coast of southern Ireland, killing 1,198 of the 1,959 people aboard. The dead included 128 Americans. There was outrage in Britain and the United States, and attitudes hardened. It became clear that the German ships in US ports were going to be there for the duration of the war.

CHAPTER TWENTY THREE

As the threat of German ships being able to break out lessened, the Calgarian was ordered to Montreal. Returning to the St Lawrence brought back Kendall's conflicting memories of Father Point: the triumph of Crippen's arrest; and the tragedy of the Empress of Ireland.

When they arrived in Montreal, they discovered that their mission was a top secret one, to escort the first four British H-Class submarines across the Atlantic Ocean to Gibraltar. These were based on a design used by the US Navy and had been ordered from Bethlehem Steel in Pennsylvania. Because the United States was supposed to be neutral at the time, the components had been shipped to the Vickers shipyard in Montreal where the 364-ton submarines were assembled.

The British government wanted to keep the existence of the submarines a secret, aiming for H1, H2, H3 and H4 to come as a big surprise in the naval war in the Mediterranean, where the Dardanelles Campaign was then in full swing.

At the time whenever a submarine was spotted it was immediately assumed that it was German. The British had long favoured surface vessels and it was felt that sailing the submarines across the Atlantic on their own was too dangerous, as they might be attacked by Allied ships. The Calgarian was to play the role of Mother Hen, even if she was much faster than the submarines, which could travel at only 13 knots.

The first stop was St John's in Newfoundland, where the

22-man crews prepared the submarines for the ocean voyage.

Accompanied by a tramp steamer carrying fuel for the submarines, the small fleet set sail for the Azores. On the way one of the submarines suffered damage to her propeller from floating wreckage and it was decided to stop behind the island of Flores, the furthest flung of the Azores, while the crews repaired the damage. From there they sailed on to Gibraltar, at one point encountering two liners, the passengers on which applauded the Calgarian, assuming that she had somehow captured a nest of U-boats. After a voyage of 12 days, they neared Gibraltar and the three healthy submarines asked Kemp's permission to go ahead. They duly frightened several small steamers which, being unarmed, turned and fled when they spotted a pack of three submarines.

The four submarines would go on to do important work in the Mediterranean, although their torpedoes were unreliable, which meant that they did not achieve as much success as had been hoped.

From Gibraltar the Calgarian steamed north to Liverpool and the crew then enjoyed three weeks of shore leave before returning to the New York patrol. The return trip took them to Bermuda, where in August they were held up by a hurricane. This swept in with 120mph winds and heavy seas, causing considerable damage on the island.

Towards the end of the year Kemp received orders to take the Calgarian to Halifax, Nova Scotia, where he received word that he had been promoted to the rank of Rear Admiral. His new job was as commander of the British forces in northern Russia. Before the war Kemp had visited St Petersburg on several occasions and spoke some Russian. He was not a man given to exaggeration and was believed when he claimed to have warned Tsar Nicholas II that there was revolution in the air. The crew had grown to like Kemp in their time together. He was gruff and had a bad temper, but when he left the ship in Halifax he was cheered by the crew, all the way down the gangway. For the captain of a ship there is no greater compliment than that.

His replacement was Calgarian's new commander was Captain Robert Corbett RN. He was nicknamed "Shackles" because of the ungainly way in which he walked. For the next few months they went back to the New York patrol on the off-chance that a German raider might break out. The war was going badly. The French and German armies fought at Verdun from February to December, with appalling losses on both sides. At Easter the Irish nationalists rebelled against the British. There was street fighting in Dublin.

In May 1916, as the Calgarian patrolled her lonely beat off New York, the Imperial German Navy's High Seas Fleet, commanded by Vice-Admiral Reinhard Scheer, finally ventured out from its bases on the north German coast. The fleet met the Royal Navy's Grand Fleet, under the command of Admiral Sir John Jellicoe. The result was the Battle of Jutland, during which 100 German ships took on 150 British. There were no fewer than 50 battleships in action, and by the end of the day 25 ships had been sunk: 14 of them British and 11 German.

Fearful of losing more ships, Admiral Scheer did not press home his advantage and the High Seas Fleet retired to the German ports, leaving the British in control of the North Sea.

Britannia had suffered, but she continued to rule the waves. Never again did the Germans attempt to challenge British naval supremacy with surface vessels. German submarines continued their attacks on merchant shipping with great effect. No vessel was safe in the mid-Atlantic, but the Admiralty refused to try the convoy system, fearing that larger concentrations of ships would provide bigger targets for the submarines, and arguing that faster ships would be slowed down by having to keep pace with slower vessels. Those in favour of the convoys argued that while the convoys offered a bigger target they also gave the British defenders the opportunity to hit back and would stop the German practice of picking lone ships, surfacing and shelling them until they surrendered. After that the Germans would place bombs on board and sink the ship. This reduced the need to use precious torpedoes.

In June Lord Herbert Kitchener was drowned when a German mine sank the battleship on which he was travelling.

A month later, on the morning of July 1, the Battle of the Somme began with 13 British divisions attacking the German front lines. By the end of that dreadful day 19,240 British soldiers were dead and 35,498 wounded. The full casualty figure, including the missing and those taken prisoner, was 57,470. These were the worst casualty figures in the history of the British Army.

That summer Kendall's commanding officer Admiral Sir George Patey wrote to the Admiralty, recommending that Henry be awarded the Distinguished Service Order. The pen-pushers in the Admiralty decided that this was too much and Kendall was given a mention in despatches and a promotion to the rank of Lieutenant-Commander.

The losses continued to mount that summer and, although the Minister for Munitions David Lloyd George managed to get the first tanks into action that summer, the perception was that the war was not going well. The Kaiser agreed to allow direct bombing on British cities and night raids by Zeppelins because a regular occurrence, until the fighter and anti-aircraft defences improved. At the end of November there were the first bombing raids on London, using Gotha aircraft.

A week later Lloyd George agreed to work with the Conservatives, in order to improve the handling of the war. Prime Minister Herbert Asquith was forced to resign and Lloyd George took over. One of the first things he did was to order the Royal Navy to use the convoy system to ensure adequate imports of food and military supplies.

The Calgarian was a fast ship and the new government began to use her to transport VIPs. The first significant passenger was the Duke of Connaught, brother of the late King Edward VII and King George V's uncle. He had been Governor-General of Canada since 1911 and had reached the end of his term of office. The Calgarian was ordered to rush him across the Atlantic, in the hope that speed and secrecy would avoid disaster. The Duchess of Connaught was by then in poor health and, although there were few comforts aboard, the royal couple made the most of the conditions. On arrival in Devonport, the Duke presented Kendall with a set of cuff links, bearing his monogram.

The Calgarian then raced back to Canada with the new Governor-General, Victor Cavendish, the 9th Duke of Devonshire. Once the youngest member of the British Parliament, Cavendish had a worthy career in Parliament and was considered a safe pair of hands. He was safely delivered to Canada and the Calgarian then returned to the New York patrol until April 1917 when she was called upon to carry Sir Robert Borden, the Prime Minister of Canada, to attend the Imperial War Conference.

The switch to convoys had proved to be a great success, and tonnage losses dropped immediately as submarine commanders baulked at attacking for fear of the destroyer escorts that would give chase when a ship was torpedoed. More and more submarines were destroyed and before long Germany was losing more submarines than it was building. The tide was turning.

The Calgarian was finally ordered to begin convoy duties and joined a westbound convoy. These tended to be less dangerous that those going east as the Germans were keen to sink ships filled with supplies. After passing through the areas favoured by the submariners the westbound convoys would break up and the ships would head off in different directions. The Calgarian was heading back to her base in Halifax, Nova Scotia, when she received word by wireless that there had been a huge explosion in the city.

"We had no idea what to expect," Kendall remembered. "As we sailed into the harbour no-one was prepared for the devastation we saw."

On the morning of December 6 1917 the 3,000-ton French ship Mont Blanc had steamed into the outer harbour, carrying a cargo of 5,000 tons of various high explosives. This was bound for munitions factories in France. Because of the submarine war, and the fear of German spies, the ship was not flying flags warning of a dangerous cargo. A pilot boarded the ship to take her into the inner harbour, known as the Bedford Basin, by way of a stretch of water called The Narrows. There was confusion in the strait and the Mont Blanc collided with a Norwegian ship called the Imo. The captain of the Mont Blanc, Aimé Le Médec, tried to minimize the damage of the impact, by turning the ship so that the bow took the blow. Unfortunately the ship was carrying barrels of benzol on the foredeck and several of these were ripped open in the collision. A fire started and, with so much fuel in one place, it was soon burning out of control. It quickly became clear that the ship could not be saved. Le Médec ordered his crew to abandon ship and to warn those on land about the danger. The Mont Blanc drifted towards Pier 6, opposite the busy industrial district of Richmond. A warehouse on the quay caught fire. Several ships in the harbour had by then sent boats to assist and the local fire brigade arrived on the scene. There were a large number of spectators, unaware that the Mont Blanc was about to blow up. By the time the French crew arrived on land there was little time left for warnings. It did not help that few people in the English-speaking town understood what the terrified sailors were shouting.

At just after nine o'clock the Mont Blanc exploded with unimaginable force. The entire ship disappeared into a million metal splinters. Parts of the anchor were found two and a half miles away from the blast, while a gun barrel landed three and a half miles away in Dartmouth, on the other side of The Narrows.

The Stella Maris, a 200-ton tug that had been trying to tow the Mont Blanc away from the pier, was blown out into the harbour. She stayed afloat, despite almost all of her crew being killed. A passing schooner called the Lola R was blown to pieces. Another called the St Bernard, which was desperately trying to get away from Pier 6 when the explosion occurred, simply disappeared, fragments of her hull later being found on shore near Pier 6. When the explosion occurred the 5,000-ton Imo was in mid-channel. She was blown on to the shore on the Dartmouth side, while the 6,000-ton British ship Curaca, which had been loading horses at Pier 8, was blown clean across the harbour and sank in Tuft's Cove. A 38-ton tug called the Hilford at Pier 9 was blown out of the water on to the pier. A dozen other ships were seriously damaged, set on fire or blown from their moorings. Railway freight cars that had been on the wharf were blown two miles through the air. The shock wave from the explosion rang church bells 60 miles from Halifax and the explosion was heard in towns more than 150 miles away.

In the immediate vicinity of the explosion nothing remained. The devastation was complete. Hundreds of people were blown apart where they stood. The few who survived the initial blast were swept into the harbour when the displaced waters flooded back. The entire Richmond district was flattened and more than 1,600 buildings were completely demolished. A further 6,000 buildings - everything within two miles of the blast - was either destroyed or seriously damaged. When rescuers arrived they were greeted with the grisly sight of dismembered bodies in the streets. Hundreds were blinded by flying glass, having been caught watching the fire from the windows of their houses or offices. No pane of glass was intact within four miles of the explosion. The blast upended hundreds of stoves and lamps. Fires spread quickly, killing many who were trapped in the rubble of their houses. No-one knows for sure how many people died in Halifax and Dartmouth that day but the estimates range as high as 3,000. A further 6,000 were seriously injured as hot metal rained down on them.

It took most of the day for the fires to be brought under control. Thousands were in shock and there were few firefighters who survived the initial explosion. By nightfall around 25,000 people were left without a safe place to live. To make matters worse, that evening a blizzard swept across the region. Sixteen inches of snow fell on the ruined city. That night people froze to death. The following morning the Calgarian steamed into Halifax. The remains of the city were silent beneath the snows.

"The scenes of distress were beyond description," Kendall recalled.

The crew of the Calgarian provided whatever aid was possible. The ship's many berths were used to provide shelter for the homeless and her galleys kept them fed. Relief trains from other cities had begun to arrive in Halifax on the evening of the disaster, bringing medical staff and supplies. It was two days after the explosion before Red Cross trains began to arrive from the United States.

Although some of Halifax's hospitals survived the blast, there were soon a large number of temporary hospitals in operation. So many people required surgery that it was several days before all the work could be completed. All the while people died, while survivors searched for missing friends and relatives in the frozen rubble. The winter weather and the snows meant that bodies were still being discovered in the spring of 1918 as the debris was cleared and a new city laid out.

If there was any good news it was simply that the waters had help reduce the destruction. Experts reckoned that the devastation would have been far worse if the explosion had occurred on land.

Eventually, there was sufficient help for the Calgarian to be able to leave. She was ordered to join an eastbound convoy, heading for Britain. On arrival in Portsmouth, she received a new captain.

Bobby Newton was a Royal Navy officer who had retired to New Zealand before the war to become a sheep farmer. They settled in to the rhythm of the convoys, back and forth across the Atlantic. Shipping losses has reduced significantly, but the U-boats were still a danger. As targets became harder to find, the U-boat commanders concentrated on locations where they could guarantee to find shipping. The obvious one was the North Channel, the 15-mile wide stretch of water which connects the Irish Sea with the Atlantic Ocean, between the coast of Ulster and the islands off the west coast of Scotland.

In the early months of 1918 this became the graveyard for several ships, beginning with the coal freighter Knights Gareth in the first week of January. It was followed by the armed Cunard liner Andania on January 27 and the Tuscania in early February, which was torpedoed while carrying 2,000 US troops to France.

Three weeks after the Tuscania went down, the Calgarian arrived from Canada, carrying 610 naval ratings. She had crossed the Atlantic as an escort for a convoy of 30 merchant ships. This was travelling at 8-10 knots and, as they neared the North Channel, Newton asked permission to increase speed to 20 knots to get through the dangerous waters as quickly as possible. Permission was granted and the ship increased speed and began zigzagging, in order to make life more difficult for any submarines.

She had a couple of destroyers with her as escorts. Standing on the bridge, Kendall remarked to a fellow officer that he would happily shake the hand of any submarine commander who was capable of hitting such a target.

Moments later there was a loud explosion amidships.

At first it was thought that the Calgarian had hit a mine, but as soon as the explosion occurred the destroyers began laying a smokescreen around the big ship, just in case there had been a submarine. No-one was sure. Reports began to arrive on the bridge that the explosion had been in the forward stokehold, where the stokers had been busy shovelling coal into the furnaces to power the ship. The compartment was flooded and at least 30 were dead. Further reports revealed that the watertight doors were shut, and although the ship had a slight list on the port side, it was decided to head for shelter.

Beneath the waters, however, lay U19, under the command of Johannes Spiess, one of Germany's most experienced submarine commanders. U19 had been in action throughout the war, under the command or various captains, and in April 1916 had been the submarine used to transport British traitor Sir Roger Casement to Tralee Bay in Ireland in support of the planned Easter Uprising. Casement had been arrested, but U19 had got away, returning to her patrols, sinking merchant ships wherever possible.

Spiess was not about the give up without being sure that he had sunk the big ship. The destroyers were a danger, but the German was soon able to get off another torpedo, and scored a second hit. After that Kendall left the bridge of the Calgarian and went below decks to make sure that all the correct watertight doors were being shut. He was there when Spiess's third and fourth torpedoes hit the ship. The order was given to abandon ship and by the time Kendall reached the deck he found considerable chaos.

He noticed, however, that off the stern of the Calgarian was an armed trawler called the Thomas Collard, which had come to assist. He realized that if he could find a rope he would be able to slide down from one of the deck installations on the Calgarian and land on the deck of the smaller ship. The plan worked perfectly and Kendall was dusting himself off, and preparing to go in search of the captain when the Thomas Collard was hit by another of Spiess's torpedoes. She was only a small 200-ton vessel and was not built to survive such an attack and she soon began to sink.

This time there would be no escape, or so it seemed. But as Kendall was pondering taking to the water, another small ship drew alongside the Thomas Collard and Kendall and the other passengers were able to scramble across to the other ship.

"The first man I met as I climbed aboard was an old Canadian Pacific employee," said Kendall. "It is a small world."

CHAPTER TWENTY FOUR

Being torpedoed twice on the same day, without getting wet, was quite an achievement, but Kendall was too busy fishing others from the sea to have time to consider his good fortune. As dusk fell the survivors watched the Calgarian disappear beneath the waves. They were then landed at the port of Larne, on the Ulster coast. The town was used to dealing with torpedoed sailors, and they were soon being looked after. Spirits were high, although the loss of two officers and 47 ratings dampened the mood. There was a memorial service for the dead in a small church on the sea front and then the survivors were put aboard a ferry to the Scottish port of Stanraer. From there Kendall made his way by train back to Portsmouth.

It was a long and complicated journey, with changes at various stations. At one point he found himself being surveyed by an elderly gentleman. They sat in the same carriage for the next part of the journey and struck up a conversation about the war. Kendall remarked that he had just been torpedoed. On hearing this news, the gentleman asked his name and, when he heard the name Kendall, explained that he had suspected as much. He had been the governor of Pentonville Prison, who had organized the execution of Dr Crippen, and was pretty sure that fellow passenger was the man who had caught him.

It was a very small world.

When he reached Portsmouth, Henry was told that the German submarines were responsible for a rather curious problem. The Admiralty had no shortage of captains, but was short of ships. There was no immediate position available for him. It was felt that the best thing was to send him to a training course at HMS Excellent, the Royal Naval Gunnery School on Whale Island in Portsmouth. Given his experiences during the previous three and a half years, this was a fairly pointless exercise. Kendall was already a highly-accomplished gunnery officer. The good news was that the government also needed King's Messengers, to carry despatches and documents to the British Embassy in Paris. Kendall was just the kind of officer needed to accompany the diplomatic bags. After years away at sea this provided Henry with a little variety in life, while at the same time making him feel that he was still helping out with the war effort. Paris in the spring was a nice place to be posted, even if it was only for a few days at a time.

Two days after the sinking of the Calgarian, the Russians signed the Treaty of Brest-Litovsk with the German, Austro-Hungarian, Bulgarian, and Turkish governments. The Russians were out of the war. This meant that the Germans could transfer troops from the Eastern Front to France. The result of this was a massive offensive on the Western Front, which aimed to capture Paris and bring down the French government. It began with the biggest artillery barrage of the war, with more than a million shells being fired in just five hours. Three German armies then smashed through the British front line near St Quentin. In the four days that followed both sides each lost nearly 250,000 men in the fighting. A few days later a second offensive began further to the north. At the end of May came a third offensive further to the south, between Soissons and Reims. The Allied front collapsed and the Germans advanced to the Marne River, within 37 miles of Paris. It was then that the Americans arrived with the US Marines turning back the German advance in a ferocious battle in Belleau Wood. This not only gave the US Marines its reputation as a fighting unit, but also showed the British and French that the US soldiers were highly motivated and competent, a major boost for Allied morale.

It was not until the start of June 1918 that Kendall received orders to report to HMS President, the London headquarters of the Royal Naval Reserve, a ship moored on the River Thames behind the Savoy Hotel. It was there that he discovered that he had been appointed a Convoy Commodore. He was still under the command of a Royal Navy officer, who controlled the escort ships and dictated the path of a convoy, but Kendall was now the man in charge of the merchant ships.

Kendall's first convoy consisted of 30 vessels, with an escort of destroyers. It was a westbound convoy, which meant that there was less likelihood of submarine attack. As soon as the convoy was past the danger zone, Kendall gave the order to allow the ships to go their separate ways. He sailed on to New York to get new orders from Rear Admiral Sir Lionel Wells, the senior naval officer in the United States.

Life as a Convoy Commodore was particularly agreeable in the US as the best gentlemens' clubs in New York had agreed to help out, and the various commodores enjoyed the hospitality of the New York Yacht Club's headquarters in Manhattan. Then it was off to the dramatic Pennsylvania Station, far more grandiose than any railway station Kendall had ever seen, and a trip south to Philadelphia, Baltimore and Washington and from there to Richmond and Newport News, where a new convoy was forming up in the harbour at Hampton Roads.

On this occasion Kendall discovered that his designated flagship was a small vessel with no great speed and immediately insisted on transferring to a bigger and better ship, a more effective place from which to operate. This was accomplished with the minimum amount of fuss and the convoy set sail into Chesapeake Bay.

Kendall, walking the decks once they were clear of the coast, noted a large number of steel drums secured on the forward deck of the ship and asked the captain what cargo the vessel was carrying. The captain informed him that the ship carried 400 tons of high explosive. Kendall, who had seen the devastating effects of big explosions in Halifax just a few months earlier, was alarmed but the captain explained that it was really nothing to worry about. If the ship was torpedoed, the explosion would be so huge that the entire convoy would disappear without a trace. It really did not matter on which ship the commodore travelled. The explosives were needed on the Western Front. The convoy could travel at only six knots, the speed of the slowest of the ships, and for 20 days the 40 vessels waited for an explosion they hoped would never come.

Kendall, who had been much impressed with his meeting with Admiral Sturdee in 1914, remembered that one of the key factors in Sturdee's victory at the Battle of the Falkland Islands had been the element of surprise. Sturdee's battle group had sailed south under orders not to break radio silence. Kendall decided that his convoys should follow similar guidelines, thus avoiding alerting any listening U-Boats to the progress of a convoy. The radio operators simply listened in to activity on the air waves, which often proved to be a harrowing experience as stray ships were attacked and sunk.

Above all, however, Kendall was impressed by the standard of seamanship as 40 ships, in close proximity, zigzagged across the ocean, their movements coordinated with light signals between them. There were many near-misses, but collisions were avoided.

By then, however, a new problem was developing with the spread of Spanish Influenza. This deadly strain of the illness had been seen earlier in the year in the United States and doctors quickly realized that it was particularly dangerous for healthy young adults. In the course of the next two years it would kill around 40 million people. Each morning ships in the convoy would be flying flags requesting that they be allowed to stop for burials at sea. On Kendall's ship there were a number of cases. There was not a single doctor in the convoy, and so the captains did what captains had been doing for years: they looked in The Shipmaster's Medical Guide and did the best they could with the supplies available. Kendall's cure for Spanish Influenza proved to be remarkably effective and involved giving patients two Dover Powders, and then leaving them wrapped in blankets in a sealed cabin. Every few hours they would be sponged down and then wrapped up again. Dover Powder was a remedy created by Dr Thomas Dover in 1732 and had served the seafaring community ever since. It was a mixture of drugs which aimed to induce sweating and thus break a cold or a fever. It also included a little opium to take away the pain. Amazingly, this seemed to work and the patients were soon back in action again.

As soon as they arrived in England, Kendall was given orders to return to New York as commander of a 16-knot convoy. This was a relief, as there was only so much luck that a commodore could have, even with radio silence. As the new convoy headed out to the

Americas, it followed in the wake of a slower convoy which had run into a wolf pack of U-Boats. They passed through the wreckage, but the submarines were gone.

From New York it was up to Sydney, a port on Cape Breton Island, the northern part of Nova Scotia, for another eastbound convoy of 40 ships and the Kendall returned to the United States again with fast convoy. It was by then October and Kendall received word that he should head to Montreal for a convoy of 30 troopships. Each was packed with soldiers for the Western Front. He discovered that on many of the ships there were so many soldiers that they slept in three eight-hour shifts, using the beds around the clock.

He did not know it at the time, but this was to be his final voyage. And in the years that followed he was able to reflect on the fact that fate took him once again to the St Lawrence, the scene of his greatest triumph and of his bitterest moments. As the convoy steamed down past the elegant Father Point lighthouse, Kendall was reminded of the awful night when the Empress went down, four years earlier. If the other officers knew they said nothing. Kendall was left with his own thoughts as they headed out into the Gulf of St Lawrence.

They hurried across the Atlantic, but this time Kendall sensed that something was different. There was less radio traffic than normal. As they neared Britain they saw that ships were lit up at night. It seemed that people were dropping their guard. The convoy continued its radio silence until they reached the English Channel and dropped anchor. The captain of a nearby fishing vessel informed them that an armistice was about to be signed and that the German government had suspended all U-boat operations against Allied shipping. The Germans had sunk an impressive 14.5 million tons of Allied shipping and killed tens of thousands of men, but it was all finally coming to an end. On November 9 the Kaiser abdicated and the next day fled to the Netherlands. At 11 o'clock on November 11 fighting stopped on the Western Front. Three days later five German Battle cruisers, 11 Battleships, eight Cruisers and 50 Destroyers surrendered to the Royal Navy.

The war was over.

Kendall was released from the Royal Naval Reserve before the end of the month. On his final day he was promoted to the rank of Commander (retired) in recognition of the services he had rendered.

The world would take time to settle down, but by the spring of 1919 the Canadian Pacific was back in full operation. Much had changed in the four years of war, but the company had grown stronger. It had provided the British government with 52 ships. Eighteen of them had been lost: 15 to enemy action and three to collisions. Thomas Shaughnessy, the company president, had been elevated to the peerage as Baron Shaughnessy, as a mark of Canadian Pacific's contributions to the Allied war effort. Having reached retirement age, he finally stood down, after 19 years running Canadian Pacific. He was replaced by Edward Beatty, the first Canadian-born president of the company.

Beatty had big plans to reorganise the business. On land there had been big changes. During the war years the Canadian Federal government had been forced to merge and nationalize a number of bankrupt railway companies. The result was Canadian National Railways, which was launched in December 1918 and quickly became Canadian Pacific's chief rival. Beatty decided that the best course of action was to separate the steamship business from the railroad company and so created a London-based firm called Canadian Pacific Steamships Ltd.

During the war the company had merged with the Allan Line, its old competitor and, despite the losses, the fleet still numbered nearly 40 ships. In the years that followed, however, Canadian Pacific was able to expand by buying three ships that would become a new generation of Empresses. When the war ended the British seized a large number of German ships and in the summer of 1921 the Tirpitz, the Kaiserin Auguste Victoria and the Prinz Friedrich Wilhelm became the Empresses of China, Scotland and India. At the same time Canadian Pacific decided to switch some of its vessels from the regular North Atlantic runs to the rapidly-expanding cruise business. This was largely the result of two factors: the opening of the Panama Canal, which made round-the-world cruising a possibility; and the decision by the United States to embark on a curious experiment, known as Prohibition, which banned the consumption of alcohol in the country. If Americans wanted to drink they either had to break the law or leave the country. Cruise ships provided the possibility to do that easily, and in comfort. In the 1920s the first purpose-built cruise ships began to be built.

Canadian Pacific switched its Empresses from industrial Liverpool to the rather more glamorous Ocean Dock in Southampton and appointed Kendall as the Marine Superintendent in the port. The Empresses were replaced on the immigrant runs from Liverpool by three new ships called the Montcalm, the Montrose and the Montclare, all of which entered service in 1922.

The Kendall children were growing up fast and Henry and Minnie had ambitions for them. They wanted them privately educated. Billy was sent away to boarding school at Ellesmere College, one of the Woodard Schools, in the town of Ellesmere in Shropshire. He was 16 when the war ended. Lily was sent to another Woodard School in Abbots Bromley. She did not settle in well and in 1919 was switched to a convent in Vracene, on the western side of Antwerp. Harry, seven years younger than Lily, would also go to Ellesmore College in the mid-1920s.

If Kendall had worries about the effect of the Empress disaster on his career they gradually began to fade, although the memories of what had happened remained with him. In 1923 he was invited to become a Younger Brother of Trinity House, the greatest honour there is for a British mariner. With his old friend and colleague James Gillies as the Marine Superintendent in Liverpool and Kendall in Southampton, his generation rose to prominence within Canadian Pacific. In 1924 Henry was transferred to the job of Marine Superintendent in London. A year later Gillies became General Manager of Canadian Pacific Steamships Ltd.

For the next 15 years Henry ran the Canadian Pacific activities in the vast Surrey Docks, on the south side of the River Thames to the east of London. This related mainly to the importation of Canadian timber and grain. In the late 1920s, as the immigrant trade began to wane, the Canadian Pacific moved more towards freight. The Empresses remained as cruise ships and the original runs to Canada were taken over by four new ships called the Duchesses of Bedford, Atholl, Richmond and York. The fleet was strengthened with five new freighters called the Beaverburn, Beaverford, Beaverdale, Beaverhill and Beaverbrae.

Henry and Minnie bought a large house in St Mildred's Road, to the south of the village of Lee, three miles from the docks. The area was farmland until the middle of the Nineteenth Century when the railway first arrived. The Kendall house was one of the first houses built in that era and still had open countryside nearby until the 1930s when development of the London suburbs engulfed the older parts of the village.

Although there was easy access to London by railway Henry had discovered the automobile and was an enthusiastic driver.

CHAPTER TWENTY FIVE

At the end of the First World War, after Henry and Minnie moved south, her family began to break up. Her brother Thomas had died in the influenza outbreak of 1918 and then Peter decided that life would be better in Australia. David Lloyd George had promised "a land fit for heroes", but the downturn in the economy created chronic unemployment, particularly in the old industrial regions, such as Liverpool. The government even agreed to subsidize the fares of those departing. May would soon follow her brother, while Minnie's youngest brother Ernie, who idolized Henry Kendall, ran off to sea. He would later write that he would return one day when he was as successful as Henry had been. They never heard from him again.

Only Dave remained. He was by then married and had two young children, but he continued to try to live off the family. In the early 1920s he convinced Minnie to let him and his family live in the top flat in the house in St Mildred's Road. Once he was installed, it seemed impossible to move him out. He paid the Kendalls minimal rent and on more than one occasion Henry was forced to pay off gambling debts that Dave had run up. In the end Henry bought a second house in the fast-developing Burnt Ash Hill: in part as an investment; and in part to get rid of Dave and his family.

Billy had proved himself to be a gifted sportsman during his time at Ellesmere College and when he rejoined the family after completing his studies he quickly became a member of the celebrated Blackheath Rugby Club, one of the first of the great independent rugby clubs of England. For several years he played scrum half for Blackheath.

Although he was by then past 50, Henry remained remarkably fit. In the late 1920s his sons Billy and Harry were goading him one day about his age, as sons tend to do. Kendall called their bluff and challenged the pair to a running race along St Mildred's Road. Much to their surprise, the boys were left behind by their father. Billy worked in London for the Imperial Tobacco Company and later moved to Malaya to help expand the business of its subsidiary British American Tobacco. When he returned to Britain he became a close friend of Irene Davoren, known to all as Bunty, who came from a well-to-do Irish family. Henry Kendall could ask no more from his son.

His daughter Lily was also doing well. She had blossomed into a pretty young woman in the 1920s and soon found herself with a handsome young boyfriend called Donald Saward, who worked in the insurance business in London, but was also an accomplished sportsman, particularly tennis. By the late 1920s it was clear to Henry and Minnie that there would soon be weddings in the family.

After so many years apart, the Kendalls now enjoyed a settled life. There was plenty of money and Henry enjoyed a solid position in the company. He travelled only occasionally and as a result was never able to fulfil his ambition to meet the man who had torpedoed the Calgarian. He was convinced that Johannes Spiess was no ordinary seaman. In 1925 the German captain published a book about his adventures called "Sechs Jahre U-bootsfahrten". It was translated into English a couple of years later and remained a popular publication in Germany well into the 1930s.

In the summer of 1930 Lily and Don were married. They could not afford their own house but Henry and Minnie were happy for them to take over the top flat in St Mildred's Road, which had by then been vacated by Dave and his family. In 1931 Lily announced that she was pregnant and in the spring of 1932 Henry Kendall was presented with his first grandchild, a boy called Michael.

A few weeks later Billy married Bunty Davoren.

Harry remained a problem. He had always been a more difficult child and while Billy and Lily had both done well for themselves, Harry seemed to have no interest at all in moving the family up the social ladder. This mattered a great deal to Henry. He had sent all three of his children to private schools in an effort to help them improve their position in society, but Harry did not seem to care. Perhaps because he could not compete with his accomplished elder brother, Harry always seemed to feel that he was second best. After a while he ceased trying and was happy to work as a clerk in the Royal Victoria Docks, never showing any ambition to achieve more than that.

He upset his father even more in 1939 when he announced that he was going to marry a working class girl called Doris Marmion, who came from Sidcup. To make matters worse, just before the wedding Harry gambled his entire life savings on a horse and lost every penny. Photographs of the ceremony reveal a scowling Henry Kendall, who had just discovered the news. Without money behind him, Harry turned to his parents for help and asked if he and Doris could move into the apartment in St Mildred's Road, which had been vacated in 1936 when Lily, Don and Michael moved to their own house a few miles away in the "garden suburb" of Petts Wood. This had a village atmosphere with wide grass verges and tree-lined avenues. It boasted its own pub, shops and even a cinema. It was a perfect place for a young family.

Kendall had no right to censure Harry for his gambling as he had developed his own betting habit. He had promised his mother many things before going to sea, but gambling was not one of them. He played the football pools, guessing the scores of a list of soccer matches each week, hoping to win the jackpot. At the time this was the only form of gambling that offered a single large prize. He regularly put money on horses and in the 1930s developed a taste for greyhound racing, after the tracks at Catford and Crayford opened for business.

While Henry's relationship Harry remained strained, he remained on very good terms with his other two children, although he saw less of Billy and Bunty after they moved to Surrey. They had become rather an odd couple who lived apart much of the time and it was clear that Bunty did not want children. Henry was closest to Lily and Don and their son Michael. On Sundays he would drive over to Petts Wood and take them for drives in the country in his Morris

Oxford. The favourite destination was The Old Barn at Hildenborough in Kent, where a former Royal Naval officer, Commander Tomlinson, had begun serving cream teas to the increasing number of motorists. This grew with a ballroom for dances and evening functions, a swimming pool and even a landing field where there was aerobatics and parachute jumping. On other occasions Kendall drove them to visit Don's parents, who had retired to the coastal town of Hythe, which sits at the edge of Romney Marsh.

In January 1939 Henry celebrated his 65th birthday. This meant that he had to retire from Canadian Pacific. He had been with the company for 33 years. In his final months before retirement he had worked with Lily to produce his memoirs and a deal was arranged with Hurst & Blackett, a London publishing house that dated back to 1812. The company specialized in biographies but also had a very clear right wing bias, as witnessed by the other offerings in that era, which included such illuminating titles as "Hermann Goering - The Man and his Work", "Behold Our New Empire - Mussolini", "Germany's Claims to the Colonies" and even a translation of Adolf Hitler's "Mein Kampf". Kendall's "Adventures on the High Seas" received many reviews, most of them saying that the book was a good yarn.

Henry's greatest joy of the era was his grandson Michael and he particularly enjoyed the youngster's adventurous nature. Early in 1939 the seven-year-old Michael learned to ride a bicycle and promptly pedalled three or four miles from Petts Woods to Lee, navigating from memory, to see his grandfather. When he arrived Henry telephoned his daughter and asked if all was well with Michael. Lily was shocked to discover that her son had disappeared from the garden.

Europe was once again drifting towards a war. In 1936 Adolf Hitler, the German Chancellor, marched troops into the de-militarized zone known as the Rhineland, essentially the German territory to the west of the River Rhine. Allied occupation forces had by then withdrawn, but the move violated the Treaty of Versailles. There was no serious reaction from the French or British. In March 1938 Hitler organized the takeover of Austria. This was followed by the annexation of the Sudetenland, areas of Czechoslovakia that were predominantly German. This resulted in an international crisis in the autumn of 1938 and the Munich Agreement, which forced Czechoslovakia to give up its lands. In March 1939 Hitler invaded the rest of the country on the pretext of restoring order after a Slovakian uprising. Hitler could no longer claim to be undoing the wrongs of the Treaty of Versailles, nor integrating German-speaking peoples into his empire. France and Britain were forced to admit that Hitler had plans to dominate Eastern Europe. It was clear that his next target was Poland and the Allies gave the Poles a guarantee that if the Germans invaded, they would declare war against Hitler.

The biggest fear in Britain was that Germany's Luftwaffe would bomb London, perhaps even with poison gas. As early as 1938 plans were formulated for the mass evacuation of children, mothers of small children, pregnant women, invalids and the elderly to the safety of the English countryside.

At the end of August the Germans staged what they claimed was an attack on a German radio station at Gleiwitz. It was made to look like the work of Polish saboteurs and gave Hitler, and his new ally Russia, the opportunity to invade Poland from east and west. Britain gave the Germans a deadline of 11 o'clock on September 3 to withdraw its troops from Poland.

Henry was worried about the bombing of London and even before Prime Minister Neville Chamberlain's radio broadcast, he had loaded Don and Michael into his new Ford Prefect and driven them to Hythe. He unloaded the car and immediately went back to Petts Wood, to pick up Minnie, Lily and her new baby called Moira. When war was declared Kendall was on the main road to London, driving like a madman, swearing and cussing at others on the road.

Michael was playing on the beach with his cousins as Chamberlain declared war on Germany. In adult life he would often declare that he was England's front line that day!

In the space of a week a million and a half people left London.

The whole family would remain in Hythe for several weeks after the declaration of war, but no bombs fell on London and gradually people began to drift back to the city. The Kendalls were no exception. The Germans completed the Polish invasion by the end of the month. In October a U-Boat sank the British battleship HMS Royal Oak at Scapa Flow, but Britain hit back in December at the Battle of the River Plate, which resulted in the scuttling of the German battleship Graf Spee. Early in 1940 Hitler struck north, invading Denmark and Norway and British troops went into action against the Germans for the first time. A month later the Germans invaded the Netherlands, Belgium and Luxembourg and advanced into France.

The Germans had plans to invade Britain, but once the battle for France was over and the British had been humiliated at Dunkirk, the German High Command insisted that the Royal Air Force be destroyed before an invasion could begin. Thus began the Battle of Britain as the Germans attacked the RAF bases across the south of England and the pilots of Fighter Command fought to turn back the aerial invaders.

In the early hours of August 25 a German plane dropped bombs in the north and the east of London. It was probably a mistake, but the British responded by sending a small force of Wellington bombers to attack central areas of Berlin. Hitler was furious and ordered the Luftwaffe to switch its bombing attacks to London.

On September 7 two waves of German bombers dropped hundreds of tons of high explosive and incendiary bombs on to the Surrey Docks. Kendall's old world disappeared. The skies were lit up for miles around as the warehouses burned. In the late autumn the Kendall house in St Mildred's Road was badly damaged when an aerial mine landed in nearby Linchmere Road, creating a huge crater and killing a number of people. It caused considerable structural damage to the Kendall home, but fortunately no-one in the house was injured.

Henry and Minnie were forced to move out of London. They found rooms in a small semi-detached house in Fetcham, near Leatherhead, in Surrey. It was in the country and away from the bombing.

Every night for the next two months the Germans bombed London. Hurst & Blackett was one of the victims, the publishing house being destroyed in a firebomb road on December 29 1940. Almost the entire stock of Henry's book and the printing plates were destroyed. Kendall's story would remain largely untold.

Don volunteered as a part-time auxiliary fireman, battling

a blaze under Waterloo Station where a store of spirits burned for days.

That winter Minnie, who was by then 64, went into decline. She had been badly shaken by the bombing and by having to move house. Her asthma was getting worse and during the winter the weather was severe, with a great deal of snow and low temperatures.

The bombing of London continued, but the attacks became sporadic as the Luftwaffe attacked other cities.

At the start of April 1941 the 29-year-old Harry was called up for military service. He was posted to a Royal Army Service Corps base near Darlington, in County Durham. Six days after his departure Minnie died from heart failure. The family gathered for the funeral in Chislehurst Cemetery, but soon afterwards Billy was called up. He was nearly 40 by then and considered to be too old for active service and so found himself in the Intelligence Corps. In 1942 Don received his call-up papers, but he too was judged to be too old for an active unit and he was soon put to work organizing supplies.

After 45 years of marriage Henry found himself alone. Only Lily was still around and she was busy with her children in Petts Wood. With more time to himself, the burdens of age and the war, Henry became more irascible than he had been when he had work to distract him. He gambled more and his temper became worse. He found it hard to be positive about anything.

In June that year the Germans turned on Russia. The British focus moved to North Africa and Harry was soon shipped out to be part of the Eighth Army. He became a corporal but suffered badly from malaria and spent much time in hospitals in Africa and Italy. By the end of the war he was in Klagenfurt in Austria.

Don, by then assigned to the 1st Airborne Division, suffered serious heatstroke in Tunisia and was sent home. He was posted to Catterick Camp, near Richmond in North Yorkshire. The D-Day landings came and went but the 1st Airborne Division was left to wait until September 1944 when the troops were informed that they would be parachuting into a Dutch town of Arnhem, where there was an important bridge over the River Rhine. Don was due to go into Arnhem once the attack had been established.

Some of the 2nd Battalion of the Parachute Regiment did get

through to the bridge, but soon found that they were surrounded by an SS Panzer Division. The planning had foreseen the entire division holding the bridge for just 48 hours before the land forces arrived, after an onslaught through the Netherlands, via bridgeheads at Eindhoven and Nijmegen. This took much longer than planned and gradually the defenders at the bridge were blasted into oblivion by the Germans. They held on for four days before ammunition ran out.

When the survivors of Arnhem returned to England, there were just 2,424 left from more than 10,000 that had been sent to the Netherlands. Nearly 1,400 had been killed and 6,400 were made prisoners.

That summer had seen the Germans attacking London once again, this time using the new V1 Flying Bombs. Further damage was done to the two Kendall houses in Lee, but it was clear as the Allies advanced across Europe that the war was finally coming to an end. The British government promised to help to repair the damaged houses, but it would be well into the 1950s before that work was completed.

In the immediate post-war period, with everyone back home again, Kendall moved into the basement of the house in Burnt Ash Hill. When repairs of the upper parts of the house were completed, he rented the rooms to tenants. Finally, when the old family home in St Mildred's Road was finished, this too was rented.

By the time all the work was completed, Henry was nearly 80, but he continued to lead an active life. Most of his generation were gone but he lived on: defying age, gambling away his money and rarely saying a positive word about anyone or anything. Before he was 90 he had two great-grandchildren, but as neither Harry nor Billy had children, he knew that he was the last of the line.

Kendall's generation had been born into a world dominated by the British Empire, and they had done their best to maintain it. To them it was a source of pride that the country had fought and won two World Wars, despite losing many of the best and the brightest.

For the survivors, the 1950s and 1960s often brought bitterness. The world for which they had fought was not the world they expected to live in. The empire faded, with country after country gaining independence. America and Russia had become more powerful than

Britain. There were new heroes. Mariners had lost their mystique and had been replaced by men with close-cropped hair and NASA space suits.

English society, staid though it still was, had rebels within: they preached peace, drugs and rock and roll. They had different ideas about what was important.

One of Kendall's contemporaries, and a man for whom he had great respect, was Sir Winston Churchill. They had been born in the same year. Their lives that had begun in a world of horses and sailing ships and were coming to an end as man was making preparations to land on the Moon. People were living longer, thanks to medical advances, but no-one could live forever. In January 1965 Churchill finally died. Kendall grew weaker and by the autumn of that year there were signs that his body was finally beginning to give out. He was in and out of hospital with one ailment after another, unable to bounce back as once he would have done. In the end the doctors recognized that there was nothing more than they could do. He was sent to the Trinity Hospice in Clapham.

The nurses there said that in the final minutes of his life Henry Kendall was re-living a shipwreck. Perhaps he was battling the ghosts of the Empress one last time.

Then he became calm - and quietly joined them.

Lightning Source UK Ltd.
Milton Keynes UK
01 October 2010

160669UK00002B/78/P